RIPPLES IN THE GENERATIONS

JOYCE K. GATSCHENBERGER

RIPPLES IN THE GENERATIONS

Joyce K. Gatschenberger

Copyright ©2019 by Joyce K.Gatschenberger

Published 2019 by Joyce K. Gatschenberger

LinesofListening.com

LinesofListeningblog.wordpress.com

DEDICATED TO:

Van, Tarena, Erica
and
Kiyah Doveanna

BOOKS BY

Joyce K. Gatschenberger

Lines of Listening: An Expose' of Generational Child Abuse and Marital Betrayal

Generations Intertwine: The Rest of the Story

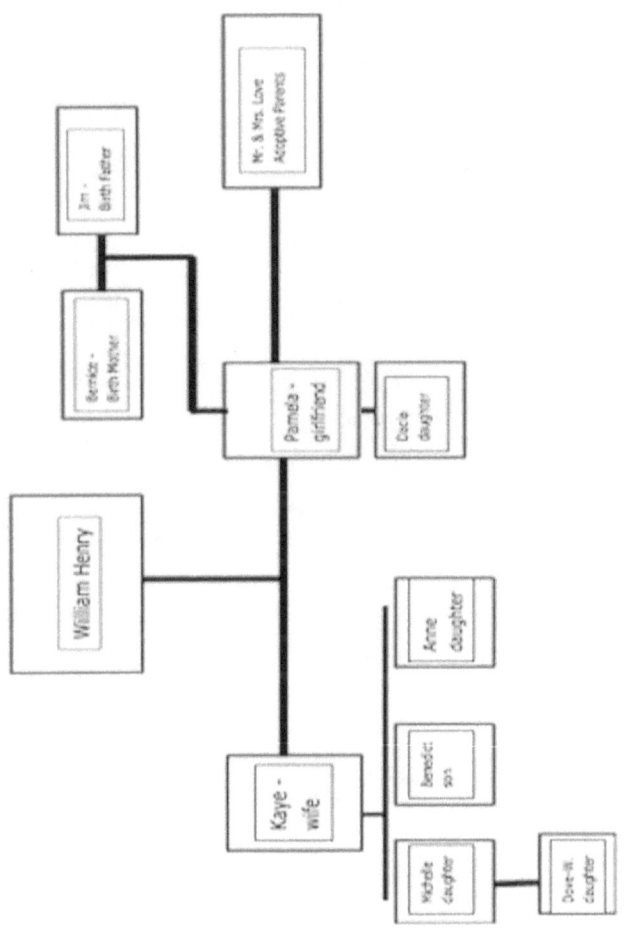

FOREWORD

Tension in the high school conference room resembles the stress of a stretched tightrope wire as Mr. Menendez strains to moderate the meeting. Divided members of the Henry family sit at opposite ends of a long conference table as the science fair judges assemble on either side.

"It's obvious why we're here this afternoon. The results of the science fair DNA tests indicate that Dacia and Dove-Whispering are genetically related. Upon learning this fact, I know that discussions are occurring to determine how this situation may have happened. I'll state the obvious; William Henry is unfaithful to his wife in Nevada and having an affair with Pamela Love here in Colorado the relationship results in a child whose name is Dacia Henri' Love.

William Henry is the grandfather of Dove-Whispering. Having moved recently with her mother, Michelle, to Colorado, Dove-Whispering enrolls at Dakota Flats High School. At this point, Dacia and Dove-Whispering meet each other through science class and become friends. Their work on a DNA project for the science fair is why we're here today.

Now, they're undoubtedly more issues concerning this situation, but these are the bare facts. I understand the emotional controversy and realize that everyone is surprised by the information. Turning back time in this matter may resolve the issues, but that option isn't possible. So, I suggest we go forward and find a positive solution. My genetic effect in this is questionable, but I do accept responsibility for developing the situation in which it occurred. I seek atonement for my part in these issues."

CHAPTER ONE

Human Frailty

"*We'd hoped for love of a different kind, love that knew and forgave our human frailty but did not miniaturize our grander ideas of ourselves.*"– Michael Cunningham

"*IT IS AN ALL-TOO-HUMAN frailty to suppose that a favorable wind will blow forever.*" – Rick Bode

HUSHED, unsettling stillness seduces the space between the tentative greeter and the suspicious guests. Rapid-fire mental, followed by visual, conversation quickly fills the void. "Well, this could be an awkward situation if it weren't for the fact that we're all here to resolve some long-held secrets." Mr. Menendez, while struggling to facilitate the meeting, steps into the pleiotropic space briefly touching mother and daughter shoulders. His position in the lives of these two women gives him a unique perspective on the possible conversation.

Bernice's baroque-designed home offers a perfect setting for juxtaposing the complex issues involved in the discussion that will emerge from this initial meeting. "Will everyone please have a seat?" She extends her hands in a welcoming gesture indicating a choice of several comfortable chairs. "I'm so happy to finally have this overdue opportunity to meet face-to-face with my family. You're aware, by now, that I've been in your lives from the beginning. I've been watching over you. It gives me overwhelming joy to stand close to you and have you realize that we're a family. You're just learning this idea, so I understand that emotions are flooding and questions are tumbling over the past years. We can talk about all of this."

While maintaining their gaze on Bernice, both Dacia and Pamela walk in a "robotic" stance and take their appointed seats in the heavily ornamented, floral chairs. While staring at Bernice, Dacia realizes that the designs inside the house match the style of "Stinky-Poo's" glasses – the sparkly, winged edges flowing freely from the margin of those heavy, dark brown frames. The next thought jumping into her already busy brain is that this rather odd woman is her grandmother.

"I'm not sure if I want to be here right now," Pamela's voice slowly stutters as she shoots a half-terrified glare at Mr. Menendez. "When you took us on this strange trip you indicated that it was a short, rather intriguing drive after the school meeting. You betrayed us, putting everyone into a situation that questions personal trust. I'm very uncomfortable right now." Pamela stands and moves back toward the front door as though she intends to leave.

"No, no wait just a minute, please." Bernice raises her hands and tentatively rushes to intercept her daughters' exit. "I know that all of this is not only a shock but unbelievable. Today you've learned that you have an extended family, that William wasn't the man you thought he was, that the entire high school staff will probably be intimately aware of your family lineage and now I'm introduced to you as your mother. You are also finding out, for the first time, that the people that you thought were your biological parents aren't. I can only imagine that your brain and heart are muddled." Bernice lowers the tone of her voice to calm her daughter's fears, gesturing for her to regain her seat.

"I don't think that I'm ready to consider this much

less talk about it with someone who has been spying on me in high school pretending to be someone that she isn't. Bernice, you have no credibility here. You can't tell me what to do. You're just an old lady who happens to be a high school counselor. You don't even know anything about my daughter and me. I don't want to talk to you about any of this, and I certainly don't want you watching Dacia behind closed doors at the high school. You keep away from her." Pamela firmly grabs Dacia's arm and escorts her to the front door. Mr. Menendez scrambles to follow the duo as they exit the house, offering his apology to Bernice. Bernice stands in the doorway of her home wondering if she has just lost the last remnants of her family just as she was enjoying the rapture of reconnecting.

THE THREE SIT quietly in the car with only the hum of the motor, and the flap of rotating tires indicating movement. Mr. Menendez knows that he's in trouble not only for making emotional presumptions but by betraying a long-held trust. He realizes that he's pushing people he loves into a relationship that they aren't ready for – there is too much to risk, too much to lose. He badly wants people who can like and support each other to meet each other, to be a family, to face the world together, to talk about the hidden past, resolve it and leave it behind, and possibly allow him to be part of their lives. However, pushing the issue will not accomplish his goal. It doesn't mean that he'll abandon his dream, it means that he'll look at the situation from a different angle. He learned by dealing with William that it's better to intervene early in a skewed relationship than to let unaddressed questions go unanswered.

"Well, that didn't turn out as expected. I imagined what would happen when everyone met; after the yelling and tears, the hugs would begin. It's too much right now." Mr. Menendez's words pierced the silence like a shower of small pebbles shooting across the surface of a calm pond. He's acutely aware that the resulting cascading ripples may continue to ruffle the surface of his human relationships. He may lose the delicate kinship of his extended family, but the risk is worth the tsunami.

Again, a repressed silence fills nooks and crannies of the moving vehicle. Dacia uses her position in the front seat to make direct eye contact with both adults. Neither one returns the glance. "I've no idea what's going on with everyone. Messing up things today seems to be normal. All of a sudden, no one likes anybody, and no one is talking about whatever we are all not talking about here today. What's going on?

Who is Stinky-Poo? Isn't she the school counselor? Why were we in her weird house? What's going on? I don't like any of this." This time Dacia prods each adult with determined direct eye contact – again receiving no verbal response. "Okay everybody what the heck is going on? I find out that dad was married to another lady and not going to tell people that I'm his daughter but what happened in that creepy lady's house wasn't about dad. It was about mom or somebody's grandma or something. Somebody tell me something." Dacia leans forward firmly placing her hands on the dashboard to rest her weary forehead in the cradle of her elbows.

Pamela gently places her sympathetic hand on Dacia's back. "I'm not sure why we went to see Ms. McKim-DePue, honey. You're right, she's the high school counselor but why she seemed to expect our visit tonight is as much a mystery to me as it is to you. Maybe Mr. Menendez can answer that question for both of us. Well, sir do you have any answers for us?" Pamela and Dacia simultaneously glare at Mr. Menendez.

"Let me start by saying that I know you've learned a lot of overwhelming information today. I also want you to understand that everything you discovered has been known to me since before both of you were born. William is only a part of the whole story. He simply added elements that make your lives more difficult. My portion of this entire human experience does need redemption; it does present me with a tug-of-war every day of my life. I want to explain every little detail to both of you. However, we are all exhausted. Today's been the longest day of my life, and I imagine that both of you are beyond fatigued. So, I'll drive you home, make sure that you're settled, and we can meet at your house tomorrow morning. My wife and I will be over about 10:00 am. Saturday morning will give us the opportunity to take our time and discuss all the issues." Mr. Memendez's stoic posture tells both females that whatever he has to explain may change their entire perspective on life.

Pamela speaks first. "Okay, you're right. We're both exhausted and can't think clearly. It's best that we continue this tomorrow. We won't sleep, but resting will give us the opportunity to sort things out." Shaking her head is all that Dacia can manage. "I still don't understand any of this, but I'll see you tomorrow." Mr. Menendez drives Pamela and Dacia to their house and watches as they give him the recognized signal that they are safely in their home. His thoughts on the drive home are atonement, regret, anxiety and downright, gut-wrenching fear.

KAYE HANGS up the telephone after talking with Michelle. She collapses into the kitchen chair realizing the full burden of secrecy and deception which has, finally and regrettably, cascaded down upon both her precious granddaughter and her new-found step-grandchild. Involuntarily, her head lowers, both hands clench to her injured breast and her dreary eyes sob. Her grandchildren are hurt; mentally and emotionally. It's a hurt that neither saw coming and an injury that neither can repair; someone they loved and trusted inflicted this scar. Kaye intimately understands this devastating realization; someone who shares your most intimate life betrays you. The fact that the betrayal occurred years ago doesn't soften the blow because each girl, each child, is just now learning of the apostate; they love the betrayer, they hate the betrayer.

At that moment, Kaye decides that she has two granddaughters – not one and an accident, not one and a maybe, not one and a question mark but two full-fledged, natural, biological granddaughters who are equal in every way. She's delighted. Two young females in the Henry family is a good thing.

Notifying Benedict and Anne is the next natural step. The kitchen clock indicates midnight. Kaye considers calling her children to update them about Dacia and Dove-Whispering. Deciding that the issue affects the whole family, she makes the late-night calls.

"I know that you and your brother have questions about this other woman, Pamela. As we all know, her daughter Dacia is your dad's child. That by now, is a proven matter. There is a new wrinkle in this whole issue. It's surely a ripple that will cascade out into our family for generations to come. Remember that everyone is human and experiences life in different ways. This human experience is one of those ripples. It seems as though the counselor at the high school that both Dove-Whispering and Dacia attend is not just a counselor but Pamela's mother. Yes, that makes her Dacia's grandmother. Yes, yes, I know it can't be true, but it is – all of it. My phone conversation with Michelle laid out some of the information when she let me know that the three of them – Pamela, Dacia and the high school counselor, her real name is Bernice, had a meeting with Mr. Menendez at the counselor's house tonight. This counselor lady, the one they call "Stinky-Poo," is Pamela's mother. Well, I can only imagine how the whole thing went." Kaye realizes that she is rambling on and not giving her daughter, Anne useful information about the meeting.

"Mom, take a deep breath. It's been a long day for all of us. I waited for your call since I know the information is still developing concerning the science fair DNA project. My concern is for both Dove-Whispering and Dacia. They're the innocent parties in all of this. It's exhausting even to think that dad was involved in this secret life and now all these people are hurting. It isn't fair. Our family will survive this, mom. You know that we will. Our history of surviving chronic diseases, hard times and other family betrayals have shown us that we are survivors. We can handle this too. You know we can."

Anne's voice reverberates with both fatigue and strength – the true mark of a warrior-survivor. Kaye nods as she listens to her daughter's profound words.

"You're right, sweetie. We can do this. We work together and get things done." The phone line quivers in suspended silence with both parties in the conversation lost in their private thoughts – only the sound of breathing occupies the ripples.

Anne tired - signs off, saying, "It's late mom, I'll call Benedict in the morning. He'll have questions. Things are still messed up in his head. Dad was someone Benedict looked to for guidance, and then he found out that his dad wasn't true. It'll be another tough conversation. Good night."

THE ANNOYING, early morning alarm statically pierces the calm bedroom mood. The resting couple quickly rises to attention. Disoriented, both realize that the alarm clock has once again done its appointed job and jarred the slumbering couple awake. "Oh, it's so early. Do we have to get up at this ungodly hour on Saturday morning, dear? Can't we sleep just a little longer?" Mrs. Menendez groans out her question while knowing the expected answer.

"Yes, dear. Our meeting this morning will change lives. There will be questions to answer. We both know that revealing some of this information may also reveal our past. It's important that we're ready and focused. We can do this." Mr. Menendez tries to reassure his wife as he walks toward the kitchen to make the morning coffee. Nervously, the couple prepares for the long overdue encounter that will articulate the lives of an extended family. Mr. Menendez feels as though he is about to breathe life over smoldering embers. The resulting flames may well burn him alive.

A knock at the front door interrupts the frantic household routine. Pamela and Dacia spent the early morning hours vacillating between periods of manic activity and somber solitude. Things are unsettled in the Henri'/Love household this morning.

"Good morning Mr. Menendez." Pamela greets the familiar visitor accompanied by his wife. Pamela is visibly nervous as she invites her longtime friends to take a seat in the comfortable living room. She senses that the kitchen table will be too barren for this conversation.

"Mom, I heard someone at the door, are the Menendez's here yet?" Dacia comes around the corner and walks straight into the face of two intimately familiar people – they have been in her life since birth. Dacia is accustomed to the social posture of these folks. They seem to occupy a common space in both Pamela's and her life. She knows them in both her personal and social life. They are comfortable. However, something seems different this morning – out of place in their demeanor. They both speak and act as though this is their first meeting. Immediately, Dacia doesn't like any of this. "Well, what is going on here. You guys act like you don't know us." Dacia isn't polite with her comment. Mr. and Mrs. Menendez avert her eye contact and switch their interest in examining the flower pattern on the couch.

"Dacia you're rude to our visitors. They're here to talk about the science fair DNA project and the discussions that have occurred at the high school. We know these people. They are our friends. They have always been good to us. Especially Mr. Menendez, he had always watch out for us and protected us." Pamela sits next to the visitors and motions toward Dacia for her to join her on the couch.

"Yeah, but he also took us to the weird school

counselor's house yesterday and said that she's related to us. He introduces her as "mom" – whatever that means. I find out that I'm related to someone at school, isn't that enough. Everyone in class is whispering behind my back. I wish that I didn't like science. I wish that I hadn't met the new girl who came into the science class. Dove-Whispering is my best friend, and now I hate her. I don't want to hear whatever they have to say." Dacia stands at the corner of the living room sobbing. Pamela slowly walks over to her daughter and gives a soft, encompassing hug. Dacia continues her sobs; Pamela doesn't interrupt.

Mr. Menendez can stand it no more. He walks toward the couple and enfolds them into a protective embrace. "Let's all take a breath. It's something that we can talk about calmly. If you sit over here on the couch, I'll start from the beginning and explain the whole, complicated story."

The three cohorts slowly take their positions on the couch. After everyone takes a deep breath, Mr. Menendez begins.

"First of all, I want you both to call my wife and me by our first names – Dale and Rose. It will make the story so much easier for me to tell. The saga of our families began when Colorado was still developing as a young state. My business partner, Jim Sleazy, and I were what today would be called speculators. We made money by working deals that gave us the most cash. Jim was not only my business partner but my brother as well. He was my half-brother - we had different fathers. In the early rough and tumble days of Colorado, families often found it hard to support themselves. My father left my mother when I was very young. I don't know if he remarried or died, but we never heard from him again. My mother remarried a man that she didn't love so that she could get enough money to survive. I ended up with a little brother – Jim. As we grow up, it's apparent that Jim and I are very different. Jim chose the quick way, the easy way for everything. If there's a short-cut, then that's the way Jim likes things. As you can imagine, he walks a thin line between legal and illegal. He drinks liquor and gets more loose with his business dealings."

Dale stands up in his recitation, adjusting his position. It's evident that revealing the true story of his family is uncomfortable – he paces the living room wringing his hands while looking aimlessly into space. Mr. Menendez feels as though he's being drawn into a sticky spider web.

"Honey, it's okay. You can do this. Remember that it's time for everyone to know the truth." Rose tries to reassure her distressed husband.

Dale regains his seat on the couch and after taking a deep breath continues with his petition. "At this point, it's evident to me that Jim's headed down a dark path in life. He doesn't care about family or honor or consequences. I decide to be his conscious, to be his monitor. Someone needs to steer him, or inevitably he'll end up dead or in prison.

Things change for both Jim and me. We develop a land-speculation business. The Colorado area is expanding rapidly, especially with the discovery of precious metals in the 1900s. Speculators, business men, developers, homesteaders, and railroad men all rush into our once sparse land to grab everything in sight. Jim intends to grab a large piece of that money. Since we have no physical resources, we spend long, fretful hours developing a strategy to achieve that goal. I want a service that supports the people as they move into the area, Jim isn't going to work that hard. The local bar is the scene of Jim's business negotiations.

We struggle but finally set up a small, shabby office on the main street here in BigTon. This town isn't far from Denver, which itself is developing quickly. We don't want to establish our business in a larger city like Denver since it may draw too much attention – don't want too many eyes on our activities. We advertise as land speculators with contacts in both the financial and legal areas; something like a one-stop for buying, preparing and developing the land. The business quickly takes off, so I decide to hire a secretary to help with organization. I'm careful not to choose a beautiful, young girl; she won't last long with Jim around. At the end of the first month interviews, a pleasant enough looking woman in her late 20's answers our needs. She is efficient, friendly, competent and reserved; almost inhibited. The office is ship-shape in no time."

Again, Mr. Menendez gets up from the couch and paces throughout the living room – his nervousness increasing as the tale develops. He feels like a grasshopper sizzling on a hot grill.

"Do you need some coffee or water Dale? I can get some for everyone." Pamela walks toward the kitchen without waiting for an answer. Dale's detailed account of Pamela's and Dacia's genealogy intermixing with the development of BigTon is visibly making everyone in the room increasingly nervous. It's like sitting next to a basket of silent Mexican jumping beans.

"Well, this next part is where the road-of-no-return begins. Jim takes a fancy to our new secretary. She, of course, fends off his advances. Jim decides that since she is female, she is available. I see the inevitable coming and could have stopped it. Sometimes you hear about people being too close to a situation that they can't see the obvious. Well, that isn't the case. I know my brother. I see the situation. I ignore the set-up hoping that my brother may eventually have some redeeming qualities. One evening, after Jim has been drinking all day, he returns to the office to sign some land development papers. I'm scheduled to meet with the newly arrived railroad manager in another building. The secretary and the inebriated Jim are together in the dimly lit office. Jim makes his move. It's a savage attack for which Jim never apologizes. I find our disheveled, young secretary in the office the next morning bitterly crying and muttering incoherently."

Mr. Menendez stops the story again and turns to take a long, questioning look into the starry eyes of Dacia who is transfixed by every detail of the tale. The child hasn't uttered a word or interrupted since the two familiar visitors entered her home. "Dacia, you're old enough to hear the rest of this story. It's about your grandmother, mom and ultimately you. Sometimes, adults, even good adults, act in bad ways. Remember, though that it's what they do that is bad, not the person." Dale breaks his visual hold on the child and accepts a cup of steamy coffee from Pamela. He'll need fortification to continue.

"Mr. Menendez, uh, Dale, I want to hear anything that has to do with my mom. What are you saying about my grandmother, what grandmother?" The information in Dacia's usually logical mind suddenly resembles the activity of a parakeet aviary that has just been invaded by a herd of wild cats.

"Child, you will soon understand about all of your family members when I finish my story. So, I'll continue. "

"He raped me; he raped me," Bernice manages to utter through her sobs. "I fought him off as long as I could but he was drunk, and this office is so small. There's no place to go. I couldn't escape. I couldn't get away. He roughed me up and pinned me in the corner over there. He tore off my clothes and threatened to kill me as he violated me. It was as if a madman or a demon or a monster was inside of his body. Nothing I said made any difference. After it was over, he ran out into the street. Afterward, I think that I passed out. Now, I can't walk, it hurts too bad." I vaguely remember covering the secretary with my overcoat before going to seek medical help.

Rose leans toward Dale and embraces her trembling husband. Dale continues. "My first reaction is disbelief, yet I know that it's happened. The quickness with which the anger swells inside of me surprises me. It's as if someone lit a short burning fuse attached to both gunpowder and hot cayenne pepper. I'm not sure how I find Jim, but I'm standing in front of him as he sits at a corner table in the local bar. He's still in a drunken stupor. His loaded gun is sitting on the table. I approach cautiously, knowing that my brother can be unpredictable. He's especially dangerous when drunk.

The closer I get, the better my view. I see another gun in Jim's right hand with the end of the barrel positioned straight into his chest. The situation is tense. I don't want my brother dead. I want to talk. Jim takes a final, haunting look at me through his dark, empty eyes and pulls the trigger. The hot-shot bullet sears straight through his black, unrepenting heart. Jim is dead."

Dale shivers as he collapses into the arms of his comforting wife. Telling the story of not only his past but the death of his beloved brother resonates throughout his trembling body and threatens to weaken his steadfast resolve to face the atonement of Mr. Menendez's life. Rose finally realizes that her husband, the strong, confident leader that she has always known, is also a fragile, tormented captive of his past. She knows the history but only now realizes that her husband carries guilt and remorse from that life – understanding that his acts of atonement may fail to wipe away his guilt. In this small apartment, it's evident that everyone involved in this intimate, convoluted tale of betrayal, sex, and family cares deeply about William Henry. William's ability to talk and persuade and conceal has affected generations of the Henry family.

Tongue-tied silence creeps into every nook and cranny of the room eventually filling each person with the inconceivable historical realization. Dacia finally breaks the hushed tentacles. "I've been listening to adults for the past few weeks and what I hear are words and stories about the past. I feel kicked around from one direction to the next. My life was beautiful, but within a couple of days, everything changes into confusion. My mother and I were living life after my father, William left. Each day gets better even though we still struggle. We had each other – mom and me, together. Then I find out through science class that I have another family – a secret family. My best friend in the whole world is related to me. Mom and I have become a public spectacle not only in school but throughout the town. I listen to gossip in the school hallways – everybody talks about me. Then I find out that the old, creepy school counselor has not only been spying on me all of my life, but she's my grandmother. A grandmother that I didn't know existed.

To make matters worse, my newly found grand-mother has a sordid past that includes rape, illegal adoption, violence, killing, and land swindles. I'm a kid – just a kid. I don't know what to do about all of this. It's too much for me." Dacia turns toward her mother, Pamela, with an engaging, pleading eye contact. The two exchange a sympathetic understanding. In an attempt to escape the entire, complicated interwoven saga, the emotional child races from the room for refuge in her bedroom. All the while, the impotent adults listen to Dacia's confused, painful cries and wonder what part they play in relieving the terrible situation that William created.

"I'm protecting my daughter. That's the bottom line. Whatever comes out of this whole situation, I'll not let any more pain or confusion come into our lives. She's everything to me. She has a future filled with goodness and wonder and happiness and no one; I repeat no one is going to do anything to change that. So whatever anyone does from here on in, remember what I say today. People think that their actions don't have consequences – but they do. Those actions hurt my daughter. I can handle when I am hurt but not when things damage my child. I hate that I can't protect my daughter from pain. I trusted a man with my heart and my property and my life – now I'm betrayed and abandoned. I agree with Dacia. It's too much. It's overwhelming. It's a crime for which there will never be any punishment." Pamela stands defensively before Dale and Rose with her face engulfed in a veil of defiance yet deference toward the couple who have guided and shaped her life since birth.

Mr. Menendez, slowly regaining his composure, rises to accept her invitation. "I have loved you since your birth, my child. I accept responsibility for William's devious intrusion into your life. My acquaintances were your biological parents, and it is only by secrecy and salvation that Mr. and Mrs. Love accepted you. William's dishonorable intentions toward you were known to me, and I did nothing to block that interaction. Knowing that his family lived in Nevada should have triggered a moral response in both William and me, yet we ignored common decency. I watch over you, yet fail you in every way. Pamela and Dacia, he turns his head toward the girl's bedroom, my wife and I are going to stand by you and support you and work with you until all these family issues resolve." Pamela, Dale, and Rose approach the center of the room and visually assess each other's conviction. Encircling each other, they respond, "we'll make this work, no more pain, no more lies." After a tearful hug, Rose and Dale leave the bewildered mother and child knowing that they're all forever bound.

CHAPTER TWO

Let's Talk

"*This is part of what a family is about. It's knowing that your family will be there watching out for you. Nothing else gives you that. Not money. Not fame. Not work.*" – Mitch Albom

"*BRAVERY IS the choice to show up and listen to another person, be it a loved one or perceived foe, even when it is uncomfortable, painful, or the last thing you want to do.*" – Alaric Hutchinson

PAMELA APPROACHES DACIA'S ROOM; snuggling up next to her confused, sensitive daughter in an attempt to soften the pain of the revealed truth. "Sweetie, I know that what's happened is overwhelming. Everyone's emotional and confused. My first reaction is disbelief especially when I learn that William, the love of my life and your father, was married and had a family in Nevada. I hate him; I love him. I want to kill him; even though he's already dead. I'm working out my feelings. When I think about our relationship, I realize that William taught me a lot. Things that I only now realize I didn't know or didn't understand. I'm experiencing the pain and hurt of our relationship, and I guess that's the reason why I'm forced to understand." Dacia snuggles closer to her mother. Dacia too is confused about her feelings, but she didn't realize that her mother was experiencing similar mental and emotional pain from living with her father. "Mom, what was it like living with dad? I always thought that you two were happy. He made me laugh. Whenever he was around it was like having a party; living on a roller coaster."

Pamela inhales deeply before answering. "That's true sweetie. William did like to have a good time. He'd come into town and bring presents and talk about his traveling adventures. Life was exciting. I believe that he truly cared for me and I know that he loved you with all his heart. He certainly was a good dad. In his eyes, you were the sun, moon, and stars." Pamela gives her daughter an extra tight squeeze as though she is trying to physically transfer the love she feels in her heart into her daughter's body. She wants her daughter to experience a physical sensation of an emotional essence. Dacia's body responds with an extra close, wiggly squeeze.

Pamela loses herself for a few minutes in the perfume of her daughter's closeness. There's much to tell her, so much for her to know about life as a young woman. "Dacia, life with your father, taught me that I'm vulnerable. I didn't know that I was. The idea never occurred to me before I met him. I thought of myself as a successful businesswoman in the community. I manage finances and run a profitable public enterprise. I interact well with city leaders. Honest people know me as an honest person. When your father came into my life, I was looking for something to fill the sensitive, emotional side of my being. I imagine that William recognized that need and saw an opportunity. I'm not saying that your father didn't care for me, but he couldn't truly love me or commit himself to me. The commitment idea was not part of our relationship. Now I understand that concept; I didn't then. I also learned that I'm strong. I'm not talking about the physical strength that allows me to lift heavy objects; it's about internal moral and emotional courage. Since learning the true story about William, I now know that I can deal with our flawed relationship and I am stronger for that knowledge." Pamela faces her daughter and straightens her body to engage eye contact so that her child may understand that out of tragedy and disappointment, out of the crisis, a person can find themselves. "I also want to pass on to you Dacia, the most important lesson of all. I realize that from this point forward, I possess the power in my hands to build the next chapter of my life. The future can be whatever my efforts and abilities make it. That is the lesson for you; from mother to daughter. Within you, my precious child is the ability, strength, and understanding to look at yourself and see the future. Imagine that you contain a crystal orb that conjures strengths and insights. This sphere gathers particles from your ancestors, mixes it with your potential and congeals the fusion into a composite that is waiting for you to develop. Dacia, you are the best of your grand-parents, me and the better part of William."

Dacia quickly breaks her mother's embrace and walks to the doorway of her room. "Mom, I know that you think that I'm some great young woman who can work through all this crazy stuff going on around here – but I'm not. I'm a kid in high school who has kinda lost her best friend in the whole world and now learns that the creepy lady at school that everybody makes fun of is my grandmother. She's a grandmother who's been spying on both of us for years. Mom, that's stupid and creepy and strange and awful. Don't you understand anything? It's not cool. So now I'm like the kid who has a weird disease and lives in a plastic bubble all their life and people watch everything. Everybody in town and the school knows our business. For god sakes mom." Clutching her favorite, soft pillow to her chest for comfort, Dacia slumps into the couch. Her fiery, bouncy curls whip across her furrowed brow, and her blazing green eyes vigorously and involuntarily begin to tear as though a generous genesis has already started.

An exhausting, involuntary breath releases from Pamela as though it belongs to someone else; someone outside of this mother-daughter scene who is exasperated by the inner workings of this intertwined generational situation. Sensing that it's better to keep her distance, Pamela tentatively sits in a chair opposite Dacia. "My sweet child, I'm not saying that I'm emotionally strong or brave. I'm certainly not. William hurt me; he hurt me to the core. His ability to detect my vulnerability and then exploit that weakness was his strength. His hidden talent of reading others emotional weakness, their needs, the voids in their lives, gave him a window into their minds and souls. He then pretended that he was the only one who could fill that void. His persona, his character, gave him a public shield that made him appear as though he was genuinely concerned for them. I now realize that for William it was a game - something or someone to conquer. He enjoyed the process, the adrenaline rush that he must have felt in pursuing something forbidden surely was enjoyable. Unfortunately, he used his talent to destroy our family." Pamela pauses at this point as though she is buried in personal thought remembering long past interactions that both inspire and sadden her. She's unable or unresponsive when Dacia tries to coax her into accepting a gentle hug. Dacia senses that her mother is remembering long-lost, naïve days with a love that both engulfed her and eventually destroyed her. After an emotional silence, Pamela's mood changes into the protective mother that Dacia knows. It suddenly dawns on Dacia that her mother may have once been a young woman just as Dacia is now. That is a thought Dacia will spend time reflecting on, later.

Dacia is jolted back to reality when Pamela continues her thoughts about William. "Dacia, I am still thinking about my relationship with your dad. He hurt me in every way that a man can hurt a woman. He presented himself as a single man available and susceptible to a loving relationship. The signals he sent to me indicated that his intentions in forming a rela-tionship were honorable. It seems as though he's an artesian collecting precious flowers to make a lei to present to Tahitian royalty. Thinking about how

William presented himself, I ask myself questions about his childhood. I still wonder what happened to him. He learned deception over time. Or was he taught to be deceitful because his survival depended on it? He didn't wake up one day and have that knack. The refinement in William's approach to people took years to develop. Maybe he felt inferior and knew that he wasn't a morally strong man or he understood that his character was weak in the area of honesty? Whatever it was, William developed a defense mechanism to counteract his faults instead of facing them. He chose to present an outward mask to the public that projected honesty, confidence, and truth. He had so defined his outward appearance that people thought that the mask of William was the real William." Pamela sits quietly on the couch with her head lowered, apparently exhausted from attempting to explain the unexplainable William.

For the first time, Dacia sees her mother through different eyes. Suddenly, her visual lenses mold into a kaleidoscope viewing her mother as a woman comprised of many parts. Pamela isn't just her mother but a vulnerable, strong, adult woman. However, one thing remains undiscussed – the marriage of her parents. Dacia decides that this is the best time to approach the subject. She feels like a foundling asking for acceptance into an orphanage. "Mom." Dacia slowly walks toward her mother and slides her arm around her relaxed shoulders to soften the impact of the upcoming question. "Why didn't you and dad ever marry?"

The question evokes an attentive response from Pamela.

"Well, it isn't because I didn't want to marry William. We did discuss marriage. When I was pregnant, William and I had extensive and heated discussions about marriage. He always avoided examining the question, and as my pregnancy progressed, it was obvious that something in his past prevented him from a full commitment to our relationship. William never told me what haunted him, but something hidden in his past was following him like a silent ghost. It prevented him from committing himself to both our family and me. Repeated attempts to approach the subject of marriage, brought William to sway the conversation. Finally, a whiff of honesty overcame him, and he told me that he couldn't, and wouldn't, marry me even though he loved both our child and me." Pamela turns to Dacia, full-on, for eye-to-eye contact. She wants her daughter to understand the gravity of their discussion and receive the message of her father's love yet understand that he was a flawed and troubled man. "It's obvious now that William's married and has a family before he meets me. He came to Colorado and entered into a romantic relationship knowing that he was betraying his family.

As we both heard from Mr. Menendez, he also knew that William's family in Nevada believed that William was faithful to them and simply traveled to Colorado because of his duties to the company. William's family never suspected that you and I existed. William refined his secret-keeping and people-deceiving talents especially toward folks who cared for him." Pamela nudges her exhausted body toward the kitchen window; having no real interest in the outdoor flora or fauna. The exhaustion of dealing with the message delivered by the visitor's, and the following discussion, has depleted every reserve Pamela's body can muster. Her battle-weary body and brain collapse inward as though she is a general who has been abandoned by their command. Pamela's long, straight blonde hair gently falls across her shoulder as though a concealing veil is being released from guard duty.

Dacia didn't know the full story of her parent's relationship. She imagined that her mother wanted to be a single, independent woman and that provoked the status of remaining unmarried. Hearing the actual, full details of her mother and father's relationship now clearly shifts the responsibility to her father, William. Dacia must face it – he's the reason that she's a bastard. He's the reason why she doesn't have a legally recognized father. All this time she believed that her mother kept her parents from a binding union. Now she must deal with the fact that it's her father, her dad, her particular person, who is the referee making an awful call in this ball game.

Dacia also realizes that she loved her father unconditionally but didn't know her father. The life that William led before he came into her mother's life was different from the one that he shared with her and her mom. Her dad hid a life that he was trying to escape. Dacia realizes that she is now thinking about personal, family things that she never spent time thinking about before Mr. and Mrs. Menendez made that early morning visit. The stuff that she studies in school is easy to figure out, especially the science class. However, the information about her father and his involvement with Dove-Whispering's family is a part of her dad's life that she still can't figure out. Why would her father intentionally hide that fact that he already had a family in Nevada when he met her mother? Why would her dad, who told her that he loved her, keep secrets from both her and her mother? She doesn't understand what happened to the relationship that wove between herself and her dad. Strangely though, she feels like she is somehow older than she was just a few weeks ago. "Mom, my head hurts thinking about all these things. My heart aches too, I think. I'm going to bed." Dacia grabs her pillow as she snuggles her chin into the comforting material. She is already asleep before flopping onto the bed and winding herself into the rumpled covers.

"HONEY, I want you to understand that you're not responsible for anyone else's actions. Whatever William did or didn't do isn't your concern. Each person makes their own decisions. You knew Bill as well as anyone could and yet even with your guidance, he chose to live his life in deceit and betrayal." Rose's attempts to comfort her husband, knowing that his inability to prevent emotional pain from entering Pamela's life still haunts him, offers slight condolence. "I'm glad though that you did relate the entire story of Bernice, your brother, Pamela and her biological parents. I can tell its lifted a heavy burden from your shoulders. I love you, dear. You're my husband, and our life together has always brought us joy. My eyes and heart hold nothing against you. Even if you don't feel honorable I know you trusted that William would be honorable and true in his relationships. You give everyone the benefit of the doubt. I remember the day you came home and told me that William was going to continue in his relationship with Pamela. Knowing of

William's marriage and family was a moral dilemma; we talked about it for hours. The wrinkles that appear at the corner of your eyes deepen whenever we discuss your relationship with William. The destruction is in your spirit. Remember, my dear husband, that it wasn't you who committed the crime of betrayal, it was William. It was William, not you." Rose's dark, loving eyes radiate uncompromising acceptance for this man that she knows so well.

"You're right, my love. It's time to face the facts, understand them as they are and try to rebuild not only our lives but the lives of the people who are still struggling" – their eyes blink in unison, then lock in a shared understanding. "I'm going to talk with Bernice about our visit with Pamela and Dacia. Knowing the full story may help Bernice to understand her part in this family that is coming together to rebuild itself. Bernice is Pamela's mother and Dacia's grandmother that forms a solid core with which to construct a strong family structure. Bernice needs to know the full story, the complete background so that all the women involved in both the Henry and Love families can talk to each other." Sentiment interwoven with determination sets into Dale and helps to refine his feelings that he can indeed reach the atonement that he so desperately desires. He will talk with Bernice, soon.

'KNOCK, KNOCK, KNOCK.' The unexpected visitor announces himself with a persistent, yet urgent sounding, declaration. "Mercy me. Who could it be at this early hour? I'm not expecting anyone this morning. I'll be right there if you can wait just a minute. I'm just not dressed for company. It takes so much time to fix my hair, and I never seem to be able to find my glasses." Bernice hurries to put herself together, making sure that her rusty-red beehive hairdo is plastered with enough super-hold hairspray so that any stray hair gets firmly set back into place. Her bony fingers perform small rippling actions as they perform one final sweep of the bouffant hairstyle. She grabs her black-rimmed glasses edged with rhinestones from the hall table as she approaches the front door. 'KNOCK, KNOCK, KNOCK.' The persistent intrusion echoes throughout the entryway. "Mercy, mercy. They sure need to keep their pants on – whoever it is." Bernice catches a final breath as she turns the handle of her large front door.

"Well, well my goodness. Did we have an, an appointment this morning? I don't remember writing anything down." Bernice stutters as she examines the face of the persistent visitor. "No, no. We didn't set anything up for today. I have just talked with Pamela

and Dacia, and now it's important that you and I talk."
Bernice steps aside as Mr. Menendez steps over the
all-too-familiar threshold into 'Stinky-Poo's' home.
"Listen, Bernice. We need to get things straight. My
wife and I just talked with Pamela and Dacia. They
know the whole story about the early days of our business here in Colorado. We all talked about what
happened between you and my brother, Jim and how
it resulted in your pregnancy. Having Pamela raised by
Mr. and Mrs. Love was also discussed. Believe me. It's
embarrassing and exhausting talking about all the
mistakes a person makes in their life. It's even harder to
talk about it with the people who have been hurt by
those mistakes. But now that the information is known,
maybe we can think about what the next step is going
to be and put this whole mess back together. I helped
create this and need to start putting things right."

"Wait a minute. First of all, have a seat." Bernice
motions to Dale, guiding him toward the overstuffed
chair situated in the front parlor. "You need to give me
a moment to catch my breath. You caught me off
guard. I don't know what to say. I thought that it was
time to let Pamela know that I was her mother, but
when we met the other evening, things didn't go well.
Now you're telling me that there has been other meetings and discussions." Bernice's unhurried gait reflects
her serious thought. She stands in front of her large

picture window inconspicuously staring in deep, reflective thought. "Dale, we all know that Pamela is my daughter which makes Dacia my granddaughter. Knowing that is different from accepting that and understanding the story behind that truth. I feel unclean knowing that I have been spying on my family for years. Even worse, the entire community now knows that I have intentionally hidden the truth from my family members. It's like a sullen criminal who waits in a dark alley for the opportunity to take advantage of a vulnerable situation. However, in this situation, I'm that sullen criminal. It's a horrible situation that's unforgivable."

Dale allows Bernice her moment of silence and reflection. God knows that he has enough for which to beg forgiveness. His conversations with not only Pamela and Dacia but school members and other community leaders have revealed to him that it is cleansing and cathartic to face the truth of one's past rather than evade the facts. He approaches his lifelong friend slowly. "Bernice, it's okay. Take a breath. You can approach this any way you choose." Bernice turns from the front window into her dimly lit living room. Comfortably positioning herself next to Dale on the couch, Bernice begins the litany of her troubled childhood.

"You never knew what my life was like before you

met me in Colorado. It's time that you know the full truth. I was not the plain, mousy, stable young woman that you thought I was. My mother was still living outside of the small town of BigTon when we met. She was a sought-after prostitute working on Holladay Street in Denver. My father was the resident "professor," – the man who served as bouncer and bartender. My mother was beautiful, artistic and could remove money from a man's pocket faster than a rat devouring rancid meat. I was born and raised in a whore house learning early that the men working on the railroad had plenty of money and were in our house for only one thing – sex. My parents worked at the business night and day. My mom and dad slept until late morning and then would entertain the lusty, loud men until late at night. Sometimes men wandered through the house alone searching for their special girl. I would hear them bellowing out, 'where is my special honey.' All at once my bedroom door would bust open and in the doorway stood a liquored-up, dirty, sweaty guy with a bewildered look on his face. About that time my mother would grab his arm and usher him down the hallway to another room. As I got a little older, I noticed that my mom hesitated as she grabbed the men's arms. My mom looked at me for a moment as though she was thinking of something but each time she would usher the men back down the hall. As I reached my teens, I realized that I was part of the life of the brothel. I accepted that it's routine was my routine. I was slowly becoming a whore, at least in my mind. It became clear to me that that look in my mother's eye was no friend of mine. I was frightened every day of my life. I knew that I had to get out or my mother would indeed turn me into one of her whores." Bernice nervously jumps up from the couch as though she is sitting in a colony of fire ants.

An emotional Bernice rejects physical efforts of comfort from her longtime friend. Dale backs away and verbally offers words of understanding and support. Since Bernice is willing to share this much of her story, maybe she will update it to the time when she met both him and his brother, Jim. So, Dale decides to probe her with a gentle question. "I know it's hard to tell your story Bernice, but did we meet you right after you left the brothel?" Bernice turns back toward the one person in her life that she has learned to trust.

"Oh no. I knew that I needed to leave Denver. The brothel that my mother owned was well known. People knew who I was. So, I decided to move to a small town, hoping to hide out and find work in a small business so that I could support myself. That's how I ended up in BigTon. However, I needed to change my appearance. People could recognize my flaming-red, curly hair. I was tall and tended to stand out in a crowd. Therefore, when I was in public, I didn't want anyone to know that I was in town. That's when I decided to start wearing my disguise glasses. People would look at the flashy glasses and not see me – only the weird, sparkly glasses. Then I saw a picture of an opera star performing at a local theatre. Her beehive hairstyle made her look older than her real age. I knew that the hairstyle would also work for me. My job backstage at that same theatre taught me that certain disguises could adjust my body image. I adopted the sparkly glasses, beehive hairstyle and wore a black, baggy dress. My life settled down.

Then one night I got the shock of my life. My mother came to the theatre bringing her fellow whores with her to see a performance of a prominent female opera singer. Before the show as I was setting up a display, my mother came backstage to meet the singer. I don't think my mother recognized me when we accidentally met in the back hallway, but it was only a matter of time before someone did. Again, I was afraid that my mother would try to pull me back to Holladay Street. That's when I met you and Jim. I appeared as a homely, inexperienced, naïve woman because that's how I wanted people to see me.

Working for you and Jim could help me distance myself from prostitution and all that goes with that type of life. Things went well, and I was feeling secure. Then came that fateful night when your brother Jim raped me. You know the rest of the story." A sense of solace overcomes Bernice. She has finally found the courage to talk about her troubled life with someone she can trust who knows her past and doesn't judge her for it. It's a freedom she has never known – acceptance for herself without wearing a costume or accepting a role in life to be able to function on the fringes of society. It's a releasing sensation to be Bernice.

Dale jumps up from the couch after intently listening to Bernice's fateful life story. "Bernice, I just realized that I'm Pamela's uncle. Pamela is my niece. I didn't understand that family relationship until this very moment. Having been concerned with unraveling everyone else's story, I didn't concentrate on my own. I've felt responsible for her safety but had never accepted or realized that I have a family relationship with Pamela. My guilt has clouded my judgment. You'll have to give me a moment Bernice, to glow in the warmth of the thought that I am an uncle. The idea makes both Pamela and Dacia more precious to my wife and me; we have an extended family. Of course, Bernice, you are a large part of this family.

I guess that talking out issues gives a person a new perspective. I came to your home thinking that you would be resistant to facing the past, but instead, find that we all have something in common; we have a shared past and future. I also understand how much courage it took for you to reveal your history to me. Pamela and Dacia only know you as the creepy, old counselor who works at the high school. A person who stands in the dark hallway at school and watches them as they walk in and out of the building. You're an invisible, background person never having a connection to their destiny. Only we know of your actual relationship.

That horrible night when my brother Jim attacked you, enraged me. I tracked him to his favorite local tavern only wanting to talk or reason with him not hurt him. He had already dug his grave when I found him. The pistol in his hand was the final killing instrument. He knew his sins as he chose to leave this world. It was a dark, fateful, sorrowful night that still grieves my heart.

You had little choice, especially in a small town like BigTon. You and your child could not have a future in this town if people knew the true story of her birth. You and your baby girl needed help. I was as responsible as my brother. After Mr. and Mrs. Love adopted Pamela, your job as a high school counselor allows you to stay close to, and watch, your child on a daily basis. Pamela doesn't know that you're her mother. Well, the relationships have come full circle and are known to the community at-large.

Who could have imagined that two young, high school girls from different parts of the country, would meet in science class and change the lives of so many people?" Both Dale and Bernice sit pensively facing the large front window of Bernice's baroque styled home. Looking at the decorations around her house, Bernice finally notices a hidden reality. She has decorated in the exact style of her mother's Holladay Street brothel. In trying to escape her past, Bernice has unconsciously recreated that exact physical environment in her everyday life. It's a stark reality that she now realizes. She will begin her redesigning tomorrow.

"Well, Bernice I'm going home. I'm tired. All this drudging up the past is exhausting. My wife will be expecting me and want to know developments with the situation and people surrounding William. I've talked to everyone involved with his story. Now, it's time for people to meet and decide how to come together as a family. We'll talk again soon." Dale gives Bernice a reassuring hug and slowly shuffles out to his car, his beleaguered body and mute mind are devoid of conscious thought.

"*M*emories are dangerous things. You turn them over and over until you know every touch and corner, but still, you'll find an edge to cut you.*"–* Mark Lawrence, *Prince of Thorns*

"WHEN YOU GIVE *yourself permission to communicate what matters to you in every situation you will have peace despite rejection or disapproval. Putting a voice to your soul helps you to let go of the negative energy of fear and regret.*" – Shannon L. Alder

KAYE HENRY SITS at the kitchen table examining her 1969 wedding photo. As she considers the man and woman lovingly embraced in the picture, she realizes that it is her trusting ability that makes her vulnerable and her naïve, tendency to love deeply – an everlasting love – that makes her unable to accept inevitable, yet foreseen relationship outcomes. Kaye is "the sticking kind" of a woman. Her marriage to, and life with, William may have been predetermined. Although there's no way for Kaye to know the outcome of her marriage on her wedding day, speckles of suspicion surround their relationship. She should have been able to see the signs – to detect the trace - of betrayal that would befall her family in years to come. She married a man she barely knew. A man simultaneously gifted at deception and love is a talented man, indeed. It's only after deep reflection on their life together that Kaye can understand the interplay between love and left-handed deceit. William became a master at the game. Kaye was unconditionally in love with William. William talked about love yet lacked the commitment of the word.

Becoming disenamoured with their marriage, William made a decision that would affect the next three generations of his family. Instead of discussing the issue with Kaye or asking for a divorce, William devised an alternate plan – he removed himself from the marriage. An affair with a vulnerable woman in another state and working in a job that sat on the gray side of legal framed the illicit escape. William's untimely death left a wake of damage not unlike the remains of a tropical tsunami. Debris litters each. There is a truth that Kaye has realized she must accept. It's a theme that must run through the remainder of her life. She must "let it go." Kaye is thinking about the emotional and psychological scars of her life with William – not the life events. If she holds on to the pain and agony of past events then that "holding on" will interfere with the business of life that continues with the next generation. There is a thread of certainty that weaves through life – life goes on. Kaye's ancestors will know nothing of the deep, intimate psychological pain that William caused so many people. All the ancestors will know is that at one point in history their grandparents were married and had a family. The family won't be curious about grand-ma's pain only about grandpa's girlfriend. They will want to know why grandpa had a girlfriend, what her name was and where she lived – just the important stuff. Holding on to grief and anger for Kaye holds her back from enjoying a full and happy life with her family. So, she must let it go. That journey will be arduous, but Kaye resolves to stay on course.

Kaye also views the 1899 wedding picture of her paternal grandparents. Reviewing her aunt's stories of the abuse suffered at the hands of her grandfather, it's evident that the effects of her ancestor's abusive and chaotic upbringing influenced the current generation of her family. Had Kaye unknowingly married a man just like other men in her family? A searing memory of her grandfather's marital betrayal still makes unwanted entries into her everyday thoughts. Kaye chillingly remembers a poignant conversation. "My mother told me of her first meeting with her father-in-law. After repeatedly knocking at the front door of my grandfather's home, my parents entered and called out his name, but he didn't answer. They searched the house, following the moans and groans until they found him in the bedroom in a sexual encounter with his girlfriend. My grandfather didn't seem to be disturbed by the incident and without moving from the bed, unceremoniously introduced his girlfriend to his new daughter-in-law. He made no excuse for his situation and didn't attempt to cover his half-nude body or remove himself from his sexual position." My mother went on to explain that my grandfather had many girlfriends and often brought them home to introduce them to his children. Kaye's aunts confirm that as they reached their young adult years, their father's abuse and sexual exploits motivated their move from the family home.

Another memory haunts Dacia's stepmom and Dove-Whispering's grandmother. When she's in fifth grade, her teacher approaches one afternoon and makes a rather strange statement. "You don't know me other than as your school teacher, but I know your father very well." The thought seems strange at the time and causes wonder for a few years until Kaye graduates from grade school. She never was brave enough to approach her teacher for an explanation. Finally, after mustering her courage at the graduation ceremony, Kaye askes the teacher if she remembered making the statement. The teacher's reply surprised her. "Well, of course, I do, Kaye. I could have been your mother. That's how well I know your father." Kaye realizes that both her father and grandfather were unfaithful to their marriages. At that moment, Kaye vows that she will never marry a deceitful man.

These probing thoughts occupy her mind as she reviews the unfolding events her family faces. The knowledge of their fathers' "hidden" family in Colorado has changed the lives of Michelle, Anne, and Benedict. Each child has responded differently. Benedict seems to be struggling and confused. His emotional bond with his father was and is sturdy. His father was a strong male role model. To learn and accept that his role model was flawed and human is not an easy acceptance for Benedict. His stoic personality won't allow him to demonstrate his feelings or talk about his concerns, emotionally. It's a complicated process for Benedict. How does he resolve the issue of honoring his father yet accept that his role model leads to a deceitful life? Benedict has always been physically strong but psychological matters are complicated for him; emotional scars are like an iron anvil pulling him back to his past. Benedict is a hefty, broad-shouldered young man. His well-groomed dark brown beard and medium length hair are streaked with slight waves of silver. These threads reveal his genetic connection to a family trait; turning gray early in life. These strands are also representative of his vulnerability. This vulnerability sometimes prevents Benedict from allowing anyone to assist him in working out his issues. This turmoil is emotionally painful for Benedict – it makes him very uncomfortable. He's willing to support his sisters in performing physical duties such as moving furniture or adjusting heavy objects in the yard. Sometimes, he will even work on their broken car. However, when it comes to sitting down at the family table for a holiday dinner, he is extremely uncomfortable and makes excuses to either not attend or leave the function early if an intimate conversation occurs. Benedict will not be emotionally open to discussing his father's life in Colorado. As far as Benedict's concern, his father had no presence in Colorado.

Anne loved her father without reserve. Her soft manner and gentle heart always brought out the protective side of her father. When William brought home a puppy, Anne knew that it was just for her. She embraced the new family pet with as much love and attention as the small animal could endure. Anne's heart was always "worn on her sleeve" which put her into positions that made her vulnerable to heartache. Whatever her dad said was a world truth. If her father told her that he was going to take her to a movie, Anne was ready to go an hour in advance. She would dress in her best clothes, make sure to complete her homework, and her shoes were polished. Her dad was her everything. Anne's crystal blue eyes and golden-white hair matched her china skin tone perfectly. She often wished that she could join her dad for long naps in the afternoon sun. However, her delicate skin would surely catch the sun rays early and turn as red as the setting sun within minutes. Although her physical features resembled her mother, there was still a large, loving place in her heart for her dad.

When it's evident that her father, her one and only, isn't an honest man, isn't a real man, she doesn't understand. How could the man who was so kind to her hurt someone else? Even though she was no longer a child and had knowledge of the world, the facts don't make any sense. She had heard her father say that he loved his family. She had seen her dad kiss her mom. She had seen her dad be happy when he was with the family. How could he love another family? How could he keep a secret bank account to take care of that "other" family? Her brain heard people talking about her dad, but her heart couldn't believe the words. They didn't sound right and didn't seem to fit her idea of her dad. It was all very confusing. Things were better when she could hold her cuddly dog and try to remember that it was a special gift from her dad. Anne always made life better for her family if she could. By making it better for them, she felt better about herself. The idea of her dad having a girlfriend and another child horrified her. It meant that her dad might not love her anymore. If her dad left her mother, did her dad also leave her? Just the thought was unsettling. Anne's heart ruled, and she couldn't figure things out with her head. Resolving the issue with Pamela and Dacia and the weird school counselor was going to very difficult for Anne.

MICHELLE'S PERSONALITY is like a tornado that sucks the air from a room when she enters. She's the child who most identified with her dad – latching onto his fun-loving ways and risk-taking adventures. William functioned best when his adrenaline was surging, and the stakes were high. If he could wait until a deadline to complete a project or file paperwork, then that was just what he did. It offered him a chance to feel alive. Everyday life was left behind, and William could, just for a moment, be faster, bigger, better, more significant and ahead of the pack. William always liked that kind of life. Some would call it an "addictive" personality. Military life offered a balanced opportunity that fit well into William's thought process. It gave him structure and routine to balance out his periods of intensity yet provided opportunities to travel and explore options away from home.

Michelle studied her father intently deciding for herself which behaviors she wanted to adopt for her lifestyle. She always struggled with the tendencies that she chose. Michelle liked the glare of the bright lights and roar of the party scene but couldn't handle the debilitating consequence of the aftermath. Michelle's soft, coffee-brown eyes are carbon copies of her father's memorable brown, almond-shaped inviting eyes - although the eyes of her father could ping-pong between laughing and predatory when he was in a pervasive mood. Michelle was also the child who inherited her father's skin. In that I mean, she could stand in the sun for a few minutes and receive a rich, lush, berry-brown tan that was the envy of the neighborhood. In that respect, she was her father's child. Michelle's soft brown curls fell easily across her strong shoulders and showcased her lovely, curvy, female figure. Michelle's resistance to learning that her father has taken a lover occupies every thought in her brain. Other conscious or unconscious brain activity doesn't occur. She begins to mentally review her entire life – her life as a daughter, worshiping her father.

Slowly, she realizes that it's possible. Indeed, a grown woman with a child that Michelle had never met would not make up a story about her father. For heaven sake, we are talking about people who are living in a different state, people who have never met her. Why would someone like that make up a silly story about her family? Michelle has met Pamela and Dacia. They are real people. Dacia is Dove-Whispering's best friend. Her daughter, Dove-Whispering, is an excellent judge of character and wouldn't befriend someone who wasn't honest. There are too many facts, and related coincidence's for the information about her father not to be suspicious. Michelle wants to, needs to, know more about Pamela and Dacia. Michelle wants to know the entire story of her dad's life in Colorado.

Dacia is Kaye's step-daughter. This fact may not be fully realized yet by her other biological children. Her three children with William – Benedict, Michelle, and

Anne, may or may not accept or embrace this unknown young woman into their established family. However, it's a truth that Dacia is indeed their sister. Dacia also is Dove-Whispering's aunt. All of these ancestors and intertwined connections smack up against a wall of the establishment: the establishment of a family of the known line of relationships, the comfort of knowing who is who and how everyone is related to everyone else. Kaye knows her children well, and each finds comfort in understanding where they fit in a particular pattern. How will they embrace the knowledge of their relationship with Pamela and Dacia? What did their father see in these two females that enticed him into sharing pieces of his life with them?

KAYE KNOWS that if each family, and each member of each family, is to approach this puzzle of needs left from William's life, she must begin the process. She was William's recognized wife; she bore William's legal heirs, she is his lawful widow. She will be the one to approach Mr. Menendez and begin the discussion. William's boss has talked with her on the phone many times, especially after her husband's death - but never in a personal manner. The two of them had a brief exchange at William's bedside when he was on his hospital deathbed - under strained pretenses. It's time to change the relationship. She will talk to Dale and Rose on a different level. They are no longer a Mr. and Mrs. Menendez, and she is no longer the wife of a former employee. She is now the matriarch of a questioning family that dearly needs to address long-held secrets, and the Menendez's have been keepers of those secrets. The parties must be on equal footing to discuss family secrets.

Kaye initiates the first step. Her unconditional acceptance of both her step-daughter, Dacia and granddaughter, Dove-Whispering is all-encompassing and absolute. Kaye is quite fond of Dacia's curly, fire-red hair and Dove-Whispering has those unique almond-shaped, dark brown eyes in which a person can lose themselves. These two young women have taken up lodging in her crumpled and aging heart in such a way as to rekindle small recesses that still harbor glimmers of hope and love. Just seeing these vivacious girls together convinces her that the next generation of the Henry family is not only surviving but is the unbroken and achieving lineage of their ancestors. These two high school friends will secure their biological line – for Kaye; there is no doubt. Dacia and Dove-Whispering know nothing of the torrid, deceitful ways of past generations, specifically

William's. Dacia knows him as her loving father; Dove-Whispering knows him as a kind and fun-loving grandpa. That's the persona he presented to each – that's the mask William wore for each girl to see. Each girl believed that she was related to a loving man that cared for her and only her. Howbeit, he was at once a grandfather and father living a lie and weaving a web of deceit that would follow the next generations of his family. William's hubris followed him so entirely that the revelation of his deception was unfathomable even to him. Dacia and Dove-Whispering bring a new perspective, a new view, of the Henry family. They each know of their relationship, but the sorted details of how that relationship wedges into the dynamics of the family, aren't yet outlined for them.

KAYE FEELS PHYSICALLY heavy and emotionally weak as she considers the next step – her husband's lover and their intimate life. Just retrieving memories of discovering the tender love script in William's brief-case burns her soul as if it is a searing dagger. Regard-less, she knows that if her family is going to reconcile, if her beloved children, step-child, and grandchild are going to enjoy a full and happy life, then the secrets of the past need to be examined and discussed. The sorted amorous affair needs to be revealed and addressed. Kaye's awareness of the history assures her that to secure a secret in silence brings searing pain to everyone. So, the decision is - Kaye will call Pamela. She will call "the other woman." Instantly, she wants to change her mind. Her heart rate increases, her palms are sweaty, her previous clear vision seems to dull, her muscles twitch ever-so-slightly, and her mental focus blurs. She's involuntarily transported back to that devastating moment when she's sitting at the desk searching through the contents of her husband's briefcase: her sensitive fingers quiver as they remember tracing the perfumed document while removing it from its' hidden creases. This illicit thought transforms into feeling as her body shivers, and she feels her spine attempting to readjust her skeletal structure.

Mustering courage that she can only retrieve from the far reaches of her stirring soul, Kaye stares intently at her cell phone. Looking at the telephone almost dissuades. Kaye clenching her fist breathes deeply. She can do this!

Blind determination guides her as she picks up the cell phone; she hasn't realized until now that she doesn't know Pamela's phone number. All of her thought, all of her concentration - wasted. What to do? She can't approach Pamela unannounced at her home.

Kaye tries to think of who she knows that also knows Pamela. The only candidate is Mr. Menendez.

She fortifies and resigns herself to contact the man who employed her husband – her unfaithful partner. Her husband's employer has been in a position to know the truth about William's double life. Mr. Menendez, Dale, knows both sides of William's story - although he's just getting the opportunity to understand the "legal" aspect a lot better. Kaye's brief encounters with the employer have never revealed suspicious information, but Dale has been a shadowy, background figure to her. Her most recent contact with him at the high school when the results of the science fair revealed familial relationships between the Henry and Love family, gave Kaye an in-depth view of how intensely connected he was to Pamela and her daughter Dacia. That thought gives her pause in continuing with the phone call. Hesitation threatens to weaken her resolve. However, she places her hand back on her cell phone. She is calling Pamela's uncle, but she will also be dialing the number of the man who holds answers to her family's past.

"Hello, Mr. Menendez, this is Kaye, Mrs. Henry, Bill's wife." Silence resonates up and down the phone frequency - anticipation on one end, suspicion and possibly terror on the other. Kaye, enduring the painful silence, assesses the tenor of Dale's thoughts when he responds. "Uh, yes. Of course, I know who you are. We have met a few times. I expected you to call. It may be time for all of us to talk about issues in William's life. I'm assuming that's why you're calling." Again there's silence on the airways. Kaye is trying not to respond emotionally to the words that are traveling through her ear canal and threatening to embed themselves in her sensitive neurons. She holds the phone away from her ear since the vibrations of Mr. Menendez's voice is almost more than she can endure. This voice is the voice of the man who employed, and talked with, and discussed issues with, her husband. She remembers hearing this voice as she greeted her husband's employer when he came to visit William on his hospital deathbed. This man may well have known that William had a family living in Nevada. He certainly knew that William was already married when he began working in Colorado.

Kaye steadies herself. "May I call you Dale? The term, Mr. Menendez sounds formal. Since we seem to have a history together, it's time for you and me to talk on a less formal basis." Kaye tries to relay a note of moderate intensity into their desultory conversation to set a clear tone for the base of their relationship. "Well, sure. Dale will be fine, although I feel a little awkward referring to you by your first name. I don't even know your full name." Kaye lets the silence linger for an appropriate amount of time to relay the thought that addressing her so informally might not be well received.

"For now, Dale, I think that if you call me Mrs. Henry, it will be fine. I don't want you to get me confused with anyone else." Kaye knows that Dale refers to Pamela as William's wife and she wants to start the relationship with a defined association. "Okay, Mrs. Henry when can we meet and begin to talk?" Dale has accepted the ground rules and seems eager to further the discussion – he may be willing to face his atonement. However, Kaye isn't interested in having "that" discussion with Dale just yet. Kaye is more interested in securing Pamela's phone number. The discussion between Dale and Mrs. Henry certainly will occur, but later. "What I want to know is the phone number for Pamela. You see, I want to talk to her about some issues. I think it's important to talk to her face-to-face and woman-to-woman.

As you know very well, Dale, both Pamela and I have a personal interest in William." Dale has learned to wait a moment before responding, especially in emotionally tight situations. "Well, yes of course. I can give you the number. She and I talk on a regular basis. She may even be expecting your call. It's good that you're contacting her." Kaye notes a veiled quivering in his voice – a vulnerable tension that she hadn't detected previously. When Kaye listened to Mr. Menendez talk at the high school, he projected forcefully and possessed almost an intoxicating tone; a man who speaks persuasively. However, when discussing Pamela, he unconvincingly tries to maintain his public persona. Kaye senses that Dale may also be detecting her vulnerability during their conversation– she anguishes over exposing her intentions. "Thanks so much for the phone contact, Mr. Menendez. I'll contact Pamela and set up a meeting."

CHAPTER FOUR

The Other Woman

"*True love should never be hid. If you're a secret then your probably just an option, not a priority.*" – Tony A. Gaskins, Jr.

THOSE WHO CHEAT *on their partners who are loyal to them; don't deserve them. It is a trashy attitude to disrespect a person who is loyal in a relationship, by cheating on ...her.*" – Ellen J. Barrier

PAMELA ABSENTMINDEDLY PICKS up her ringing telephone without much thought toward the caller. She and Dacia have been trying to rouse themselves from a fitful sleep. Both seem to have experienced a night filled with weird dreams and upset stomachs. Pamela feels that their late night conversation was the cause. Dacia senses that the inability to understand her father is the real reason for her sleepiness. Whatever the motive, both are caught off guard by the early morning call. "Hello, this is Pamela." There is a sudden silence on the other end of the call. Pamela hesitantly removes the phone from her ear as though she perceives the call to be from someone calling a wrong number. Then she hears a pleading voice call out – "No, don't hang up." Pamela replaces the phone to her ear; curious about the message but more cautious about the caller. "This is Kaye, Dove-Whispering's grandmother, and Michelle's mother. We met at the public meeting at the high school when we discussed the results of the science project." Kaye nervously waits for an answer. "Yes, I remember you. But why are you calling me?" Pamela doesn't want to offer too much information until she knows the true reason for the call from this suspicious woman. She instantly senses her heart rate increase, her breathing becoming short and rapid, her eyelids twitch and palms sweat. Her voice may reveal her body tension. She is acutely aware that she, Pamela, is the "other woman" in this conversation. "Well, Pamela, you and I both know who we are. We both cared deeply about William. I am his widow, and I know that you were his, well what do I call you, his girlfriend. Let's start this conversation by being honest with each other." Kaye realizes that she has been holding her breath and after speaking, takes a deep, lung-filling breath. Not a zephyr breath but a fortification that a person needs when they brace themselves against an oncoming storm. This phone conversation could be the beginning of a verbal understanding between, the "other women," each one connected to opposite sides of the same man.

TENTATIVELY LISTENING TO PHONE SILENCE, neither woman initially speaks. Pamela is the first to respond. "Well, I don't know what to say right now. My emotions wrap around my words, like the claws of a large eagle. I need to center myself." Sensing hesitation, Kaye continues. "Mr. Menendez and I had a short talk – that's how I got your phone number. He knows that I'm calling. It's important that we talk, Pamela. My family is important to me; precious gems hold less value for me in this world. That's why I'm making this call. You and I know about each other. It's time that we know each other. We are both aware that our relationship affects the entire family. I'm not saying that I want to get to know you – I need to know you, for my family." Kaye is feeling calmer now that she is talking about her reason for calling. However, her true emotions and motives must remain hidden until she can determine this woman's inner character. Kaye's year-weary lines around her mouth deepen as she struggles to hold back the true direction of her words. "Well, Kaye. Can I call you Kaye? Or would Mrs. Henry be better? I'm not sure about this entire experience." Kaye senses an opportunity to take the psychological upper hand at this point, so she takes a moment to consider her answer. "Kaye will be okay, for now." Pamela breathes deeply. "I'm relieved Kaye that you made the first call. I saw you at the high school meeting but knew that it was inappropriate to approach you at such a public gathering. Even though the community knows our family situation, we haven't had the opportunity to meet much less talk to each other." Pamela is desperately trying to maintain an even status with Kaye even though she senses that Kaye has the upper hand, at least legally. Kaye finds herself clenching her fist as she listens to Pamela. "Yes Pamela, everyone does know both of us and everyone connected to us – no thanks to William and his wayward ways." Kaye surprises herself with the last half of that statement. She has revealed more than she wanted about her feelings. Pamela listens with a heavy heart. She's reminded of Kaye's pain by the simple existence of both she and her daughter, Dacia. Their presence is a physical reminder of William's lies and betrayal. Pamela carefully considers her next statement.

"Kaye, I want to say that I truly didn't know that William was married when I met him. He told me that he was single and didn't have any children. I believed him. He was as convincing as a preacher in a pulpit. His ability to spin a tale was spellbinding. It's not an excuse; I'm just trying to explain. I was vulnerable, and he picked up on that fact." Pamela wants to say what is obvious; to say what Kaye is thinking. Again there is phone silence.

"Pamela, I'm wedged between hatred, anger, and forgiveness. The only reason I even considered calling you is to ease the pain for my family. Benedict, Michelle, Anne, and Dove-Whispering need to understand William's life in Colorado. They also need to know you and Dacia; since you are now part of our family. William is dead, but as usual, we are all left to deal with the issues he created. I can't deal with this alone. It's got to be a family function. Even though I don't like the idea, we need to arrange to meet and talk about William and our family." Pamela relaxes her shoulders and considers her answer while twirling her long, golden hair; an annoying, nervous habit she recently acquired.

"Kaye, I'm not sure what you want me to do.

Should we meet somewhere or talk about things on the phone?" Kaye feels her frustration growing. She's not sure if it's from talking with 'the other woman' or because the entire subject still causes her such pain. She does know that she's aggravated that William is still negatively influencing her family's life long after his death. The pain and intensity seem to be getting greater. Maybe it's because the issue causing the pain is getting closer and closer. She also senses that Pamela is on the other end of the telephone waiting for an answer.

"Even though I don't want to Pamela, we should meet each other face-to-face." Kaye sensed that her phone call to Pamela would end in just this manner - Kaye would be forced to meet Pamela. Maybe she wanted it that way? Now it was time for Kaye to face the difficulty of differences. She knows that this woman is the source of her family's psychological pain, and mental distress and the shredding tightly held familial bonds. "Pamela, before we go any further in this discussion, I need to say that our talk will help me to examine and release what I have been holding onto related to my life with William. It's for my sake and emotional survival. I also need to know how I missed the signs of betrayal. Even though I was married to a man for thirty-five years, I didn't know that man. It feels like I have been intimately painting a mosaic picture yet I failed to understand that the paint, the medium, was manipulating my brush strokes instead of me controlling the paintbrush. The portrait was determined long before I picked up the brush. I'm doing this for me, not for you. Right now, I don't even like you."

"I don't know how you feel Kaye. I can only imagine a reverse situation. Right now, that's all that I can say – other than to say that I'm sorry." Pamela's voice slowly trails off since she understands that there is no expected or appropriate answer. Once again the phone line is quiet; snuffed out of audible noise – human or otherwise. As though communication is being held, hostage. Ever so slowly breathing is detected on Kaye's end of the conversation. Her words startle even her by their intensity and sharpness.

"We'll have to meet each other, Pamela. You know Colorado better than I do. I'm willing to come to where you are and sit down in a public place so that we can talk. I can spend some time visiting my Michelle and Dove-Whispering. However, I don't want you to think that this meeting is in any way a social gathering. It's just you and me sitting down to examine each other. I don't want anyone else at this first meeting. It's important to me that you understand. I'm sure that you are brave enough to present yourself for that kind of session." Kaye wants to present herself as someone in charge of the situation before they physically meet each other.

"I'm open for that, Kaye. You're right. I do know this area of Colorado very well, and I'm sure that I can locate a public restaurant where we can arrange to meet. Let me know when you'll be in town, and I'll decide on a good meeting place. I'll make sure that it is between my house and Michelle's house. That way neither one of us will have to travel very far." Pamela wants to appear congenial in this situation so that the tense conversation continues amicably. She's acutely aware that this phone exchange sets the tone for the upcoming meeting.

"Alright, I'll arrange a visit with my daughter Michelle and let you know when I'll be in Colorado. Goodbye." Pamela is startled by the abrupt ending of the conversation but then realizes that she has been talking with William's wife – the mother of William's children, William's widow. Pamela senses an invisible veil covering her face that threatens to thicken her vision. Her perceptions of her life with William is set. She loved him; he loved her. It's simple. Their love produced a beautiful daughter, Dacia and their family life was loving and real. However, that unforgettable day when Dacia's science project revealed family secrets is still haunting because the secrets are still revealing and revealing and revealing. Each revelation seems to bring pain and discontent. Pamela is slowly becoming aware of the true consequences of being the 'other woman.' She has just agreed to meet the person who ranks Pamela as the 'other woman.' The status is real for her. This awareness brings the full weight of William's weakness crashing through Pamela's pretense. Pamela is the 'other woman.'

Pamela's thoughts absorb her so intently that her daughters' words only now become audible to her. "Mom, mom I have been talking to you for five minutes. What did you talk about on the phone? Who was calling you? The conversation was so intense I thought that someone was dead." Only now does Pamela realize that her daughter, Dacia was standing next to her trying to discern the substance of her telephone call.

Still half in deep reflection, Pamela responds. "That was William's wife, Dove-Whispering's grandmother" – was all that she could whisper.

"Oh my god. Oh my god. She called you. You're kidding, right." Dacia flops down on the couch next to her mom, reeling from the news. "What did she say? What did you say? Was there yelling? Did you talk about dad, I mean her husband, I mean dad? I don't know what I mean anymore." Dacia grabs and cuddles her favorite soft, squishy pillow that she rescues for situations just like this – untangling her fiery-red locks as they mingle in the folds of the material. The sparkle of her usually bright green eyes seems to be hidden behind a screen of scrutiny. Pamela differs from her daughter in one respect. When her emotions rouse or issues become intense, Pamela's bright, blue-purple eyes brighten with an intensity that would challenge a deep, tropical sea. Her polished stare is a reflection of her mental existence into the world of uncertainty. The full realization of being on the fringes of marital legalization hadn't been real for her until this conversation with Kaye. The full impact of that status upon her daughter is also just now cascading down upon her. The 'other woman' status is not the ending she had envisioned – yet that's where she finds herself. She cared for William exceedingly well, and for that attention, the legacy is a public admonishment. It may not be her relationship with William but the realization that there's a family attached to William's betrayal that is finally coming to light which causes her so much uncertainty. Pamela snuggles next to Dacia fully embracing her and sharing comfort from the soft, squishy pillow.

As MICHELLE ANSWERS THE PHONE, she recognizes

her mother's phone number displaying on the screen. "Well hello, mom. What's up?"

Kaye waits a few seconds so that her message receives its full measure. "I talked with Pamela." Michelle is at full attention. Dove-Whispering previously occupied with organizing her wardrobe, notices the difference in her mother's awareness. Both mom and daughter are now attentive to the phone call. Dove-Whispering knows that when grandma calls something important will probably be happening.

"Well, I'll be coming to spend a little time with you guys in Colorado. Pamela and I are going to meet in person. Our strained phone call could start a process of discussion for all of us."

"Well, I don't know how to respond to that mom. We've met publicly but taking this conversation down to an individual level could bring out information that would cause you concern. We all know the basics of the relationship. Do you want to know intimate details of Pamela's and dad's affair?"

"No, I don't want to know. I have to know."

Dove-Whispering can wait no longer and jumps into the conversation. "What's going on? Why is grandma calling? Why are you talking about Pamela? Is there something wrong with Dacia?" Dove-Whispering is excitedly standing next to her mother as though they are Siamese twins.

"Shush, girl. I'm trying to hear what she's saying." Michelle returns to her mom's conversation.

"Don't worry sweetie. I'm able to talk with Pamela. I need to understand this woman so that I can understand myself. It will be okay." Just talking with her daughter seems to give Kaye a renewed strength and purpose in her mission – fully face her husband's life. "I'll be at your house in a few days and probably stay for a couple of weeks. It will be okay. Don't worry." Kaye's voice has a new sense of strength. Mother and daughter end their conversation on an uncertain but determined note. However, the scene is just beginning for Dove-Whispering.

"Mom, what did grandma say? When is she coming? Is Dacia in trouble? Am I in trouble? What's going on?" Michelle hugs her excited daughter as much to calm her as to reassure her.

"Don't worry sweetie. Grandma is coming to stay with us for a couple of weeks. She and Pamela are going to meet each other and talk about your grandpa." Dove-Whispering's body assumes a staunch, silent position.

"Mom, if they talk about grandpa then everybody will know about the things that he did. I loved grandpa; he loved me. People shouldn't talk about him; he's dead. He did some bad things, but he wasn't bad for me. I know that he hurt grandma, but I can't forget the nice things that he did." Michelle tries to soften her daughter's posture and console her fears by offering a tender embrace. However, Dove-Whispering is distraught and retreats into her pensive thoughts which have always assisted her in mentally resolving her emotional issues. The two women part company with Michelle wondering how she can support her daughter to deal with matters that stab at the core of her emotional and psychological attachments – especially those relating to her grandfather. Dove-Whispering resolves to talk with her best friend, Dacia so that they both can discuss the real issues of their relationship, not the emotional barriers conjured up by all the adults in this situation. Dove-Whispering is positive that both she and Dacia can resolve any issues – they're best friends forever, and related. Besides adults have old ideas and don't look at all of the problems. She and Dacia can always discuss these family things with Ms. Walters, their science teacher; nothing's too much for her.

CHAPTER FIVE

Poking Skeletons

"*We dance round in a ring and suppose, but the secret sits in the middle and knows.*" – Robert Frost, *The Secret Sits*

"I NEVER UNDERSTOOD *why Clark Kent was so hell-bent on keeping Lois Lane in the dark.*"
– Audrey Niffenegger,
The Time Traveler's Wife

"YOU CANNOT GO POKING *skeletons in the closet without making maggots wriggle.*"
– Salena Godden, *Springfield Road*

"WELL GIRLS, it's good to see you. We haven't had a chance to talk since that public meeting to discuss the science fair DNA results. How are you doing these days?" Ms. Walters greets her two favorite science students with outstretched arms – expecting a positive response. Dacia responds for both girls.

"Our families are talking about the results all the time. People are making phone calls and visiting each other. All we hear is the tail end of whatever is going on with everyone." Dove breaks into the litany with her remarks. "If we would have known the raucous that this project was going to cause we surely would have chosen another idea to test. People seem to forget that we are also involved with the test results. We didn't know that we are related. It doesn't change the fact that we'll be best friends forever." Both girls take a seat in the classroom indicating that they are here to do more than visit their favorite teacher and relay a quick, friendly greeting.

"Uh, what we want to know is how the tests prove that we're genetically related. Don't care, but if everyone is going to be all upset about the results, then we want to make sure that things are right. We want to be able to talk about the DNA tests and what they mean." Dove echoes Dacia's words with an affirmative nod and shoulder shrug.

Ms. Walters slowly walks over to the classroom

smartboard to outline the issues of DNA – knowing that she has her students' full and undivided attention. Even though the class has discussed the guidelines, Ms. Walters wants to review specifics with these two students. "As you remember DNA testing was initially used in the early 1990s to identify historical figures such as the Romanov family, Thomas Jefferson and Charles Darwin. In the early 2000s technology had advanced sufficiently to make individual testing available to the general population. Present-day tests are refined and specific to not only test for genetic connections but can track regional and continent locations. The extended results may also reveal links to health and illness conditions."

Dove interrupts her science teacher as though to indicate that the teacher is reviewing known information. "Yes, we know all of that. What we want to know is about Dacia and me."

Ms. Walters shakes her head in understanding. "I know girls. Be patient; I'm getting to that. I can't pass up an opportunity to do a little education for my favorite students. I don't often get a chance like this." Each girl waits impatiently. "Now, as I was about to say. Our cells use DNA to control its' function. A small part of the deoxyribonucleic acid, the genes, carry the instructions for the blueprint - molecules of DNA pair-up to form chromosomes. Each cell has 23 pairs of chromosomes. Those chromosomes are what the lab examines when we sent in your buccal swabs for the DNA science fair project."

Dove can't endure the lesson any longer. "Yes, we know all of that too. We memorized that information to prepare for the competition judging. We need to know how the lab determined that Dacia and I are related."

Ms. Walters, sensing the frustration that her favorite students are experiencing, grabs a piece of paper and a pencil to draw out in an elemental way the results of the DNA testing. "Come here girls; I'll draw out the results. You'll be able to see the connection." She knows that the two girls normally wouldn't need a physical graph, but this particular science project was very close to their hearts and causing emotional unrest for both of them. The teacher begins by graphing the marriage of Kaye and William complete with the outline of their three initial children – Benedict, Michelle, and Anne. Both girls agree with this graph. The science teacher then tentatively pushes the envelope by penciling-in the relationship between Wiliam and Pamela. After graphing this outline, Ms. Walters halts and waits for feedback from the students.

Dacia responds first, - "Well, it is more upsetting when I see things written out on paper. I don't like to see my mother penciled in like this. She looks like an afterthought. I know it's true, but I don't like it. My dad never told me. I want to cry and be angry and talk to my dad." Dacia's face flushes, and her piercing green eyes resemble fresh, swaying Kentucky bluegrass. Sensing her best friends' distress, Dove comforts Dacia. Ms. Walters waits for the girls to console each other.

"Let's continue with the chart. I know it's difficult, but both of you will have a better understanding of your family structure." The science teacher then completes Doves' relationship to Dacia on the family outline. Both girls gaze in amazement at the completed genealogy chart. Ms. Walters gives them a moment to analyze the results. Two things are initially clear: Dacia is listed on the same level as William's acknowledged children, and Dove is drawn below Michelle – one of William's daughters. It takes a few minutes for her struggling students to understand the graph. Ms. Walters finally states the obvious – Dacia is Dove's aunt.

This time it's Dove who responds. "It can't be! It can't be! We are best friends. She can't be my aunt. Something is screwy with the printout. I don't understand. How can my best friend be my aunt? We never met each other before we started coming to this high school. This chart isn't right. I can't look at this thing." Dove reaches out her arm and shoves the paper to the floor, stepping on the pencil as she races from the room – followed quickly by her best friend. Ms. Walters is distressed by the manner in which she has had to relay her students' family connection. The science teacher assumes that each of the student's families explained the more delicate details of the DNA results. She now knows that the opposite is true.

———

THE SCIENCE TEACHER watches as the two friends walk hand-in-hand down the hallway toward the front door of the school. They're so absorbed in their conversation that they ignore a greeting from the school counselor as they pass. The friends are walking so closely together that their long, flowing hair intermingles to resemble a loosely interwoven, multi-colored braid as they exit the school.

"Well, I imagine that those girls are so involved in a personal conversation that they failed to notice that I was trying to talk to them." The counselor, who has been absent-mindedly talking to herself, is interrupted by Ms. Walters. The science teacher, watching the interaction at the front door, wants to solicit the counselor's help in supporting the girls through their transition into a blended family. Little does the science teacher know that 'stinky-poo' is already intimately involved in the transition. "Good morning Ms. McKim-DePue how are you this morning?"

"I'm doing fine Ms. Walters." Each of the school employee's attempts to glean information from the other without revealing information – each is an advocate for the two students, and each has watched the pair exit the building. Since the daily school schedule allows for a short break in the routine, the two employees decide to spend a bit of time 'farming' information from the other.

"Well, Ms. Walters, I guess that people are still talking about the results of the science fair projects?" Bernice tries to get the upper hand in the conversation. Ms. Walters, being tight-lipped about personal information, isn't about to spread any idle rumors, real or imagined – about her students, especially her favorite ones.

"Everyone knows the state lab delivered all the DNA results. Everything checked out. I'm sure that you're referring to Dacia and Dove since we both watched the girls walk out of the building together. The entire community knows that they're related. It's no secret." Bernice is intimately aware of the information. She's checking to see if the science teacher discovered the in-depth connections of the Henry family – especially her place within the family. Bernice softens her speech knowing that Ms. Walters holds a special position in her classroom for these two girls.

"I watch the students in school, and everyday something unfolds that tells a story. Seeing the graduates move on always gives me pause to reflect on my own life. However, these two students occupy special positions in my life. I can't explain any more than that right now. Maybe the entire saga will be revealed, maybe not. Whatever the story, I will only do things that help those girls."

'Stinky-Poo' hesitates to make eye contact with Ms. Walters because the science teacher has come to know the counselor all too well over the years. A suspicious look in 'Stinky-Poo's' eyes could betray her at this moment, and the full sorted, concealed, convoluted story would be known. Bernice hesitates to reveal her intimate connection to these two special students even though she does trust Ms. Walters. The school counselor offers a polite good-bye to her fellow staff member and hurries to follow her younger family members as they exit the school building. Although Bernice isn't brave enough to approach Dacia individually just yet, under the camouflage of her school position, the curious grandmother intends to continue her surveillance. She observes the two best friends standing in the parking lot absorbed in deep conversation. They're unaware of her presence. Even if they knew that she was there, she's almost a fixture of the school premises – something to be dismissed. Bernice decides to slowly walk up behind the girls and unofficially eavesdrop on their discussion. The tone of their conversation gradually increases. "I don't care what she said, that DNA stuff can sometimes be wrong. Just because she's a science teacher doesn't mean that she's an expert in genetics. It's not that I wouldn't like to be related to you, but I don't think that it's true. My grandpa was a good man. He wouldn't do things to hurt other people." Dove's voice intensity escalates to match her emotions. Her dark raven hair and warm brown eyes seem to deepen with energy - matching her concern. Dove harbors fond, loving memories of her grandfather. Learning intimate family secrets in such a public manner is indeed distressing. Her grandpa loves her, and it's not fair for him to spread his love around to so many people without concern for her. Her grandpa was supposed to love her, not everyone – mostly just her. Dacia is tuned into her best friend and understands that their discussion with the science teacher has been the most upsetting interaction of both of their lives. Her father not only has other children but was already married when he met her mother – plus, she is Dove's aunt. How can she be an aunt to her best friend? Dacia suspects that most of the stories her dad told her weren't true. The stories were merely things that made her and her mom, Pamela, feel better. Dacia also is emotionally nervous since she learned that the spooky school counselor is indeed her grandmother. The late night visit from the long-time family friend, Mr. Menendez was not only traumatic but changed the entire direction of Dacia's life. She has not yet told Dove about that visit or the visitor. However, Dove's keen eye and sharp, perceptive skills sense that her friend's, and now she must face facts – her aunt's, usual cheerful attitude has changed. Dacia has become watchful, secretive and suspicious without an apparent reason. Dove is ready to ask Dacia about her behavior when someone approaches that they know intimately well.

"Hello, girls, having a little girl talk? It's a nice morning for such a thing." Both girls turn in the direction of the greeting only to stare smack into the eyes of 'stinky-poo.' Dacia and Dove freeze in place. If they could both be Lot's wife as the family is fleeing the biblical city and be turned into pillars of salt or stone - or whatever the solid, mute material was - then that is their wish. However, this is the present day, and they live in a thriving city.

Bernice, the school counselor, pretends to be oblivious to their reaction and continues her greeting. "I noticed that you met with Ms. Walters this morning. Did your discussion about the science fair go well?"

The expression on the student's faces suggests to Bernice that her abrupt approach isn't welcome. However, she detects a slight accepting glint in Dacia's eyes that she hadn't seen in any student in the school. Usually, when she approaches students, they spend an enormous amount of energy making excuses to avoid interacting with her. Dacia is the first to acknowledge her presence. Words slowly tumble from Dacia's mouth.

"Uh, uh, yeah it was okay. We talked about a lot of stuff." Dacia deliberately lowers her head so that her sharp green eyes avoid direct contact – still not believing that this odd counselor is her grandma. However, for the first time, Dacia notices that her ruby-tinged hair matches the amber streaks in the counselors greying hairstyle. Even in a dated beehive hairdo, the comparison is suggestive. Dacia doesn't like the queasy feeling in her stomach. She senses it's related to the close physical presence of the counselor. Dove decides to rescue the pair.

"We need to get back to class. Ms. Walters wants us to review plans for the regional science fair. Since our project has such unexpected results, school administrators scheduled the project for the regional contest. Our science teacher wants to talk to our parents about the trip. We don't want to travel with the project, but Ms. Walters convinced us to explain the process and unusual results to the judges. All the adults seem to think that it's a great opportunity for the school." Dove grabs Dacia's arm, and both girls huddle back into the high school. Bernice watches the science students hurry away. The girls seem to be escaping an uncomfortable situation and walking into an undesirable position that holds more significant implications. The counselor follows them into the high school recalling all of the unfolding family situations. She wants a sense of direction for not only her daughter and granddaughter but all of the extended family members. The events of recent days have cast her family into a sense of aimless drifting that resembles an empty quiver searching for amenable arrows and a balanced bowman.

Ms. WALTERS MEETS the counselor as she re-enters the school. "Can we talk for a minute Ms. McKim-DePue?" The science teacher moves close enough to 'stinky-poo' in an attempt to shift her direction so that the counselor has little chance to suggest otherwise.

"Well, I do have some duties in my office, but I can spare a few minutes. What do you want to talk about?" Ms. Walters wants to set the tone for a friendly conversation.

"We have been working together for many years Ms. McKim-De-Pue, but I don't know your first name. After all this time I would like for both of us to get to know each other better. Generally, the school staff gathers in the employee break room, but I noticed that you don't use that room. You don't take your breaks or lunch in that area. So, we haven't had the opportunity to talk." Ms. Walters waits for the school counselor to reply. An instant stab of panic shoots throughout Bernice's body. Thinking is impossible; muscle movement resembles mortar. Mental chaos instantly ensures in Bernice's brain: 'What could this woman want? What information does she already know? All of the hidden events in Bernice's past life instantly spring into focus. All is lost; all will be revealed. Lies and false stories will be revealed. This science teacher is brilliant so she must already know all the hidden information. The teacher has never talked like this to me before today. What makes today different? Does she know about my connection to Dacia and Pamela?' Bernice is so utterly lost in her mental fog that she's not aware of Ms. Walter's persistent nudge on her arm.

"Excuse me, excuse me. Are you okay? Do you feel alright?" A familiar voice gradually comes into audio focus, and 'stinky-poo'recognizes it as words of the science teacher.

"I'm okay. I just lost my concentration for a

minute. Now, what were you asking me? Do you want to know something about the teacher's lounge?" Bernice is still trying to regain her verbal skills.

"No, No, Ms. McKim-DePue, I want to get to know you better. We work together every day, and I don't even know your first name. Do you mind if we exchange first names'? My first name is Erica. What is yours?" Bernice has never intentionally shared her name with anyone for many years. She is uncomfortable revealing even this small bit of personal information.

"Well, I don't get personal with the people at work." The school counselor feels like this lady is asking her to strip off her clothes and parade around naked in the science classroom. Shivers quickly vibrate up Bernice's spine.

"Well, I must confess to you that I already know your first name, it's Bernice. I found out your full name when we were arranging the science fair committee. The school secretary keeps a roster of all the personnel and Mr. Menendez, and I reviewed the list when we were nominating individuals for committee judges. It was Mr. Menendez who decided that you would not want the position. He said that it had something to do with prior, personal commitments. I didn't mean to pry; I read your name on the personnel list."

The school counselor's fears quiet, and she feels

herself taking a deep breath which lowers the position of her elevated shoulders. "You're right; I'm Bernice. Now I know that you're Erica. I don't mean to be rude but is there a reason why you wanted us to exchange first names?"

Ms. Walters begins her speech slowly. "As you know, I have two brilliant and special students in my science class. As you also know, as everyone does, they are genetically related. I believe that the DNA results prove that Dacia is Dove's aunt. Well, I have been teaching and watching students in this high school for almost as long as you. That means that I am a pretty good judge of people and can tell when something unspoken is going on. I am an honest person, so I'll tell you what I see. I have watched you observe the students particularly Pamela, and then as the years have gone by, her daughter Dacia. You have watched those girls with a passion. Not the caring concern of a school counselor but the guiding, watchful eye of a mother hen. Yes, that's a good analogy. Like a mother hen watching and guiding her baby chicks to keep them out of danger."

Bernice can hardly believe the hard, plain talk that is coming from this science teacher. She's about ready to interrupt.

"No, no don't interrupt me just yet. I have more to say. I am a science teacher. I study forensics. I look at facts because the facts tell a story. I keep an artificial human skeleton displayed in the classroom. I keep it there because it not only gives the students a lesson in anatomy but offers other lessons that they can learn when they poke a skeleton. Poking the skeleton makes it shiver and shake. The students learn that all of the bones are connected. They observe that the muscles help to connect the joints and the joints help the bones to move. Then they learn that the muscles need blood and nerves to function properly. So every time one of the students pokes the skeleton, they learn intimate details about the body – mainly that every part is connected." Ms. Walters waits for the delivery of her message to be received and the analogy to situations surrounding the DNA project for the science fair. Bernice instantly grabs the significance of the similarity but is not about to share any family details with this forensics fortuneteller.

"Well, it's nice that you have a skeleton in the classroom for the students. I'm sure that they enjoy working with it – especially when you poke it and everything that's connected shakes and rattles. Also, I have enjoyed meeting you on a more personal basis and enjoyed our little chat. When we meet each other in the hallway, I will be sure to say hello. We can greet each other as fellow school employees. It's also nice to know your first name, Erica. I'll have to get back to my paperwork, but we can talk again. Bye for now." The counselor makes a quick exit because she feels the urge rising in her to lower her secretive guard and begin the fragments of friendship with another human being. It's an unfamiliar and uneasy feeling. A feeling that Bernice is sure will end up in compromising her position with Pamela and Dacia.

"Well, it was nice to have this little chat. Maybe, we can do it again sometime?" Ms. Walters walks 'stinky-poo' to the classroom door and bids the fellow school employee good-bye.

CHAPTER SIX

The Male Perspective

"*A son is not a judge of his father, but the conscious of the father is in his son.*"
– Simon Soloveychik

"*WHAT WAS silent in the father speaks in the son, and often I found in the son the unveiled secrets of the father.*" – Friedrick Nietzsche

---

"WHAT IS this I hear about you making a trip to Colorado?" He intentionally places his hands on his hip to strengthen the delivery of his message. Benedict can be an intimidating figure with his tall, broad stature filling a door frame when he enters a room. His powerful, muscular jaw and thick neck naturally match his imposing physical structure. Only his slightly greying, wheat-colored hair and piercing blue eyes betray a faint inner softness which Benedict struggles to hide.

"Mom, I was talking to Michelle, and she says that you're planning a trip to see her and Dove-Whispering. Why would you go to Colorado? I know you're involved in that big squawk at the high school, but it's all a farce. The results of the science project that Dove-Whispering is doing is all bunk. There's no truth to any of it. You know that dad didn't mix with any women when he worked there. He certainly didn't have any other kids with anyone." Benedict's voice vibrates with an intensity almost to the point of being a challenge as he addresses his mother. There is no tender embrace or loving kiss from her eldest child only a threatening accusation that his mother is inching into tentative emotional territory that may challenge his father's memory. "There's no reason for you to pry into something that you don't understand." Benedict has walked further into the kitchen area so that he is now standing a couple of feet away from his startled mother. Kaye senses that her son wants to portray anger, but she knows her eldest child well. Her boy is showing his vulnerable side and expressing fear and uncertainty just as in his youth when he felt threatened. Benedict doesn't want anyone to know, not even his mother, that William's only son doesn't trust the full truth about his dad. Besides, he's held the memory of his father in select parts of his brain and his heart. It's the naïve collection of childhood memories that he trusts. If his mother rifles through hidden family secrets and finds that what is known isn't true, then Benedict's father-son past won't be real; for Benedict that unacceptable.

Benedict stiffens his massive body as Kaye offers him an enveloping hug. "I do love you, son. Your father's death has been hard in so many ways; he left unresolved issues that we're all trying to work through. I wish that I could make the process easier for you but if I talk with the people in Colorado, then maybe we can all learn the truth about our family."

Benedict intentionally places his hands firmly on his mother's shoulders and gives her a slight shove – just enough pressure to make his point. Kaye's apprehension turns into concern as she senses physical danger from her son. This threat never existed between them until the discovery of Pamela Love. "I don't want to hear any more about anything. You have been talking crap about dad since he died. None of what you say is true. He was a good dad, and you're hurting his memory. Stop all this talking to people. I don't want any of this in my life. He didn't have a girl-friend and didn't have a child."

Kaye braces herself against the kitchen cabinet – unsure of her son's next reaction. For a brief moment, Benedict hesitates before stepping back from his mom – surprised at himself that she's evoked such a physical response in him. "Mom, I'm not sorry that I touched you in that way, issues swirling around dad make me so mad. I don't know what to believe anymore. I want to remember dad in my way, not the way things might have happened."

Kaye steadies herself. "Son, you're out of control. What you just did is unacceptable. It changes our rela-tionship. Even if you're feeling bad, it doesn't permit you to be abusive to me. It's not okay. I'll remember this forever. I'm dealing with your dad's betrayal, and you always make things harder for me. You, my son, should be helping me, supporting me when I'm trying to figure out a challenge. Instead, you make my life more difficult. You're old enough to know better. You're a man. It's time that you look at life from an adult point of view."

Intensity consumes Benedict's piercing, blue eyes with such emotion that it's difficult for the openings to contain his inner explosive feeling. Kaye knows that if her son is going to follow through on his physical threat, it will be at this terrifying moment. She catches her breath, waiting with both fear and determination. Kaye intentionally avoids direct eye contact, yet something tells her that for the survival of this encounter, close scrutinize of her son is crucial. A glance in Benedict's direction is all she can manage. Benedict stiffens his muscular body while clenching his fists – he holds this frozen position for an eternity. Palpable intensity vibrates between mother and son. "I don't need you in my life." The scathing words saturate Kaye as though they're progressive, sharp nails slowly scraping down a slate blackboard. Benedict turns and quickly storms from her house – intentionally slamming the front door, leaving a weak door hinge to flap in distress. Kaye lowers her shoulders and inhales a deep, lung-filling breath realizing that it's the first cleansing breath she's taken in the last few minutes - then she pauses and takes another. The tense scene seems to have held the room air captive and his leaving releases a fresh spring breeze. The distraught mother collapses into her kitchen chair sobbing uncontrollably; not only has she lost her husband but now, her son as well. Her tears release the romanticized image that Kaye has held of her beloved, eldest child.

COULD the view she held of her husband also have

been romanticized? Kaye loved William with blind attention usually reserved only for tightly bonded mothers and newborns. Every like and dislike of her lover was known intimately. His moods and attitudes were ingrained in her so deeply that she could almost sense before he walked through the door how their evening would unfold. Kaye knew what kind of bread William liked to eat and how high he would pile the lettuce on his sandwich. The strength of his coffee was something that William knew Kaye would always get just right. William's military fatigues always pass inspection with just the right amount of starch – Kaye perfected the technique after their first few months of marriage. Kaye cut William's hair, so it conforms to military code – high and tight.

Still, she wonders. What did William see? From his male perspective did he automatically expect her to know these things? Since Kaye did these personal care duties without thinking and because she loved William, was the rest of their relationship also expected – at least from his point of view? Did William assume that Kaye fit into a military wife stereotype? Was that the big mistake of their marriage? William believed that he could take Kaye for granted knowing that he already has her undying love. Kaye is a "known" for William. The male ego of William doesn't need to keep winning the female in his life because she's conquered, she's already his. Why should an adventurous man who likes adrenaline rushes and new adventures be concerned with a conquest that's achieved? William won Kaye. Kaye is his. William is looking for new conquests. Kaye needs to be honest with herself; she never considered this viewpoint in their marriage. She assumes that since she loves William totally, he loves her, totally. Looking back on their relationship together, Kaye's only now entertains the idea that William's male perspective wasn't her perspective. William didn't love her with the same kind of love – it's conditional love. A love that not only fades over time but conveniently wanes when they are not together. A bigger question now enters her mind. Is this the difference between male and female love? Is there a difference between the female perspective and the male perspective? All of this rational conversation is as exhausting and threatening to Kaye as her recent physical encounter with her son.

Finally, Kaye understands the reason for her mental anguish. It has little to do with the female/male perspective as it has to do with the fact that she has a female body. It's biology. She's a female and William was a male. She and William looked at the world differently. This one fact sets the tone for their marriage. William was looking at the world with male eyes. He was using his male brain to develop their relationship. William's idea enveloped the fact that women do not offend men – in any way. The structure of the world, in fact, all of society, is built toward a male perspective. The legal system, public sentiment, the business environment, and even public restrooms are all designed to accommodate the male perspective.

This male perspective in society reinforced or formed, William's attitude of a man's superiority. Add in William's unrealistic bent toward adrenaline rushes, and risk-taking behavior and the picture is slowly coming into focus for Kaye of a man who's involved in the fantasy of pursuing "the woman who got away." All woman naturally would be sensitive to his male charms and vulnerable to a relationship with him. Since women, in general, don't "offend" men, there should be no issues with his wife, Kaye. William was already involved with Kaye and their family – that pursuit is over. Therefore, engaging in a tantalizing quest with a gorgeous young woman fits perfectly into William's personality. When Pamela succumbs to William and agrees to their relationship, it was another conquest for William. The problem arises when Pamela wants to make the partnership permanent, especially when she becomes pregnant with William's child. Kaye imagines that William feels trapped. Even when Mr. Menendez approached William about the tenuous aspect of his relationship with Pamela,

William's obvious response of anger reveals that there's a slight crack the veneer of his male perspective. Never the less, William maintains his precarious relationship with Pamela and their child, Dacia. The situation resembles a grizzly bear destroying a busy beehive to steal the sweet honey. The bear knows from experience that he'll encounter a painful situation because the bees will sting multiple times, but he also remembers that the savory taste of the succulent honey is well worth the excruciating pain. The bear rushes in – blinded by luscious lust.

Of course, all of this refrain is speculation. Kaye can only surmise the issue that exists between William and Pamela and Dacia. William's no longer here to explain or defend himself. No one knows with certainty what the man at the center of this controversy thought when he waded into this grizzly tale. What would William say? What would William do if he had the opportunity to redo his initial interaction with Pamela? What would William tell Mr. Menendez if he were offered the job in Colorado, today? If William had not taken the position in Colorado and continued to live with his wife Kaye in Nevada, he wouldn't have met his girlfriend, Pamela and they may not have had a romantic relationship. The child, Dacia, from that liaison, possibly would not have been born. Therefore, Dacia wouldn't be Kaye's, step-child. If Dacia hadn't been born and subsequently grown into a teenager who entered a Colorado high school, then she may not have met and become best friends with Dove-Whispering, William's granddaughter; who also entered the same Colorado high school. If Dacia and Dove-Whispering hadn't both loved science, they would not have met Ms. Walters, the high school science teacher. If the two best friends hadn't met Ms. Walters, then they may not have developed the DNA project for their science competition. If their science project wasn't considered for the regional program, then Dacia and Dove-Whispering may never have known about their genetic relationship. These two best friends mothers', Michelle and Pamela, became involved in this family saga during the science fair committee meeting. This committed genetic relationship forced the high school counselor, 'Stinky-Poo,' whose real name is Ms. Bernice McKim-DePue, to reveal her sorted past and family relationship to Pamela, Dacia and Mr. and Mrs. Menendez. When Kaye's son, Benedict, becomes aware of this interwoven, biological Scrabble-game he not only denies its' existence but refuses his father's participation in it or cause for it. This denial leads to a fierce and permanent separation between mother and son.

Kaye looks at this situation from a female perspective which admittedly is different and maybe opposite from the male perspective. The result of Williams' intentions is clear; the extended Henry family is experiencing emotional pain, psychological anxiety, and uncertain genealogy patterns. However, the uncertain environment is also a time of change for Kaye's extended family. Positive things can occur when change is in the air. There's a new and flexible generation within the family – best friends, Dacia and Dove-Whispering. These intelligent young women don't carry the negative, heart-crushing memory of love's betrayal within their consciousness. Both girls seem to look at their place in the family as a positive, friendly process. This fresh viewpoint may be the new beginning for this beleaguered clan. Kaye knows that beginnings launch when attitudes are open and fresh – when views come from fresh eyes and new concepts. That's why the next generation will be the saving grace of the Henry family. Dacia and Dove-Whispering like each other; they are best friends. That's a strong foundation on which to build a sturdy family structure. Kaye will foster and maintain the relationship between her step-daughter and granddaughter. They're the building blocks of the family that she and William began. Kaye's heart is broken, and her trust seduced, but expectations for the future look bright.

CHAPTER SEVEN

Mother-Daughter Talk

"*His leaving wasn't about you. It was about him.*" – Iyanla Vanzant

"*My father died many years ago, and yet when something special happens to me, I talk to him secretly not really knowing whether he hears, but it makes me feel better to half believe it.*" – Natasha Josefowitz

Sensitive conversations all usually initiated by her mom. Dacia isn't comfortable talking about the softer, emotional side of life; especially with her mom about her dad. There have been plenty of hushed dialogues in this house swirling around her mom's relationship with her dad: all of them resulting in closed doors and emotional exhaustion. Dacia's conversation in the science room with Ms. Walters about the DNA project was a stark reminder of her position in the Henry family relationships. Dacia knows the scientific aspect of DNA and how it endeavors to reveal the genealogical connection of family members. She has heard the school board and science committee discussing the results of the project. However, she isn't prepared for the reality of the information. When Ms. Walters draws out the physical outline of the DNA results showing her not only as a legally, fatherless child but the aunt of her best friend, Dacia can't comprehend the vast reality of it all. Her heavy exhaustive exhale is an outward symbol of Dacia 's emotional uncertainty. She tentatively approaches her mother intent on having "that" talk with mom about dad.

"Mom, can I talk to you about something?" Pamela turns away from her bookkeeping duties at the hotel front desk to have a face-to-face conversation with her beloved daughter; giving Dacia an engrossing hug.

"Sure honey, what do you want to talk about?" Dacia raises her chin so that her inquisitive green eyes match the crystal blues of her mother. Dacia hadn't noticed the slightly visible age lines at the edge of mom's eyes until now.

"I know that everyone has been talking about the results of our DNA science project. Understanding the science is pretty clear to me. What I don't know is what it means for me." Pamela takes ahold of her daughter's shoulder and walks her back to a more private area of the office. Pamela knows that this conversation is important to her daughter.

"I'm sure that you're thinking about your father. You loved him deeply. You saw him through a loving daughter's eyes. I understand that. You certainly have been exposed to a lot of adult ideas in the past few months. I would say that you have grown up quickly because of those ideas." Pamela takes a deep breath when she realizes that she has monopolized the conversation and not given her daughter a chance to ask her original question.

"I'm sorry Dacia. You wanted to ask me a question, and I just offered you information before you had a chance to say anything." Dacia lowers her head in agreement, with a slight knowing smile appearing on her face and a loving twinkle in those captivating green eyes, understanding that her mother automatically offers protective information whenever subjects of her daughter occur in a conversation; even if it's her daughter who initiates the inquiry.

"It's okay mom. I love you too. What I want to know is about your relationship with dad. When you first saw him, what did you think? When he came into the front office to rent a room, what did he say to make you like him? Was he attractive to you? Do I want to know what made you like him? So much has happened because of that first meeting between you and dad, I have to know why you liked each other." Pamela takes a moment to realize the transition that has occurred in her daughter. The vortex of emotional events surrounding the science project has so intently occupied her every waking moment; she hasn't realized the emotional and psychological effect that these same events have germinated within her daughter; Dacia is growing up.

"Well, when William walked into the front office that shifting day I didn't view him differently than any other potential border looking to secure a rented room. He mentioned a personal referral from Mr. Menendez, so I assumed that my life-long friend had already secured a completed review of his background. When someone that you have known your entire life gives you a personal assurance of credibility for someone you take it at face value; you believe it. So I assumed that William was a credible person who was working with Mr. Menendez. It's a cruel twist of fate that I now know that Mr. Menendez is not only a life-long friend but also, my uncle. However, you already know that story. Anyway, back to your question." Pamela takes a quick, pensive moment to reflect on the irony of the convolution of her extended family connections.

"What I didn't notice about William's innate ability to 'read' people. By that I mean he would watch a person to determine their weakness; something that he could exploit. It wasn't necessarily a bad thing; just a knack that William used to make himself personable. A trait that he could work with to start a conversation or develop a relationship. It made him a good salesman. That trait is what Mr. Menendez saw in William. That ability helped to make William a top salesperson in the insurance recovery business. Mr. Menendez exploited that tendency in William and overlooked his reckless unfair advantage in business dealings. It helped their business expand into previously unworked areas. That is why Mr. Menendez assigned William to work in the Colorado area. William surely did a good job here for his boss." Dacia is quickly becoming bored with her mom's long-winded explanation of irrelevant facts. Dacia wants to know about the mushy, lovey stuff between her mom and dad, not all the other stuff. "Mom, why did you like dad?"

"Okay, okay, I understand. Your dad found me lonely and vulnerable. He wanted a romantic fling. He was married but wasn't satisfied with that relationship and needed some zing or forbidden rushes to make his life a little more interesting. I don't think that love initially had anything to do with it. He 'worked' on me slowly." Dacia looked square into her mom's dreamy eyes,

"What do you mean, mom 'worked' on you?"

"Well, I was vulnerable. Being a young, single woman sends out a beacon to certain men, saying; 'I'm available.' Married men are supposed to ignore that signal because they're committed to a romantic relationship with someone they love. Some men disregard societal norms and take a calculated risk of emotional encounters. William, your dad, was one of those men. He complimented me on my physical attributes; blond hair, blue eyes, good physical figure often taking small opportunities to touch my hand and slide his arm next to my shoulder. He would initiate a conversation about physical interactions between young men and women thereby creating opportunities where we could physically talk and touch in a private or secluded fashion. Slowly, I began to understand his words and actions more than his physical appearance. I'm not saying that he wasn't personally attractive, it's just that I didn't notice slight bodily signs that I should have seen; a tan line on his left ring finger, an in-depth knowledge of young children's development and growth patterns, etc. I accepted him for what he appeared to be – an attractive, professional, single man who cared for me. I liked the easy manner in which my hair was stroked, the gentle way he hugged my shoulders, the concern he showed when I was upset and the fashion with which he caressed my hand while helping me sort the office mail. Our relationship grew closer when he rented a room and received his mail here in the hotel." Dacia wasn't only engrossed in her mother's description of her relationship with her dad but realizing that her mother was once young like herself. The thought of her mom being an attractive young woman hadn't occurred to Dacia much less that her mother would be romantically involved with a man.

"So, what you're saying mom, is that you didn't like dad right away; at least as a boyfriend. He liked you first and chased you."

"Yes, I guess that's true. You're old enough to know the rest of my story, sweetie. When your dad suggested that we share an apartment here in the hotel, it was a turning point in our relationship. I wasn't sure how I felt about your dad at that point. His proposal that we move our meetings, our interactions to another level forced me to examine my feelings for your dad. It took time for me to decide my intentions.

Once determined, I was committed to a full romantic union. I loved William and was willing to give myself physically and emotionally; he was the man of my future. He kept his private mail address, but we lived together in the same apartment. We were living as a married couple in every way except legally."

"Mom, are you saying that's when you and dad first had sex?" Pamela physically jerks as she considers the unexpected question from her daughter.

"Uh, well, uh, I'm a little uncomfortable saying yes or no to that question, sweetie. Your dad and I did love each other enough to engage in sex, but exactly when that happens is a little tricky for me to explain to you. But yes, we did have sex and did love each other very much."

Dacia looks at her mom suspiciously, "If dad loved you, why didn't he marry you?"

"As you know now, sweetie, your dad was already married at the time. If he married me, he would have to divorce his wife in Nevada. That would involve telling his family about me. I was the 'girlfriend' the 'other woman.' His family didn't know about me or William's relationship with me here in Colorado. When I learned that I was pregnant with you, the relationship between William and I became strained. I wanted to marry, William wouldn't."

"That's how I became a fatherless child; a bastard."

Again Pamela's body jerks from the stark and forceful words spoken by her sweet daughter. Dacia's intense facial expression reflects an emotional response not witnessed by her mother in any previous discussions.

"Sweetie, do you hate your dad?"

"I hate the situation that I'm in because of him. I think that I love him but am confused about my feelings. That's why I'm asking you about your relationship with him. I need to understand."

"I'm sorry for any pain you have because of me."

"It's not you, mom, it's what has developed because of what you and dad did. All the adults in my life seem to know everything about you, me and dad. It's like my story's written before I came into this life. I thought that I knew dad and how I feel about him. I love him and hate him all at once." Pamela takes her daughter in her arms and offers a reassuring hug. Dacia initially resists but relents to her warm, comforting parent.

"Dear, these feelings are normal. You're moving emotionally between childhood and adulthood. You're dealing with both sets of emotions, especially about people. Looking at your dad through the eyes of a child is different than viewing him as an adult male; different values apply."

"Mom, the idea of truth shouldn't matter whether you are a child or an adult. That value should always be the same."

"I agree. However, your perception of your father

in your eyes is changing. It makes you angry. He no longer is the pure, honest, all-good man that you imagined as a loving child. That was a romanticized view. Your anger may be coming from an adulthood viewpoint where you're understanding your dad as a human being capable of human actions and emotions." Dacia quickly releases her mother's embrace, not wishing to accept her logical explanation; even though she suspects its precisely correct.

"Okay, mom. You could be right, but I don't want to tell you the other thing. It has to do with my feelings about you. I've been thinking about things that I shouldn't think about a mother." Pamela attempts to offer her daughter another hug, is quickly rejected. "Mom, don't try to make this mushy and lovely, I want to let you know how I feel. It's hard for me to talk to you about this."

"Well, Dacia what do you want to say?"

"Why didn't you do more to make dad marry you? I don't understand something. If you are so dedicated and focused on your business life and knowledgeable in your community service, why weren't you like that in your relationship with dad? Why were you so permissive with dad? Why did you agree not to get married? Why didn't you think about me? What about me, mom, what about me? Weren't you supposed to do something about me?" Pamela identifies with her daughter's pain but hasn't truly understood until now that her past actions impacted her child's life more dramatically than she ever imagined.

"I always think about you, sweet child. My whole life is about you. My relationship with your father began with desire, ran through affection and then blossomed into true love. I asked I pleaded; I begged your father to marry me so that we could have a 'proper' family. He wouldn't do it. He refused to marry me. Even with my pleading and cajoling, your dad refused marriage. It was embarrassing for me. I was in the position of begging a man to marry me, and he refused. Even after you were born, William still refused to marry. I thought that he was concealing a terrible secret in his past that he didn't want to expose me to. But now I know that he was already married and unwilling or afraid to face his family and get a divorce. Dacia, sweetie, I made a choice – a compromise. If I wanted to have William in our lives, to enjoy his presence or occasional visits, then I would have to be content with the position of 'the other woman.' This choice, unfortunately, relegated you to the permanent position, the eternal stain, of being a fatherless child. It's true; I could have told William to leave our lives. I could have cut off my relationship with him forever. However, you would never have known your father. William would never have been part of your early life.

The look in his eyes when he first held you was protective; I knew that he truly loved you. Love filled his whole being, with every fiber of his person. He was your dad. I knew that, and he accepted that. I don't know any other way to explain it to you."

Dacia slowly walks away from her mom, intentionally showing her back toward her mother. Pamela, tempted by the silence, doesn't hasten a response from her daughter. Turning, the expression on Dacia's face betrays her thoughts.

"Mom, I hate the decision that you made. You could have sent dad away and told everyone that he died. You could have raised me as a single mom. You had this hotel for income. You had Mr. Menendez and the Chamber of Commerce people to help you out. You could have made things work. You would have been okay. I would have been a child whose father died or something. You could have told everyone that you married dad, had a child and then he died. Then things would have been okay for me. Since you didn't do that, things are all mess up now, and I'll always be a 'marked' person; someone who doesn't belong."

Pamela faces Dacia full-on. "My dear child. You belong to yourself, and me and Mr. Menendez, your grandmother 'stinky-poo' and your family and this entire community. Think of your best friend Dove-Whispering and all the students at the school. They're all part of who you are. After the recent developments of the science project, you've gained a whole new family. There's a lot of people involved in your life because William was your dad. You have an extended family that is excited to know you."

"I hear what you're saying, mom. But I don't like what you're saying. It doesn't erase the fact that I'm a bastard and always will be. Can you imagine the kids at school talking about the fact that I'm my best friends aunt? Do you know what it's like to go to school with someone who you thought was your very best friend in the whole world wide world and then you have to talk to her like both of you are weird because now you are her aunt and she is your niece? Mom, that is messed up. Neither one of us wants to do that. This whole situation causes a lot of pain for me." Pamela listens as her child recites a litany of insults she has suffered in the past few months since the results of the DNA science project have been made public. Pamela is in pain for her child. If she could turn back time and make different decisions, she would, but that's impossible. All she can do is try to explain to Dacia what the atmosphere was like between her and William.

"Dacia, in today's society no one seems to care if a child doesn't live with both their mom and dad. Children live in all kinds of different families. Some kids even have two or three fathers and don't live with their biological mother. It's okay to be a child without a mom or a dad."

"But mom, it's not okay for me. I'm mad at dad for not publically claiming me as his daughter. He's dead, and there is no one to be angry at now. I don't want to be mad at you but seems like I'm taking my anger out on you. I wasn't angry at first when everyone was talking about the results, but now after I have had time to think about it, I'm upset. I guess because I didn't have any say in the decision making but the result affects me for the rest of my life." Pamela quietly listens to her emotional daughter since she has learned not to hold and cuddle her while she is expressing her intense feelings. However, Pamela's nervous habit of twirling her long, blonde, curls not only occupy her busy, dominant hand but obscure and cloud the sound of her daughter's pleading words.

"Mom, mom are you listening to me? I'm trying to tell you how I feel about this situation with dad and the DNA science project and all of the talk about you and me. For god sakes mom, who is the weird lady at school? Everyone says that she is the counselor but now all of a sudden she's my grandmother. How goofy is that? What the heck is goin' on mom?" Dacia walks toward the wall, turns around, straightens her back, stiffens her posture, slams her body back against the wall, crosses her arms across her chest and assumes a stance of defiance - yet appears vulnerable and child-like. It only takes a few seconds for the tears to flow and flow freely they do. The salty cascade billowing from Dacia's luxuriously green eyes seems indistinguishable from a succession of small waterfalls following the irrigation of lush fields of growing vegetation. Pamela hesitates before approaching her distraught daughter. When she does, it's with softness and trepidation.

"I know that things are confusing right now. You know some of the information; the remainder must seem extremely unlikely. You are changing from a child into a young woman. At the same time, you're exposed to an extended family that has been intentionally hidden in the shadows and is now not only being revealed but connected to you in a very public fashion. Dacia, there is no part of this that you can deny or avoid. It's coming at you all at once, and every part of it is important. I can't keep it from you, but I can help you deal with all of it."

"Oh mom, It's all so much. It's all too much. I don't know. Kids aren't supposed to have to deal with adult stuff; not even big kids." Pamela and Dacia embrace firmly and passionately as though each wants to melt into the others' body. Their hug meshes not only their flowing tresses, making a braid of blond and amber, but their intertwined limbs resemble a mangled handful of partially cooked pasta. Tears flow and hugs embrace until feelings of intensity and anxiety drain from the consoling couple.

"Mom, it's so hard growing up."

MICHELLE'S WORK day has been busy and hectic. When she gets home, all she wants is to take her tight-fitting shoes off, change into her 'comfy' clothes and slow-sip on a chilled glass of her favorite wine. These ideas occupy her thoughts when entering the front door. Struggling with the door key seems to be the final challenge to her restful retreat. Exhaustively, she sets down her large bag and cumbersome purse. Her teenage daughter, Dove-Whispering is laying on her bed absorbed in finishing a homework assignment on her computer in the back bedroom. However, she turns off her computer and when she recognizes that her mom is home. Dove-Whispering has been waiting so that she can discuss with her the surprising revelation in the science class with Mr. Walters.

"Mom, mom, is that you?" Dove-Whispering runs to meet her mom who is now relaxing in the living rooms most comfortable chair.

"Yeah, it's me, sweetie. Do you want something? How was your day? Mine was very busy." Dove-Whispering hurries to sit on the arm of the chair so that she can talk with her mom and not disturb her. The two females enjoy a quick, loving embrace – their usual greeting. Dove-Whispering speaks slowly at first so that she can get her mom's attention but not disturb her mental rest. She runs her fingers through her long black hair as if it is a calming effect for the question that she is about to pose.

"Mom, today in science class, Ms. Walters drew out a graph showing us the relationships of everyone in my family and Dacia's family. We ask her to do this because Dacia and I wanted a picture of what everyone has been talking about when they refer to the DNA science project. We both understand the science stuff, but we wanted someone to draw out a map for us so that we could see the hard stuff – the people stuff. Mom, it's awful. Dacia can't be my aunt. She's my best friend. It also showed that she's like me; neither one of us had a real dad growing up. We want to see our birth certificates to know who is listed as 'father.' It can't have happened to both of us." Michelle hadn't realized that her daughter was experiencing the results of the DNA science project so deeply. As a mother, she's caught up in her adult version of the prodigy controversy, and she just realized that the two people who were most intently affected, Dacia and Dove-Whispering, had gotten little psychological support or mental mediation assistance. Michelle grabs her daughter from the arm of the chair and snuggles her with a hug so smothering that Dove-Whispering starts choking and spitting – which instantly releases Michelle's hold.

"Oh dear, you have a father. Just because he wasn't in your life to help with your everyday issues, doesn't mean that he wasn't available. He couldn't make a commitment to us as a father and husband. He loves you." Dove-Whispering stands up and raises her arms in the air so that her next statement gets her mom's full attention.

"I'm talking about that. Dacia's dad, my grandpa, I mean her dad couldn't make that commitment thing either. I don't understand adults. If someone loves you, they should stay with you and be in your life. I have a dad and Dacia had a dad, but neither one is here. Neither one put their name on the line of our birth certificates that says 'dad.'" Michelle breathes deeply, realizing that her answer holds a very emotional aspect.

"Honey, your father loves you. I'm sure that if Pamela were having this same conversation with Dacia, she would tell her the same thing. Sometimes adults have issues in their lives that they can't deal with – issues to too big to handle. When that happens, they try to avoid making a decision hoping that the issues will go away. In your and Dacia's situation, the entry on the birth certificate is blank. I can't answer for your dad or your grandpa – Dacia's dad – but I know that they loved both you and Dacia." Dove-Whispering doesn't seem satisfied with her mom's answer.

"I know that grandpa was a good man. He showed me a lot of good times when I was a little kid. I liked to laugh with him and go to parties. When he picked me up from school, we would have all kinds of adventures and meet interesting people. When he went to work here in Colorado, I thought that it was for a job with his friend. I didn't know that he was messin' around with Dacia's mom."

"Wait just a minute. When your grandpa met Pamela, she wasn't Dacia's mom, yet. Pamela was just a single businesswoman. She didn't become Dacia's mom until your grandpa, and she had a romantic relationship. Sweetie, you are old enough to know all of this, and I am sorry that I didn't take time to have a personal talk with you about how you fit into this story."

"Well, mom, Dacia and I have been watching how you and Pamela are handling this whole situation. It seems like everyone is either not talking to each other or blaming the other person for something that they didn't do. Grandpa caused this by acting out and not telling the truth. Now Dacia and I have to deal with all the crap." Michelle wants to orient her daughter back into a time when the communication between people was more personal and face-to-face. To a time when during a conversation if someone told another person something, that fact was taken as truth.

"Well, Dove-Whispering things were different when grandma and grandpa met each other. It's a time before instant cell phone calls and worldwide webs that operate with split-second timing. Computers, i-phones, androids, A.I. formats, wide-ranging T-broadband devices weren't created or even available to the general public. People talked to people. Because of that intimate contact, if someone told you something and they presented themselves as a credible person, then you accepted what they said. They were a credible person in every way. Therefore, there was no reason for Pamela or even Mr. Menendez to doubt anything that William had to say about himself or his life. People were less suspicious about each other. Times were more socially naïve, and people had an innate feeling of trust and honesty toward each other. Sweetie, it's only been less than two decades since Pamela met your grandpa but you know yourself how much technology has changed in that time. Remember that I tell you stories all the time about the fact that I didn't have a computer or cell phone when I was growing up. You know yourself that we didn't have either one of those things until just a couple of years ago. Even if all of those electronic devices were available, they were still too expensive for most people. Even now a cell phone can cost a few hundred dollars. Yes, it was a different time and so were people. Even you and I interacted in a different way before cell phones. We never 'text' each other until we both had a cell phone – remember."

"Mom, you always get on this 'kick' about me spending too much time on my phone, but I never thought about life without one. I guess people did talk to each other – it's scary. Living life without my phone? I don't like the feeling I get just thinking about it." Michelle wants to make this talk about cell phones relevant for Dove-Whispering, so she switches the conversation to her dad - grandpa.

"Remember sweetie; your grandpa was my dad. Everything that you and Dacia are feeling and thinking about him and because of him, I'm thinking and feeling also."

Michelle nudges her daughter toward the living room couch to relate an 'adult' story that it's time for her blossoming young daughter to hear. Michelle starts slowly.

"That's how this whole story about you and Dacia began; with a cell phone and a hand-written letter." Michelle breathes and relaxes her shoulders as she gets comfy with her daughter to tell a story that is long overdue in the telling. "Grandpa William and Grandma Kaye both got cell phones right before grandpa traveled from Nevada to Colorado so that they could stay in touch. Grandpa was going on a short business trip for his friend Mr. Menendez to expand his insurance business. Both grandpa and grandma knew that the regular mail would be slow, so they wanted to use their new electronic phones to keep in touch quicker." Michelle pauses a second to reconsider delving into family skeletons but then decides that since Dacia and Dove-Whispering are dealing with the consequences of decisions made a generation ago, both girls need to know the full story of those resolves. "This is the story as Grandma Kaye told me, so I'm passing it on to you from that experience. When grandpa first arrived here in Colorado, they talked every day. Grandpa described his job duties and how he was meeting new people. He would call her when he found a new museum or car show located near his new apartment. Grandma Kaye planned to visit him as soon as he got settled. Mom, Grandma Kaye, had met Mr. Menendez only once before grandpa left for Colorado, so grandma thought that things were going well in grandpa's new job. After a few months, things began to change. When mom would call grandpa in the evening, he wouldn't answer the phone. She would leave a voice message. He would call her back, but it was late at night after she had gone to bed. Sometimes she would miss the call. When grandma did talk to grandpa on the weekends, he said that he was getting busy with his job and was working very long hours. Then grandma decided to make flight reservations to see grandpa in Colorado so that they could spend some time together. When she told grandpa, he hesitated and told grandma that he was living in a cramped apartment with a few other guys and it would be uncomfortable for her to visit. He added that he was using an old car that his boss loaned him and it didn't work very well. Therefore, he couldn't pick her up at the airport. You need to remember Dove-Whispering that this is a time before alternate travel – no Uber, or Lyft or AirB&B or auto drive cars. So, grandpa was telling grandma not to come and visit. At first, grandma believed grandpa about his living conditions and thought that he was considerate. He didn't want grandma inconvenienced. However, grandma started finding it increasingly difficult to reach grandpa by cell phone even on the weekends – grandpa didn't call her anymore. She was always trying to reach him. Grandma assumed that the business must be expanding rapidly and that grandpa was the manager of the new territory. So, grandma made an airplane reservation for Colorado for a visit to see grandpa. She wrote a handwritten letter to let him know when she was arriving. The letter would take about three days to arrive in Colorado and grandma was sure that she would get a call from grandpa. Well, the days passed and no word. Grandma was worried that grandpa was hurt or sick. She packed and was scheduled to leave the next day; she had one more day at the medical clinic. Grandma was rushing to get to work, and as she ran out of the door to get into her car, she was surprised to see grandpa standing on the porch with their son, Benedict. Grandpa smiled and said, 'surprise, I'll bet you didn't expect to see me here today.' Well, you can imagine my mom's reaction – you know grandma when she gets excited. Unfortunately, the clinic was short-staffed, and grandma couldn't stay home that day and had to rush to work. She got another surprise when she got a call from grandpa later that day at the clinic. He had come back to Nevada because he had a doctor appointment at the clinic – not to see grandma."

At this point, Dove-Whispering interrupts her mom. "Wait a minute. I have all kinds of questions. What was grandpa doing all this time in Colorado? Why didn't her call grandma back? Didn't you say that he had a cell phone? Didn't he know that grandma bought a plane ticket to come and see him? Why did he fly to Nevada anyway? What's going on here, mom? I don't like this. Grandpa is up to something. It's not like him to do this. Something's wrong here." Michelle strokes her daughter's arm as Dove-Whispering wiggles away from her mom's embrace – as if Dove-Whispering is trying to avoid the next chapter of the story.

"I already heard the next part about grandpa being sick and not going back to Colorado. Is that what happens next? I don't like this story. I thought we were talking about cell phones and writing letters." Dove-Whispering is now sitting across the room from her mother and assumes an almost fetal position in the corner of an over-stuffed chair.

"We're talking about letters, dear and this is where the most overwhelming part of our family story takes place. Grandpa had a very aggressive illness; one that he couldn't overcome. You know what happens in that part of the story. What I want to tell you next is something that I don't think you know. After grandpa passes away, grandma goes through his briefcase – the one he used for business in Colorado. She found account files that were returned to Mr. Menendez in his Nevada office. But, there's another piece of paper in the brief-case. It's an intimate handwritten letter from grandpa to Pamela. In the letter, grandpa writes that he loves Pamela very much and looks forward to their next loving time together."

Upon hearing this, Dove-Whispering jumps from

the chair. "No, no don't say it, mom. Don't say that grandpa and Dacia's mom were making love. Don't say that."

Michelle waits for the shock of the obvious to sink into her daughter's consciousness. "It's a biological fact that for Dacia to be the child of grandpa and Pamela, they would have had at least one sexual encounter, you know that sweetie." Michelle tries to calm her daughter. However, when Dove-Whispering hears the words being spoken out loud by someone that she knows intimately, a shiver is sent down her spine.

"But grandpa is old, and Dacia's mom is young and pretty. Why would she like somebody who is old? Why would she want to kiss my grandpa? Ms. Walters drew out a graph of our family, but she didn't say anything about old people having sex. I know about sex; but not grandpa. Yuck, yuck, mom, no, no." Dove-Whispering flops back down into the welcoming chair – is this her last bastion of comfort?

"Sweetie, you have to realize that grandpa could be very charming when he wanted to be and could weave a story that rivaled the best-known storyteller. So, when grandpa wanted to make the acquaintance of a beautiful young woman, I'm sure that he was gracious and gregarious – that means that he could get what he wanted. Also remember that from all that we have heard, grandpa told Pamela that he was a single man without any children. Can you imagine how I felt, knowing that my dad was telling people that he didn't have a family? It's painful, I know. But it's the truth. You should remember that Pamela is not yet Dacia's mother. Dacia wasn't even thought of yet – she doesn't exist. I know that you have seen this on our family chart but William is not only Dacia's dad, but my and Auntie Anne's and Uncle Benedict's dad, grandma's husband, your grandpa and Pamela's boyfriend. Grandpa did something that still affects our entire family today."

Michelle draws closer to her daughter so that the implication of her message is well received. "This next part that I'm going to say to you is as important as what I just shared. You and Dacia are the next generation. You and your best friend don't carry the physical and mental scars of what your grandpa did. It's true that you know your family's past, but that is different than living through the pain and suffering of that experience. Therefore, you and Dacia can be the healing for all of us. I know that both you girls watch Pamela and me interact. It's true that we don't seem to be doing anything positive about all of the DNA science project information, but we are. We're doing a lot. It takes adults more time to get things done. Adults are more set in their opinions and have to work through more memories to move forward in a positive direction.

That's why it can take longer. But you and Dacia are young and have fresh eyes and soft hearts. As both of you look at the relationships in our family, you can begin a new direction for our whole family – all of us. Neither of you experienced the original trauma connected with this emotional situation. However, you are forced to deal with its' consequences. I'm sure that both you and Dacia can see it from a different perspective than me, or Pamela or Mrs. Henry or Mr. Menendez. We are adults; old people in your eyes and have crystalized lenses that distort our vision when we look at a problem. You are young adults; youngsters in our eyes, and look at a tough situation as a challenge – something to figure out or overcome. You and Dacia will serve our family well in finding a new path for yourselves and others that will follow you in dealing with these unfortunate ripples, in our generations."

"I don't care about the people who will be born later in our family. I care about what happens now and how we deal with it now, not generations from now." Dove-Whispering looks at her mother with her wide, teary, brown eyes as if to say 'protect me now mom, not later.' Little does Dove-Whispering realize that's what her mother can't do. The two best friends must hold on tight as they careen through the ripples of their generations – much like riding the dangerous rapids of a raging river. Because, if the Henry family is to survive the emotional perils of their newly discovered connections, then it's the faith, persistence, and love of these two young women that will see them through to the other side of the river – to the calm, clear waters of the life-giving stream. The way Michelle looks at the situation of the Henry family is like everyone is in the middle of both holy water and firewater. The generations that have come before both Dacia and Dove-Whispering have made less than wise choices in their relationships. Secrets, lies, hidden adoptions, betrayed relationships, and lost opportunities have all plagued individual family members. The DNA science fair reveals the affliction of these choices in the most public manner. Unfortunately, the youngest members of the Henry family are bearing the visible burden as the very private family secrets are publicly revealed.

"I care so much for you dear that I'm showing you the path to your future. I wish that I could avoid this journey for you. I wish that the secrets of our family would have been revealed sooner so that I, and the others of my generations, could have addressed and resolved them but that didn't happen. I didn't know what was going on behind the scene. Relationships in our family appeared to be normal. I wasn't aware that there was another part, a fragment, or our family unfolding here in Colorado. Knowing the information now makes me angry, but I'm going to use the energy from that anger to help you and Dacia work through the scandalous issues and emerge with a new understanding and hopefully embrace our extended family members. I'm talking about forgiveness. Certainly, not for your grandpa because his actions were intentional, but for all the others involved in developing this situation into a public spectacle that has embarrassed and hurt you and your best friend. I know that I have talked a lot about you growing up in the past few weeks but, it looks like I've been doing a bit of that also. I guess that extending forgiveness is in the near future for both of us." Dove-Whispering and Michelle sit quietly next to each other on the couch, each absorbed in their thoughts – unsure of the future or their part in it. Dove-Whispering emits a low, sorrowful, pleading sound which slowly cascades into a full-blown, tearful sob while softly laying her head down on her mother's lap. "Mom, it's going to be so hard. I don't want Dacia ever to have any pain. She's my best friend, and I love her so..." "I know dear, I know. It will be okay." The two women console each other in a rhythmic embrace.

CHAPTER EIGHT

The Meeting

"*I bought the place because it had that door in the patio. I had no peace until I bought the house.*"

– Georgia O'Keeffe, describing - In The Patio VIII – 1950

"*EACH MEETING OCCURS at the precise moment for which it was meant. Usually, when it will have the greatest impact on our lives.*"

– Nadia Scrieva, Fathoms of Forgiveness

"I'M GOING to pick your grandma up at the airport. Do you want to come with me?" Michelle knew that the drive to the Colorado airport was at least half an hour and she wanted to meet her mother's plane on time.

"Mom, I don't know. Is Uncle Benedict coming with her? It's been such a long time since I've seen him. He's my favorite uncle. I love him so much. He's a nice guy."

"Well, I don't think that he's coming. Mom, uh, grandma said that he came to her house and was angry that she was talking about grandpa and Pamela. Uncle Benedict doesn't believe that grandpa ever met Pamela or had an affair with her. Uncle doesn't believe that Dacia even exists." Dove-Whispering lowers her head as though she's deep in thought - stroking her long, dark hair to comfort herself.

"Well, what about Auntie Anne, is she coming?"

"No, this trip's a special trip. It's a time for grandma to meet with Pamela." Dove-Whispering would like to have some comforting quiet time with her favorite aunt, especially if all this family time is going to be another rehash of the science fair.

"Sometimes grandma talks about family and all that lovey stuff about everybody. Why can't we bring her home here and visit with her? Do we always have to talk about everything? You said that she was going to stay for a short visit. Why is she coming here anyway?" Dove-Whispering isn't excited about meeting her grandmother not because she doesn't love her deeply but because Dove-Whispering knows that the topic of conversation will be the issue that the family always talks about – the connection to Dacia and her mother. "Yeah mom, I'll go but don't get grandma talking about the DNA science project."

Michelle looks at her daughter with a sigh of disbelief. "You know that grandma told us about the meeting with Pamela. Grandma and Pamela may be meeting when she comes to visit. We need to remember that grandma was married to grandpa for a lot of years and when she found out that grandpa had a girlfriend, it was a shock. It took courage for grandma to agree to meet with Pamela."

Settling into the car, Dove-Whispering takes a minute to ponder her mom's statement. "I know, but grandma's an old person. It doesn't matter if she feels bad. The thing between her and grandpa is already over. Dacia and I are still young; it's important for us."

When she hears that unexpected statement from her daughter, Michelle stops the car in the middle of the street, "What did you say? What did you say? Are you saying that old people's feelings don't matter?" Michelle releases her seatbelt and moves toward the passenger seat facing her daughter in a face-to-face approach.

"Uh, no mom. I didn't mean that. I just meant that

sometimes older people forget easier than we do. Gee, don't get so touchy."

"I'm not touchy. I want you to know that everyone in this issue is dealing with a lot of emotional turmoil. The one person who has the biggest load is grandma. She loves our family and is trying hard to keep everything and everyone together."

"Okay, mom. I guess that I forgot about grandma. So much is going on between everyone, I think about Dacia and me."

Michelle hugs her daughter and finishes it with a neck zerbert – 'which means I love you.' "We better hurry up, or we'll be late in meeting grandma's plane."

After settling into Michelle's home, Kaye sits down with Dove-Whispering to discuss her upcoming meeting with Pamela. "Sweetie, you know that I'm going to meet with Dacia's mom. Pamela and I shared a romantic relationship with your grandpa. I say this to you because you're old enough to hear someone say this to you. Since it involves me, it should be me that says it. The other reason is that I want to talk to Pamela and see if we can find a way to resolve our uncomfortable positions about your grandpa."

Kaye grabs her granddaughter closer knowing that their subject of discussion is not only sensitive to them but is the latest topic of conversation for the school staff and city officials as well. "Everyone is talking about us, grandma. Everybody knows our business. Dacia and I walk down the school hallway, and even the creepy school counselor looks at us like she wants to be our long lost friend. Everything has changed – ever since that darn science fair project. I wish that we would have chosen to do a project about plants or something else – anything besides people and DNA."

Kaye gives her special granddaughter an extra tight hug as she delivers a juicy zerbert on her neck – meaning 'I love you.' "Well, after my plane ride, I'm tired. After a good nights rest, I'll be able to call Pamela in the morning, and we can arrange our meeting. I want both you and your mother to know that this meeting is only between Pamela and I. It's not a time for others' prying eyes and ears. There are some things which need to be said between Pamela and me that aren't for others to hear. It's not that I don't love you guys, but this will be an intimate talk about grandpa and Pamela and me." Dove-Whispering and Kaye walk arm-in-arm into the kitchen where Michelle is filling water bottles.

"I thought that after we drop you off for your meeting with Pamela, Dove-Whispering and I might take a short walk to that new hiking trail that we discovered the other day. We have wanted to take Kiko out for a good walk and tomorrow is a good time for that. She's a dog who always enjoys a good romp outside."

"Well, I guess that Kiko does enjoy going on the trails and we haven't been out for a good walk in a while. Okay, mom that will be fun. Let's do it." Dove-Whispering grabs the water bottles and sets them in the cooler making a mental note to add ice packets in the morning before their walk.

"Mom, do you need me to do anything for you before you contact Pamela? I can help with whatever you need."

"No, Michelle. Pamela is waiting for my call. She is going to reserve a place for us to have a secluded meeting." Tomorrow will be a big day for many members of the Henry family.

"Hello Pamela, this is Kaye. Mr. Menendez gave me your phone number. I know that you're aware that I was going to call. I'm here in Colorado. Where are we going to meet?" The long silence that occupied the phone line in their previous conversations has shortened to a series of brief, heavy sighs – progress.

"Good morning, Kaye. Yes, I was waiting to hear from you. A friend of mine from the Chamber of Commerce owns a small coffee shop – it's public yet secluded. We can meet there if that would be okay with you? My friend knows our situation and has arranged for the shop to close early; we can meet in the late morning."

"That will work with my plans. If you give me the address, I will meet you there. We will each have personal transportation. I'm more comfortable with that arrangement." Kaye still wants to extend a bit of caution when setting up this appointment with William's girlfriend.

Pamela touches base with Dacia before leaving for her meeting with Kaye. "Mom, why are you so nervous? What are you doing? You're sweating and shaking. Are you sick? Did you have an accident?"

"No dear. I'm upset and feel like a whirl of dust in a vacuum cleaner bag because I'm getting ready to meet with Dove's grandma. She's in town and wants to talk about your dad.

"Oh, mom. You can't go by yourself. Last time that we saw her at school, she looked furious when she saw you. She may want to hit you and yell at you. Where are you going to meet her?"

"Don't worry Dacia. We are both adults. Even though I'm sure that we both feel like we're about to put our hands into a buzzing beehive, we'll be at my friend's coffee shop, and my friend is going to look out for me."

"Can I go? Can I go with you?" Dacia is now visibly concerned about her mother's safety.

"No. Dove and Michelle know about the meeting, and they aren't going either. I'm sure that they are just concerned as you are. However, if you want, I can call Michelle and ask her if you can go hiking with them this morning. We've met them once before, and they seemed okay. You get along well with Dove at school, so if you feel okay about it, I'll give Michelle a call and ask her."

"Huh, I don't know." Dacia sits quietly on her bed twirling her fiery red curls, which always helps her to think and figure out problems.

"Okay, give Dove's mom a call. If she says that it's fine then maybe she'll pick me up on their way to the hiking trail. Besides, I always love spending time with Kiko; she's so fluffy and soft. "

Pamela arrives early at her friend's coffee shop; it's more of a quaint cafe. She wants to calm her nerves and arrange the chairs so that her back isn't facing the front door. "Pamela, relax it will be okay. I know that it's a big meeting for you today, but nothing dramatic is going to happen here today. I'll be in the back and be checking on you on a regular basis. I don't want to eavesdrop on your conversation, but I'm here if you need me." Pamela's friend from the Chamber of Commerce has come to her support in the past. She's the friend who was at the community health fair and helped her the day that Pamela discovered she was pregnant with Dacia.

"I know that you're right, girl. You're right. I'm just nervous. I have so much to answer for; so much to explain."

"Take a deep breath and sit here in the chair for a few minutes. You'll feel better. I'll get you a cup of hot tea. Besides, you have a couple of minutes before 'that' woman arrives." Pamela's edgy demeanor is evident to her friend. However, a few sips of warm tea seem to soothe her skittish feeling. Waiting and anticipation are always difficult for this woman who lives between two truths – the lure of everlasting love and the reality of scandalous disgrace. It's like sitting on top of an ant hill holding a handful of thick, golden honey – you know that the ants will come but not sure from which direction.

Kaye lingers as she approaches the café. Now that she is about to have a face-to-face meeting with the woman who occupied William's heart and sexual desires, there is an awkward, unnerving feeling in the pit of her stomach. Kaye will walk into this café and meet her romantic inadequacies. She also will look at the woman who gave birth to William's child – the precious, illegitimate child that Kaye has already accepted into her heart, into her family. With all the courage of a mute canary, Kaye approaches the café and opens the door to her future.

Pamela's anxious eyes focus on William's wife. Pamela has seen Kaye at the school meeting to discuss the science fair and has accompanied her daughter for a house visit, but this is the first time that she'll have a conversation with Kaye. Kaye is apprehensive but walks up to Pamela and rigidly extends her right hand – as though to offer a 'business-like' greeting. Pamela's first thought is: 'to blurt out a litany of apologies related to her amorous relationship with William, and explain how she is eternally sorry about ruining, the life of his children, and that she honestly didn't know that William was married and that she would never hurt Kaye for anything, and she will never do anything like that again and, and, and, ...' Pamela bluntly realizes that her mind is rambling with incoherent thoughts that she hopes Kaye hasn't heard.

"Good morning, Kaye. I'm glad that we could meet this morning." Pamela realizes that her palms are sweaty and she 's excitingly shaking Kaye's hand as though it were the pump handle of an old fashion blacksmith forge.

"Yes, Pamela, I've been waiting for this meeting for a very long time." Definite animosity veiled by foreboding seeps from behind Kaye's public greeting. Pamela makes a move of conciliation by suggesting the couple take seats at a table in the back of the café. Pamela's friend has arranged a closed schedule for the business today so that the two women can sit and discuss their concerns.

"Sure, sitting here will be fine. I see that you're enjoying a cup of tea. That would be nice. A cup of tea can be refreshing." Kaye sets her purse down and settles into her chair. She doesn't assume a comfortable posture because she wants to guard against making this an informal meeting between friends. An outside observer may liken the scene to a subservient, prodigal member requesting returned to the family unit.

"I'll get you some right now. I'll be right back." Pamela wants to set the scene comfortably. "I hope that the temperature is okay. Do you take sugar or cream?"

"Just a little cream will be fine." Kaye stirs her steamy, milky drink with deliberate, slow motion – looking into the cup but not focusing on the refreshment.

"Well, I have to tell you, Pamela, that I don't enjoy being here. I'm doing this because my family is the most important thing in life. We both know that William is at the center of our concerns. I know now that our marriage was a lie. However, I'm not going to let that issue mar the future of my children. They are the future, and the future of the Henry family must embody honesty and progress. William lacked these qualities; he was a fun-loving, morally weak man. His children loved him, and his granddaughter carries his memories and genealogy. I want it to be a gentle genealogy filled with forgiveness and moral strength; only a strong person can forgive." Kaye realizes that she's taken a standing position beside the table and is waving her hands upward as though a preacher is leading their congregation in a persuasive oratory. She quickly sits down; embarrassed that she has unintentionally revealed her thoughts to Pamela so early in their discussion. Pamela sits silently, absorbing the ideas of her romantically connected cohort.

"You love your family and want to protect them. The betrayal that you must have felt when you learned of my existence must have been shocking and unbelievable. It's natural that you hate me and the relationship that I shared with William; I understand. I can't defend that relationship in your eyes, but for me, it was mutually loving and caring and produced a beautiful, tenderhearted baby girl. For a short, memorable time in my life, William brought me love, companionship, and tenderness. It's only now that I realize the horrible price that was paid by others for my brief bit of happiness." Pamela places her weary head in her hands, trying not to mentally relive the moment when she first learned from Mr. Menendez that her beloved William was dead; followed by the equally crushing flash that William was already a family man when she met him. Kaye initially watches Pamela with disdain and mistrust; yet slowly glimpses her heartache as Kaye notices Pamela's body tremble and detects the sounds of heartfelt sobs emanating from Pamela's bowed head. Kaye hesitates, not knowing if she should act on her first primal instinct. With reluctance and unsteadiness, Kaye lightly places her well-worn hand on Pamela's lowered head. The passing years had not been kind to Kaye's gnarled fingers, and they sit in stark contrast to her gentling touch. The two women, the two contentious lovers, spend a few moments in the throws of connection and understanding. It's Pamela who breaks their tenuous bond.

"It wasn't supposed to go like this. I was going to meet you in this neutral place and show that I was brave and in love with William. Then I was going to bring out pictures of our beautiful daughter, Dacia. After that explanation of how William seduced me into a relationship. I rehearsed the plan in my mind; it was evident. There's always trouble when my heart takes over my mind. That's what happened with William. He captured my heart right away, and then I allowed him get away with stuff that I normally wouldn't consider. William liked the weakness that was showing from inside my heart. He went after it, and he got it; all of it."

Pamela searches for a handful of tissues from inside her purse to soak up the tears produced by her emotional outpouring about her involvement with the love of her life; William. Her hesitant speech is still peppered with spits and sputters as she attempts to regain her composure and present some presence of humanity before facing the judgmental attitude of her lover's wife. "My life and Dacia's life is tainted with the stain of transgression. Time won't change that fact. I'm here today not for forgiveness but to meet you and let our eye-to-eye contact start some understanding." However, Pamela can't bring herself to look into the eyes of the woman she has hurt and betrayed – the woman who still holds the legal title to William's love.

"Pamela, my anger, and rage won't let me listen to you. I'm not sure if it's emotions that I harbor for William or you, but these feelings occupy so much of my mind and thoughts that there seems to be no space for even listening. I've had so many days of anguish and nights of sleeplessness that my body is breathing from memory at this point. The moment that changes my life is still vivid - words in the love letter written in William's hand to you, explode off the page as though they are shrapnel. These words of endearing love puncture my heart as though they are chards of glass.

Anger and rage race through me." Even though finding the letter happened a few years ago, Kaye is still experiencing the raw emotions of that discovery. She too is now haphazardly searching in her purse for a handful of tissues. "My god, Pamela, he was my husband, he had kids. What's wrong with you? Don't you care?" Kaye's rage and sorrow spill over once more as she gets up from the table and walks over to the café window, attempting to settle herself from the intense flow of emotion. Whenever she remembers her life with William, her emotions always rise to the surface. She feels like her grandmother's old-fashion pressure cooker on 'canning' day. The large, steamy pot sits on the hot stove spitting and sputtering, signaling to all concerned that to open the lid would be disastrous. "I knew William inside and out. He loved the adrenaline rush from the search, from the hunt. I don't know how to be delicate about this or any other way to say it, but William was about the fucking. He was about the chase that leads to the fucking. I'm not necessarily talking about the physical act of sexual intercourse between partners; although I know that was in his purview, I'm referring to messing with someone's life and personal self. I can't be delicate I need to be powerful so that you get my message; so that it comes across to you. Wiliam didn't 'love' me; he didn't 'love' his children, he didn't 'love' you or your child. William 'loved' the chase, the hunt. He was addicted, if you will, to the rush that he got from pursuing the forbidden. He had to go after the thing that he shouldn't have or shouldn't want to possess. I will say that William cared deeply for his family. It was the one thing in his life that kept him even; at least as straight as he could be within the guidelines of his life. His military life also gave his structure, gave his focus. However, his military discharge ended the structure that William relied on for his inner sense of moral radar that kept him within society guidelines. I saw him struggle with the challenge, but he wanted no advice about how to face the issue. He lost direction; he lost his touchstone for tapping into the adrenaline he loved so much. There were no more TDY trips for the military or avenues to quickly escape his routine of family responsibilities. However, he did have a friend; Mr. Menendez. The two men had done business in the past, and William knew that Dale was always looking to expand his business. After a discussion, William announces that he's going to work with Dale and briefly moves to Colorado. That is when you, Pamela, come into our lives." Kaye turns away from the large café window. It's as though she has used the window to throw out, or throw away, the harsh words associated with William. In doing so, she's sent the words away into an unknown space where they can scatter and cause harm to no one. Could it be that the chards of cutting glass that sliced her heart while she read that hidden amorous love note also have cut through this glass window making it possible for her to release the words of anger, of sorrow, of pain connected to that noxious note? She slowly returns to the table where Pamela is sitting.

This bewildered woman, this taunting target, listens to Kaye's emotional outpouring related to her tumultuous life with William. She frantically looks for more tissues for both herself and Kaye. Pamela's friend, the café owner, tentatively approaches the couple to see if they are doing okay and if she can refresh their hot tea. "Yes, that would be just the perfect thing right about now, thank you so very much." Pamela hugs her friend and accepts the fresh box of soft tissues.

"Kaye, I sit here still reacting to the review of your life with William. My first thought is: You must have loved each other when you first met. There must have been something in William that sparked an interest in you, something that eventually turned into love. When I first saw him, there wasn't any particular feature that caught my eye. It was something in his character or his manner that I remembered. It's like the essence of perfume, every time you smell it you envision the very first time that you inhaled the fragrance."

Kaye listens to this woman who has caused consternation and gnashing of teeth for such a long time. Maybe it's her words or the sound of her voice or the way in which she describes her first meeting with William, but for the first time, Kaye looks at Pamela in a different light. The picture is still fuzzy; out of focus, but there's a realization that the anger she directs toward Pamela is appropriate for William. There's a question forming in her still scrambled thoughts. What would Pamela look like to Kaye if Kaye was standing on the other side of this situation? What if, just what if, Kaye was a personal girlfriend to Pamela when she meets William? One day Pamela comes to her telling her that she's met a wonderful man who's changing her life most gloriously. He's someone who makes her feel loved and treasured and desired. What if Pamela tells her that this man also is a colleague of a life-long friend and has a personal and professional guarantee of integrity? Wouldn't I, as a loyal girlfriend, be happy for my friend? Even after personally meeting William, wouldn't I be impressed with his manner and attitude? He always did have a knack for 'reading' a person and knowing their vulnerability. The new person in my friend Pamela's life is welcome. There is no obvious objection. The only sadness in the situation comes later when we learn that the love of Pamela's life is dead. Our hearts grieve for both Pamela and her young daughter. It's evident that he was the air and breath that sustained them.

"Well, I don't remember anything particular about our first meeting." Kaye doesn't want to identify with this tempestuous torment. "William and I met by accident. He was persistent about what he wanted; that's what I remember." The women are sitting across from each other, trying hard not to look at the other. Both are fidgeting with their teacup, holding the teaspoon and stirring their, now cold, tea.

"That's how it happened with me. I met William by accident. He was referred by Mr. Menendez to my hotel to rent a room. At first, I wasn't sure if he was lost or confused. There were other cheaper accommodations closer to his office, but he said that he wanted to rent a room in my hotel. The more we talked, the more I understood that William was very determined to not only rent a room but to have his mail delivered there also. He wouldn't accept objections. He just kept talking and talking. After he rents his room, he starts coming by the front lobby to pick up his mail. Unfortunately, you probably know the rest of the story."

Kaye doesn't like the familiar feeling in her stomach - the creeping sensation of understanding. There's no room within Kaye for sympathy or self-identification with this woman. However, she also harbors an intense desire for love and protection of her granddaughter and step-daughter. If there is to be a future for the Henry family, it will be through the consolidation of the lives of these two young women. The two realities; understanding betrayal and the desire for family survival are competing for Kaye's moral conscious. The battle is intense; the decision should be clear – love and protection versus understanding and forgiveness. Kaye's first thought is to hand-off the decision, someone more qualified to decide the thorny verdict. That's not logical. Then it becomes clear to Kaye. Pamela isn't asking for understanding or forgiveness. She's merely giving information and explaining her reaction. Kaye could take this opportunity to 'make her pay' for every single, terrible, awful, horrible, intense, crappy, shitty, negative thing that William ever did. Kaye is enjoying a moment of forbidden mental pleasure when her adult, moral compass kicks in – full blast. Of course, Kaye's heart is softening; she loves those two girls.

Kaye pulls her chair closer to Pamela's and sits down. Both woman still clutching their handful of partially used tissues in case there's a future need. "Listen, Pamela, we both cared for William. He entered our lives, captured our hearts, fathered our children, gave us memories, told us stories, made us promises and then disappeared and left our families to deal with the result of his deceit. I'm angry about the destruction that William left, but mostly I'm upset that I was naïve enough to believe that he was truly in love with me. Since I loved him forever and totally, I assumed that he felt that way about me; about our family. Right now, I don't much like you. It's not you specifically, but 'you' in general. You represent all the women William couldn't resist; all the woman that he had to chase and overcome. However, I am starting to understand. I'm beginning to identify with the agreement that William had with himself. When he could capture something unattainable, experience the adrenaline rush that he's searching for, then bathe in the uplifting sensation until it fades, then have the renewal feeling wash over him, he's happy. It's a renewable cycle. Pamela, you're just a woman who came into the circular spiral at the wrong time."

For the first time, Pamela listens with attention instead of anxiety and intensity. She's formulating a question as she attends to Kaye. "Kaye, one thing has been bothering me. As you know, I'm well acquainted with Mr. Menendez. I now understand that he knew William before William moved to Colorado. The thing that I don't understand and is bothering me down to the base of my moral code is that Mr. Menendez knew that William had a family and a life in Nevada. I consider Dale Menendez, my substitute father. He's known me since I was born. Mr. Menendez watched my relationship with William continue; he was aware that William and I were going to be parents, he watched Dacia fall in love with her father. Mr. Menendez never told me about William's children; even though he knew that they were in Nevada waiting to see their dad. Just how far was Dale willing to take his part? I still don't understand. He and Mrs. Menendez always said they loved both Dacia and me, yet they chose to cooperate with the lie. They kept the lie. Were they sworn to secrecy? Was there some hidden agreement between the three of them? Maybe they were concerned that if they released the truth about William, they would also have to tell the truth about my parentage; about my mother's childhood in a whore house and my father being a land swindler and drunkard. Where's the loyalty to me?"

The two contentious women, absorbed in their recitations, were unaware that the sun had released its hold to the evenings' cooling blanket. Possibly, an analogy for the upcoming conversation. Pamela's friend approaches quietly, not wanting to disturb the open, friendly atmosphere. "It's getting late ladies. I prepared a little meal for both of you. I'll just set it here on the table. If you need anything else, just let me know. I'm glad to get it for you. I'm happy to serve you a hearty meal." Both women thank the café owner and heartedly dig in; neither realizing until now how hungry they are. Eating hungrily, both women resemble devouring birds just discovering fresh spring flowers heavy with nectar. Sounds of culinary contentment drown out any conversation of betrayal or mistrust.

As the meal is consumed, the adverse conversation is less attractive to the women. Each one takes a few quiet minutes to contemplate their previous remarks. It seems that the questions posed by Pamela represent the first time Kaye hears Pamela examine interactions in her small cloister of friends. Kaye's next thought is: How did Pamela find out about her true parentage and why is she now willing to share this sensitive information with a woman who is not her friend? Could it be that Dale Menendez shared that information with Pamela about her mother, the school counselor, 'Stinky-Poo'? If so, why didn't Pamela know that William was married? It seems like there was a lot at stake for Mr. Menendez if he shared Pamela's history but nothing at risk if he kept William's secrets. Mr. Menendez made personal choices that affect the entire Henry family.

"Pamela, since we're together we have an opportunity. I'm uncomfortable. Oh man, am I uncomfortable saying this to you. I still don't like you or what happened to my family because of you, but I'm looking toward the future and the lives of the young women in our family. That's the motivation behind my thinking. You'll always be the 'other woman' to me. I love my granddaughter, Dove-Whispering and my step-daughter, Dacia because they are part of William and me and they're the future. I, never in a million years, thought I would say this to you. Pamela, you and I can at least acknowledge that we don't like each other and then start working together to resolve our emotional issues. So, let's go forward, not forgetting but trying hard to forgive." Kaye feels as though she's a vulnerable chameleon lizard whose background color has instantly changed from concealment to, sky-blue-pink; for which there is no changeability option.

"Oh Kaye, I'm so sorry that this has happened. Believing William and his story of being an unattached man will haunt me forever. Even greater sorrows are the lies and secrets clenched by my relatives that permeate my family. I have a diverse lineage, but I would never have imagined that my daughter has equally diverse ancestors. I've come to believe that all of this intrigue enriches our family. By 'our family,' I'm referring to the blending our your family and my family. Because, as you know, the family is much like gravity, it's always there; whether you want to embrace it or not. I also know that William did some tricky things. However, he did have one redeeming factor. The man thought enough of both you and me to not marry me. It's true that he loved my daughter, Dacia, but I believe that he also loved your children. From my point of view, he was a good dad. He may not have been a good husband or a moral man, but he possessed the ability to embrace his children as a father. Maybe it's because he identified with himself as a child and he saw that part of himself in his children. Therefore, he understood childhood. Maybe, he couldn't or wouldn't face the choices of being an adult. Wherever it was that motivated him to lead a double life and develop another family, will forever be held in his mind. We, you and me, are left here to deal with forgiveness and truth so that our children can see us as an example to move on with repairing our family."

Kaye momentarily collects her thoughts. Pamela is an unexpected woman and someone who Kaye isn't readily prepared to deal with approvingly. However, Kaye finds herself reluctantly identifying with this 'woman of easy virtue.' There are aspects of Pamela's life that resemble Kaye's life; that's an unexpected occurrence in Kaye's eyes. "Pamela, you give me a lot to think about when you mention family. It's obvious that we both love our children. You are right about the preservation of our family. Since our generations are already intertwined, it's obvious that there are ripples in the waters of our genealogy. I feel that you and I are beginning to comprehend the importance of working together for the good of family; even if it's for our self-preservation. If we don't, our descendants will be at odds for generations. I can see now that what we decide here makes a difference. When I entered the café today, I think that I hated you. However, now that we have talked openly and truthfully, I understand you and the relationship with William. I still don't like it, but I now understand it."

"Kaye I'm relieved to hear you say that. I truly believe that if I were to meet William or someone like him, today I wouldn't be seduced by his attitude or his charms. I've learned the hard way to be smart about people and monitor myself in matters of romance. I'm less naïve about infatuation and 'first-love.' William didn't realize it, but he taught me to reserve my feelings for someone who, not only loves me but also respects me. It's a hard lesson to learn but one that I can pass on to my daughter, Dacia. Hopefully, she won't make the same mistake."

Both women hesitate to make the first move. These concierges of arbitration have been sitting for hours expressing their intimate feelings to someone they didn't initially regard, yet here they are face-to-face, considering a handshake of conciliation. Anticipating acknowledgment, Pamela tentatively extends her right hand. Kaye's initial instinct is to behave in a confronting manner. However, family pride inhibits that natural aptitude and she graciously expands her reach to grasp Pamela's outstretched hand.

"Well, I see that you women have ended your discussion. Is there anything else I can do for you today"? Pamela's friend, the café owner, offers a friendly approach to two weary arbitrators.

Answering in unison, both women offer a half-worded sentence of gratitude. "Do you have a ride home? The day has passed since you came here, if you need a ride I'll let you use the telephone. This café's in a secure neighborhood so you'll be safe." Each woman states they'll have no problem finding their way home. The three stand for an awkward moment, each sensing that the other should be the first one to move.

"Kaye, we should make arrangements to contact with each other later. You have my phone number, so call me, we can exchange information. Does that sound like a good idea?" Pamela isn't sure about Kaye's response.

"Yeah, that will be the best way. We can talk on the phone and decide." Kaye feels uncomfortable about being too friendly with Pamela. The women leave the café, each mentally reviewing the day's discussion. The café owner tidies the lobby area, turns out the lights and locks the front door.

CHAPTER NINE

From my Perspective

"*Perspective is the way we see things when we look at them from a certain distance, and it allows us to appreciate their value.*"

– Rafael E. Pino

"FORGIVENESS DOESN'T SIT THERE *like a pretty boy in a bar. Forgiveness is the old fat guy you have to haul up a hill.*"

– Cheryl Stayed, *Tiny Beautiful Things: Advice on Love and Life from Dear Sugar*

"YOU WANT *to come in my life; the door is open. You want to get out of my life; the door is open. Just one request. Don't stand at the door; you're blocking the traffic." –* Unknown

---

"WELL, girls it's time for the science fair regional competition. To say that this particular project has been a learning experience would certainly be an understatement." Ms. Walters is standing in the science room with her two favorite students. Dacia and Dove, who normally stand so close that the teachers use the term "connected-at-the-hip," position themselves at opposite ends of the science experiment table – each girl looking a little lost and bedraggled. "Come, come now. What is all this? My two best students not even wanting to stand next to not only me but each other. Girls, what is going on with you?"

After an uncomfortable silence, Dacia speaks first. "It's because of our parents and the whole talking thing. Everybody wants to talk to everybody else, and then they get emotional, and then everybody has meetings and then everybody talks again. Can't we go back to the way it was before we did the science project? We want to go back to when Dove and I were just best friends, and 'Stinky-Poo' was just the creepy school counselor, and our mothers didn't know each other. Can't we go back there?"

Ms. Walters, the science teacher, invites both girls

to the front of the room to take a seat by her desk. She's leaning against the front portion of the counter so that she can comfortably talk with the girls. "Facing adult issues is hard especially when you aren't yet adults. That's the situation in this case. Unfortunately, everyone and I mean everyone, in the school and half of the community, also knows the situation within your families. It's a hard road that you both are following. However, you have each other, and you'll go down the road together. You have a strong bond, I see it. Also, you now know that you are genetically related. Both of these factors are strong elements of support as you enter not only the regional science competition but your family struggle to integrate these ideas into a blended unit. I have also seen and worked with the adult members of your family, and I can personally vouch for the strength and tenacity of their wish to make both of you happy. Again, I do understand your desire to return to a simpler time when both family and personal matters appeared to be clear and known. However, you are no longer there. Both of you have grown up a little; seeing life from a different perspective. To look at this situation from a science point of view, I would say that you are particles colliding and forming a new substance that hasn't yet received a scientific name or category. Therefore, you are the young scientists who will decide where each part of this new substance fits and eventually there will be a distinctive new element; your new blended family."

Ms. Walters waits for a response to her forward-looking message. She knows that both of these students understand the nuance of what she's saying. The body language of both Dacia and Dove betrays their shared thoughts. Collectively they approach Ms. Walters and begrudgingly offer an accepting and understanding hug. "You're right; it's hard. We just want our parents and all the other people in this to get rid of their old ideas of hurt, and pain and anger and get along. If we all have to do this family thing, why don't we do it?" Dacia speaks for both girls while they nod in unison. They resemble a pair of bobbly-head carnival dolls vibrating to thematic music. The girls leave the science room arm-in-arm, as best friends usually do.

"OKAY MOM, tell me how things went. What did you say and then what did she say and then what happened? Did you hit her, did she cry? Was there any new juicy news that you didn't know? Come on mom tell me absolutely everything. You were at this meeting for hours. Something must have happened; it always does when we talk about dad." Michelle couldn't contain her inquisitive excitement when drilling her mom about the meeting between Pamela and Kaye.

"Well, no one stood in the way of anyone else, if that is what you mean. We were both nervous. We both guarded our information. The owner of the café was gracious and arranges privacy for Pamela and me for our meeting. I appreciate that." Kaye knows that this is not the information that Michelle is anticipating; Michelle wants to know the "juicy" stuff. Michelle and Dove-Whispering are both waiting to hear the news of Kaye's meeting with Dacia's mother.

"Pamela and I met at her friend's café. My first thought was one of anger. I was reaching the source who ruined my family and destroyed my marriage. The intention of revenge was clouding my thoughts. My physical energy and mental reasoning so filled my consciousness that there was no room left for me to consider another point of view. However, when I saw this cautious, anxious woman approaching me, the hint of a feeling began to whisper: 'go slow.' The suggestion annoyed me. I was primed to exert my energy for destroying not for considering. A body twitch followed the feeling. The annoyance grew and even momentarily distorted my hearing until I realized that Pamela was talking to me and offering to share a cup of tea before we began our conversation. Our exchange softened as we sipped our warm tea. Pamela sat and listened as I spewed out my litany of insults toward her and William. With each barb that I hurled, she physically lowered her shoulders and bowed her head as though a skilled archer was aligning their slender shaft and directing the chiseled head of a focused arc. My intensity demanded that I stand up from our table and face the window to address my fervor outside away from the café. It was cathartic, exhausting and even unexpectedly humiliating for me. However, Pamela listened and also exchanged sentiments during my rantings. The hours passed unnoticed. Pamela proved to be honest, sincere, apologetic and understanding. When I realized that the focus of my anger was involved and engaged with my outrage, I was again upset that she understood. So, I would say to you that unexpectedly I found Pamela to be the right person and someone I couldn't continue to hate."

Michelle listens to her mother and is in awe of her recount. "Mom, you mean to tell me that you are considering forgiveness? I can tell you, mom, that once you understand a person's point of view, then you can understand the person. No one loved dad more than me, but I now understand that he was not a good husband. I'm also learning that he was not a good man for Pamela. He was never going to tell her the truth about his family; about us. Dad wanted to live two lives, and then he got caught. I still love him dearly, and maybe I keep a romantic view of my relationship with him but what he did has hurt many people. So, when I hear you say that you can even consider understanding and forgive the woman with whom he betrayed you, then I believe that our family can truly begin to heal from the terrible wound inflicted on it. Mom, it makes me angry that I didn't know that all of this was going on but I didn't and now I can't go back and fix it. However, I can be part of our family moving forward and being whole again. Dove-Whispering and I have talked many times about trying to get past this hurt and pain. Maybe now we can."

"I know that I may be the key for this process, but I'm already exhausted; physically, emotionally and psychologically. I still don't understand why the man I married couldn't love me and take care of his family. It will always be a mystery to me. William was searching for something that he already held in the palm of his hand; his loving family." Kaye hurries to call Auntie Anne and tell her about the meeting with Pamela.

"Mom, was she like you expected? I have been waiting for you to call. I thought for sure that you and she had a fight or something. When you didn't call after a few hours, my imagination went wild. Tell me everything. Did you talk to Michelle? What does she think? Tell me everything. I can't want for you to get back to Nevada. Tell me now before you get back home." Auntie Anne's excitement lights up the phone transmission as though the conversation is being attacked by a flurry of agitated ravens.

"Well, I have to admit that you were right. Pamela is a nice person. Anne, you always take a kind view of people. In this case, you are right. After Pamela and I talked for a few hours, I realize that I should direct my anger and frustration toward William and focus my understanding toward Pamela. I wasn't ready to do that when I first walked into the café, but after meeting with her for most of the day, my emotions softened into understanding and forgiveness."

"Oh mom, I know that you feel better about meeting with Pamela. I also know that it was so hard to do that. You have hated her for a very long time. I see how you feel when you think about dad and Pamela together. It bothers me that the whole situation gives you pain. Maybe now you can feel better and let go of the pain. I sure hope so, for your sake. Love ya mom. I'll talk to you more when you get back to Nevada. Bye." The click, ending the phone conversation, sends odd sensations of warmth and security through Kaye, both are such unaccustomed feelings.

"Michelle, I'm booking my plane trip back to Nevada. This trip and my conversation with Pamela have been exhausting but fruitful. Somehow, I feel lighter, or maybe something's removed from me that I didn't need. I'm not sure what it is, but something's gone from my 'self.' Anyway, I feel like it's okay to return to Nevada and work through the issue with William and Pamela. Also, as I told you, your brother Benedict threw, what I would call, an emotional "fit" when he and I discussed this same issue. He refuses to approach the idea of his father's double life or see how it affects our family. He doesn't want to see us or talk to us. His anger tells me something else. It tells me that he feels guilty about something. Just what the issue is, I don't know, but I'm sure that it has something to do with William. We will probably never know Benedict's secrets. He holds onto his anger." Kaye descends into a ferociously deep sleep; her body is unresponsive to light, sound or temperature variations.

***

PAMELA DOESN'T KNOW how to relate her experience of meeting Kaye to Mr. Menendez. Pamela's acutely aware that her lifelong friend is also the holder of secrets in her past that is just now unfolding. He's withheld vital information from her all of her young life. Can she now trust this man with her intimate feelings and her most guarded thoughts? Questions concerning loyalty and honesty and truth swarm through her mind. Mr. Menendez is the second man in her life who she has trusted with her intimate confidence and later discovered that he has willfully betrayed her. Yet his treachery is more profound since her relationship with Dale Menendez has lasted since before birth; he has known her since her conception. Mr. Menendez, her mentor, her father-figure, her protector, her business escort has guided both her personal and professional life. This man even introduced her to William, the man who would ultimately betray and abandon both her and her child, Dacia.

However, in the past few weeks, Pamela had detected a strange calmness in the man she had come to know and trust; a trust that swayed recently. Pamela is occupying herself with mundane tasks at the front desk of the hotel when a familiar visitor enters the front door. "Good morning my dear. I'm glad to see you here this morning. You are looking busy and involved in business affairs. I came by today to drop off a few flyers for the upcoming Chamber of Commerce mixer. I'm sure that you will be attending. You always come to the social functions." The frequent caller exudes such a familiarity with both Pamela and the surroundings that anyone would assume that he either owns the hotel or knows the proprietor on a first name basis.

Without making eye contact, Pamela answers offhandedly so as not to offer too much attention to the visitor's presence. "Well, I usually do attend Chamber functions. I don't see why this one should be any different." However, the statement lacks Pamela's usual tone of enthusiasm When Pamela does look up, her sharp point of focus is on a void between the visitor and herself. The visitor quickly adjusts his position to be directly in Pamela's line of sight.

"Come on sweetie, are we going to play this little game all morning. I want to talk to you. You know that I care deeply for both you and your daughter."

The silence of indecision sits on Pamela's tongue like the undertow of a tsunami following an underwater earthquake. "You want information. Curiosity overwhelms you, Mr. Menendez. Questions fill your head about my meeting with William's wife. You want to know how much information she told me. You want to know how deeply you are involved in William's secrets; in his betrayal. I would think that after knowing me all of my life, you would be more concerned about my welfare, about my feelings. Maybe I was expecting too much from a man who I loved and trusted. Maybe I was naïve to believe that a man who I have known since my birth has my best interest at heart." Again Pamela stares blankly at the stark space occupied with words between herself and her lifelong confidant.

"You're right. I kept secrets about William that I

should have told you. He was married when he came to work for me. He had a family when he met you. He was legally bound to another woman when he vowed a loving relationship to you. He was a father to other children when Dacia was born. William was a liar, a cheat, and a risk-taker. I knew all of this, and I let my precious Pamela walk naively into a doomed romantic relationship; this is true. I'm guilty of letting you experience pain and endure betrayal. I watched your heartbreak and break and break. I am culpable. Pamela, I admit I'm a weak man. I've done devious deeds that make this issue with William seem insignificant. My brother Jim and I dealt with the scum of the early in the early days of Colorado, and those deeds are following me to this day. They'll likely be sitting on my chest when I'm lowered into my grave. I can't change that idea. However, from my salvation and for your family preservation, I must, do you understand me, I must apologize wholeheartedly for crimes that I've committed toward you and your precious child. When I made easy choices, they seemed to have no consequences. I never dreamed that others, people who are innocent, would pay for my decisions. Even now, years later, I view the destruction that those decisions are having on people I love. My heart and my soul will forever be in turmoil for those actions."

Pamela pushes away the chore of sorting the

morning mail and is now looking at her lifelong friend with meaningful direct eye contact. The sincerity evident on his face and the intensity flickering in his eyes quickens his speech so that his vocabulary is mumbled resembling rough marbles rotating in a sand polisher. His speech is incoherent, but his message is direct. Mr. Menendez is attempting to apologize and bearing his broken heart. The process is, in turn, breaking Pamela's heart. She's holding back a torrent of insults aimed at destroying the soul and dignity of a man she knew all her life. However, her memory is sharp of how it feels to be on the receiving end of hurled hate and insane insults. Her recent meeting with Kaye has put her in just such a position. Even though Pamela had seen herself as the injured party in the case of William and Mr. Menendez, she now realizes that Mr. Menendez is himself hurling the arrows of agony inward and doing more personal destruction than she could ever do in all of her revenge toward him. The idea of forgiveness instantly enters her consciousness. She's not sure if it's because of the pain that she's witnessing on the face of a man she does care for or because her inner embers of care and concern aren't extinguished. Again, indecision floods her thoughts. Pamela thinks of her child. Pamela thinks of the future. She frantically searches deep into the crevices of the respective eyes of this intimate, lifelong champion to detect his true inner soul. He is a self-professed betrayer. He has made choices that protect himself at the expense of others. Pamela's childhood is clouded with suspicion due to the actions of this man. Yet, here he stands offering repentance and apology without discrimination. Pamela knows that forgiveness is different than forgetting. Pamela makes a decision.

She uses both hands to deliberately pick up the stack of daily mail that's been absent-mindedly sorted and forcefully slams it down on the front desk. Her words quickly follow her actions. "I hear your sorrowful words, sir. I see your tearful eyes. I listen to your reasons. I watch you perform punitive penance. What I don't understand is why you don't have to pay for your misdeeds. You are sorry for what you have done, but there is no consequence for you. You haven't physically lost anything. The community still holds you in high regard. The insurance business that you expanded with the expertise of William is profitable. The school district values your judgment. Married life seems to be stable for you and Mrs. Menendez. The confidence that you share with 'Stinky-Poo' remains intact. The deeds to the property that you acquired under your questionable land deals in the early days of Colorado still hold your name. I am genetically still your niece. So, Mr. Menendez, what exactly have you lost in your devious, nefarious dealings? What exactly do you have to be sorry about?"

Moments of reflection threaten to wizen the measurable distance between this dame of determination and the apologetic apostate. Both participate in the widening gap until the deafening silence threatens to cloak their relationship which now resembles a pair of staunch oaks hidden in the dark grey clouds of an upcoming storm. A furrowed brow and slumped shoulders accompany his reply.

"You are right, my dear. I haven't lost my physical possessions. My outward standing in this community is stable. We share a firm genealogical relationship. My land titles reflect my ownership. The school counselor still holds my confidence and counsel. Movers and shakers in this community respect my leadership. All of what you say about me in this respect is true. However, if you ask Dacia how she sees me, I'm sure that her response would be one of mistrust and uncertainty. Just from our talk here today, I know that your respect for me has evaporated much like blowing away the dry seeds of a dandelion; the remnants are left to find their own resting place. It's also true that I'm intensely curious about the contents of your meeting with Kaye Henry. However, that issue is now unimportant. I sense from your attitude that the discussion generated a path for understanding, if not acceptance, between you and Mrs. Henry. The most devastating aspect of my relationship with not only William but your true parentage is that I can't go back and redo my actions. The decisions that I chose at the time were easy for me because I was scared and in pain. There is a streak of spineless greediness running through me that taints every part of my life. My brother, Jim, fell prey to its spell more fully and earlier than I. Attempts to overcome my tendency are dismal. Mrs. Menendez and 'Stinky-Poo' have been my confidants over the past years and have helped to steer me back onto a better path when I veer toward my old habits of greed and total self-consumption. Meeting William tapped into my basic tendency of craving and longing for the 'good ole' days." He had a natural gift of reading people and finding their weakness and then exploiting it. I think that is what he did with Pamela too. It's no excuse for my behavior, but it's something that I now realize, is a weakness of mine; one that always brings me down to a degraded level that I operate on to take advantage of other people, usually the people that I love."

Pamela moves from behind the front desk and motions for Dale to take a seat in a chair in the front lobby. Momentarily she considers asking the man she has known her entire life to share a cup of tea but then her heart hesitates and her brain quickly rejects the generous offer. "Dale, I don't trust you. I loved you, I trusted you, I confided in you, I admired you, I believed you. However, the cascading events show me that you're willing to protect yourself at the expense of others. The image I have in my mind's eye of you whispering to William while he lay dying in his hospital bed sears into my brain. I can only imagine the words that you two conspirators exchange at that most precious and precarious moment.

Had you no concern for Dacia or me much less the Henry family? My god, Dale, William's wife was standing right in front of you. She knew that William was dying. Was there no pang of remorse in your soul? Didn't you think about staying in Nevada for a while to offer consolation to the Henry family? Listening to you describe your weakness, your infirmity it's obvious that you had no intention of revealing the truth until you were forced to do so. The high school DNA science project reveals family connections that I'm sure you would prefer to keep secret forever.

You're forced into being a 'good guy.' Your choice is to keep the secrets of our family just that way, a secret. Dale, you cause pain; you keep secrets. I would use the term 'Mr. Menendez', since it's a term of endearment that I have used to address you since my childhood, but that intimate feeling is fading. I trust, you don't. I believe, you don't. I honor, you don't. Mr. Menendez, we are growing apart. Maybe we see the world from opposite perspectives, or we interact with others on a different level, but since I'm working through family relationships and clear about protecting my daughter, I'm not willing to tolerate people who keep secrets, especially when those secrets damage people's lives."

Pamela sits back in her chair obstructing her heart by crossing her arms over her chest indicating 'our discussion is closed if you don't share my point of view.'

"You're right, Pamela. I've hurt people. I keep secrets. Have I ever truly loved anyone? I don't know anymore. My wife, may God bless her, urges me to examine my behavior; I'm unable to do that effectively. Am I standing on the last rung of my 'ladder?' When I was working with my brother Jim and then with William my perspective, my angle, in life was to persuade people to take the easy road. If making a buck is possible, or possessions can be grabbed, then I focus energy on getting that 'thing' whatever it is that stands in front of me. It didn't matter if it was money or land or people. My brothers got that same risk-taking behavior; it killed him. The passing of years seemed to quench my desire for such ventures. Then along came William. I saw in him aspects of my brother and myself. I knew that he was nefarious; he didn't hide his compromising attitude from me. William didn't personally know my brother, but they shared personality traits. Jim was your father and William was your lover, and I stood by and let both men cause you pain and agony. Now the menacing of both men is affecting the next generation. Both Dacia and Dove-Whispering are enduring public ridicule and even teenage suspicion from their classmates. The ripples of my wicked deeds are influencing the next generation of our family. I can't wiggle out of this transaction, all I can do is ask for understanding and forgiveness."

Pamela, consumed with swirling emotions, sharply rises from her chair. Visions of her recent meeting with Kaye starkly fill her thoughts. Her first inclination is to scream and yell at yet another man who has betrayed her. First, it was her father Jim, the drunken conman; then it was her doting adoptive father who concealed her true ancestry; then William, the deceiving lover; and now Mr. Menendez, Dale, the man who cradled and protected her since childhood. The personification of emotional and physical betrayal is standing in front of her in a public space during a very civil conversation asking to forgive all the past transgression hurled toward her. Dale has undoubtedly chosen his location well to foster his agenda. At least Kaye arranged to meet her in a quiet café and notified her in advance concerning the topic of their meeting. This man approached her without mental reservation expecting a total resolution for a lifelong betrayal.

The act of rising from her chair signals a physical transition in Pamela. A sheer veil of fixed determination encompasses her heart. Her standing offers a position of dominance over this bemoaning man. "I'm a woman and a mother. Living through betrayal has shown me that I can experience a full range of emotions ignited by the most intense sentiment. However, being a survivor also shows me that dealing with and facing the betrayal is a picture of my past. You, Dale, are that reality of my past. However, we, you and I, will maintain a different relationship now. You are my uncle. Your brother is my biological father who left me a legacy of turmoil. My mother, 'Stinky-Poo,' disguised her voyeur activities to serve some motherly desire, all of which I'm sure you arranged. I will see you, Dale, as a person in my extended family; someone invited to Thanksgiving dinner and Christmas celebrations. Sharing of personal confidences or intimate conversations are past activities between us. I'm relieving myself from the burden of secrecy and isolation and emotional anxiety and relationship starvation. I permit myself to define my own reality. Dale, you want to promote forgetting and usher in forgiveness, I offer you an arms-length relationship on an acquaintance basis. The forgiveness effusion will have to fester and foster within yourself."

Dale struggles to rise as though he is attempting to counterbalance oscillating realities; forgetting and forgiveness. Neither of which have been granted to him this day. His constant desire to alleviate, or at least mitigate, himself from the burden of his actions has failed; he's etched as a perpetual perpetrator. His inner confusion is now apparent. He feared this day would come. However, the etching of his eulogy is completed by his precious Pamela; the daughter of his heart. Although she isn't his biological child, Pamela holds that self-adopted place. Dale believed that if he plays the part of a pseudo-parent, it will balance out the absence of his brothers' presence. There would still be a family aspect in the young girls' life.

"Well, I'll leave now and await my engraved invitation to your Christmas party. It will be a much-anticipated request. Mrs. Menendez awaits my return. You and I have talked at each other today. Maybe as time goes on we will find a way to talk to each other; as we have done in the past. Pages are turning in our relationship; I will think deliberately about our words." The dual contenders of self and opinion stand on a ledge of ice waiting for an early spring thaw.

BERNICE IS STILL CONSIDERING her brief yet accusative conversation with Ms. Walters. The science teacher indicates that she, the school counselor, has been using her school district position for personal reasons. The interchange occurs when the science teacher observes 'Stinky-Poo' talking with both Dacia and Dove in the school hallway. Bernice tries to imagine how the situation must appear to an outsider; someone not genetically related to the Henry family.

Bernice's thoughts wander to her childhood and its unusual setting. The brothel didn't seem to be a peculiar or strange family setting to young Bernice. Her mother treated Bernice with love and kindness. Being an only child gave Bernice a position of attention that she relished. The lavish attention of frequent visitors indicates that the young child is a budding beauty. The only confusing occurrence is her mother's command that she spend extended time in her room when her mother throws lavish parties in the homes elegant front room. However, when Bernice reaches her teen years, her mother became more aware and is attentive to Bernice's type of dress and education in the social etiquettes; especially when entertaining men. Bernice wasn't sure when her awareness became clear concerning her mother's intentions. Maybe it was when she ventures into the local community and realizes that her family environment is extremely different from the accepted norm of the neighborhood. Whatever sparks her curiosity, Bernice realizes that her mother's loving attention is a grooming technique to fashion her into a prostitute for the whore house. Bernice's calculated escape from the infamous Denver brothel is accomplished under cover of night and possibly just in the 'nick-of-time.' Remembering her mother's words as she falls asleep that fateful night: "you've almost finished your education, sweetie." The word 'education' occupies her thoughts as the school bell signals the change of class. The intensity of the clang startles her back into reality just in time to avoid students hustling in the hallway.

'Um, using my school position for personal reasons,' could that be true? Bernice never looked at her counselor position as exploiting the school district. Her only desire was to be in her daughter Pamela's life without her knowing Bernice's true identity and torrid past. Mr. Menendez's role in securing a solid adoption for Pamela with prominent parents secured Pamela's future. Bernice hadn't anticipated a blessed grandchild. However, Dacia brought joy and captured the future for Bernice.

The science teacher, Ms. Walters, has said many times that both Dacia and Dove are her favorite students. Naturally, she observes them as they interact not only in her classroom but as they pass in the

hallway and become influenced by the support personnel. Ms. Walters wants to protect them; that's under-
standable. Bernice decides to approach the science
teacher to discuss her concerns. Entering the science
room Bernice speaks first. "Ms. Walters do you have a
moment? Can you spare some time to discuss something that is important to both of us?" The response is
rebounding.

"Of course, Ms. McKim-DePue, come in. I'm
grading some papers from the last class, but it can wait
until later. What did you want to talk about?"

Bernice positions herself in a seat of equal status.
"I have been considering your statement the other day
concerning the interconnection of the bones of a skeleton. Were you making a comparison to real life? Was
there something that you wanted to tell me about your
observations?" Bernice quietly waits for the usually
demonstrative science teacher to respond. However,
Erica's body language indicates a different attitude.

"I'm not sure how to word my response to your
question. I believe that your secret observations of both
Dove and Dacia have a far-reaching indication. There
may be more to your actions besides simple concern
for a students welfare." Ms. Walters' disquiet is
evident in not only her choice of words but her uneasy
tone.

Bernice unsuccessfully attempts to adjust her position and finally stands up and begins a slow, pacing sojourn around the science room. "Well, I appreciate your concern, Erica. However, you can't image the story that accompanies your forensic observation. I'll start where you began. You mention your concern about my observation of Dacia and Dove. Also, you indicate the skeleton analogy. In reality, the two situations are interrelated. Oh my, again, where do I begin?" Sensing her reluctance, Erica offers a solution. "I have a suggestion. Let me tell you what I think is going on, and you can confirm or deny what I say. Does that sound like a good idea?"

"Sure, that helps me to begin the story."

"Okay, then I'll begin."

"I know that you were a counselor at the elementary and middle schools. So, you have experience in your field. There's no doubting your credibility. I observe you watching and helping all the students without injecting yourself into their realm of interactions. However, you provide extra attention to both Dacia and Dove. I don't want you to be alarmed, but I asked the assistant principal, and he told me that you also watched Dacia's mom, Pamela, when she was a student here in high school. I truthfully don't understand your fascination with the Love family. They are a prominent community family with extensive ties to this area. Pamela's parents were trailblazers in developing the Denver wilderness and contributed greatly to the professional enhancement of the Chamber of Commerce. Honestly, Bernice, your attention to these two girls is getting a little embarrassing. The students are whispering about 'the creepy counselor lurking in the shadows.' Dacia and Dove haven't noticed your attention yet because they're focused on their friendship and the upcoming regional science fair competition. However, since they are both intelligent young women with inquisitive minds, your attention will soon be evident and possibly unwelcome. I'm saying this to you because I know that you also are an intelligent professional and don't want to cause these students any undue concern." The science teacher tentatively takes a seat on a stool next to the lab experiment table waiting for the weight of her words to yield a response.

"As always, Erica, you have an adequate grasp of the facts. Doing your homework has given you some basic information. Before I proceed with my response, I want you to know that I respect your investigative skills and believe that you too have the girls' best interest at heart. I have hidden the secret from Dacia and Dove and Pamela and myself for many years. It takes a real sleuth to uncover something that fights to remain hidden. The truth wouldn't be revealed if your prized science students hadn't chosen their DNA project. The conspiracy would have continued for generations and possibly remain buried forever."

Unable to remain composed, Erica verbally confronts Bernice. "Are you saying that your skulking in the corners of the school hallways has something to do with genetics?"

"Yes, exactly." Bernice walks over to the science classroom skeleton and stands behind the calcium configuration. "When you talk to me about this framework being connected, you are indeed referring to Dacia and Dove's family. Your observation of my observation is very astute. I do watch the two students. I'm interested in their relationship. It's important to me that the girls remain friends. Hopefully, they will form a friendship that will last their whole lives. There is an important reason why I'm concerned about their welfare. You see, I am Pamela's mother and Dacia's grandmother. Dacia is Dove-Whispering's aunt. Additionally, another bit of shocking news is that Mr. Menendez is my brother-in-law; in a way."

Upon hearing the astonishing news, the science teacher grabs the edge of the lab experiment table; it's an anchor to fortify against her wobbly knees. "I don't understand what you're saying. I've known you for years and have never heard you mention a family. You never show pictures of your children or husband. There's never been any tale of an exciting vacation.

Are you saying that for all these years you've been hiding your family? I've seen Pamela Love here in the high school, and I don't remember seeing you talk with her or hug her or sit next to her during a school celebration. I certainly don't remember hearing Dacia mention you in our discussions. Your observation of the girls is curious, but the reason for it never ran along the vein of being family related. I hear what you're telling me, but I don't understand what you're saying."

The school counselor sits quietly while the unblemished information saturates into understanding for the science teacher. Bernice knows that Erica is analytical and often uneasy with emotional or sensitive knowledge. Bernice is the first to elaborate on the shared secret. "I have a scared past with some delicate issues. This environment affects not only Dove and Dacia but Ms. Love and Mr. Menendez as well. The results of the DNA science project didn't reveal the complete structure of the Love family. It was a sentinel event that precludes the story of betrayal and deceit. My part in that story, my covert actions, and my indecent decisions have affected the relationships for three generations of my family. Only recently, through the friendship of your two favorite students, has this cloistered family secret been brought to light.

The discussions evolving within our lineage is like wandering blindly through a boulder-spiked cave. You can imagine the potential harm for Dacia and Dove. They're just learning entry information into their ancestor's background. It's now evident that they share DNA. However, their actual involvement within the web of distortion in their bloodline isn't realized by them. They're viewing the situation with 'child' eyes. They don't carry the scars or baggage of the actual occurrences that were perpetrated by each other on each other in our family. These two precious young women see the controversy as something to discuss and overcome, not something that is hand-wrenching, or intensely soul-searching like the adults are viewing our lineage. I believe that they are the future for us. They don't understand past transgressions and the need to guard them as sources of secrecy." Revealing her motive for years of significant actions reveals the unvarnished truth about Bernice. She carefully considers her next words to Erica.

"Unbelievable history for all of us; your background completes the story. As a science teacher, I look at situations from an analytical point of view, and I guess that I evaluate people from that view also. You're right; I do tend to shelter Dacia and Dove and watch their conduct. My interest is peaked when I notice anything different in their routine. You as the school counselor are fairly obvious in your observation of not only the girls but Dacia's mom as well. I couldn't figure it out. The pieces of the scene didn't fit. The idea of stalking flashed through my mind but then I quickly dismissed that idea because I know you too well. Bernice, you'll have to give me time to scrutinize all of this. Of course, I'm relieved to know the truth of why you're so concerned with both girls, but this information is just sinking into my head." The science teacher resumes a relaxed posture on the science room stool.

"Bernice you're going to have to give me time to understand. I'll sit here and think." The school counselor slowly leaves the science room wondering if her revelation of the truth was wise. Whatever becomes of this interaction will surely blend into the full story of the next chapter of the Henry family.

"DID YOU HEAR, mom went to meet with Pamela. They met in this cozy little café and talked for hours about dad and their relationships and a lot of stuff. Mom came back, and she was different; not so upset, almost like she was thinking about forgiveness or something. It was bizarre. Have you seen her yet? You have to talk to her; you'll see what I mean. Just talk to her." Michelle can't wait for her sister, Anne to see the change in their mother's attitude.

Anne and Kaye are sitting at the kitchen table going through household expenses when Anne brings up the subject of her mom's recent trip. "Well, I guess that you were pretty busy in Colorado. Meeting with dad's girlfriend surely was a big deal for you. I know that you wanted to really verbally attack her or just let her know how she has hurt our family in so many ways. You and I talked about what to say before you went there, so I'm wondering how your visit went, mom." Of all her children, Kaye knows that Anne is the most kind-hearted and emotional. What's said next, Anne will hold in her heart for an eternity as the gospel. Therefore, Kaye considers her words carefully.

"Well, both Pamela and I were nervous. I went into the meeting with an intense feeling of right-eousness, and I needed retribution. There was going to be no weakness in my heart for a little bitch who not only had a romantic affair with my husband but trau-matized the lives of my children. I was finally going to meet William's girlfriend, and I was looking for fire and brimstone. I'll tell you that it was good that Pamela's girlfriend arranged for a quiet, café for the meeting because I didn't want onlookers around when I approached that scarlet hussy." Kaye quickly searches the face of her youngest daughter to assess the intensity of her message. Anne's perceptive eyes and furrowed brow tells the story of her reaction.

"Mom, I know that we're all hurting, but you especially have endured betrayal by someone that you loved and trusted. I've watched you. Your reaction to this whole terrible mess has been both sorrowful and inspiring. I noticed that since you returned from your trip to Colorado where you met with Pamela, you seem calmer and more focused. It's true that I love my dad. He was and is a special man for me. I will always love him. I also know that what he did by having an affair with another woman hurt everyone in our family. However, he always did stupid stuff just because he wanted to do it. When I was in the hospital, he always made me feel better when he came to visit because he would act like a clown. That part was good. When it came to family or business stuff, he wasn't good at keeping things in order. He just wanted to play and have a party. That part wasn't good; hurting you was his worse thing. It will be in your heart forever. I noticed though that since you have come back from your trip, you are different. You aren't as rough around the edges. You don't talk so loud or use words that are rough or abrasive. You even walk differently and hold your body more relaxed. Something pretty powerful must have happened at that meeting." Kaye acknowledges her daughter's statements and gives her an encompassing hug. Anne accepts with voluntary love.

Dove-Whispering is sitting in the waiting room of the veterinarian office with Kiko. It's time for the dog's annual checkup. Dove-Whispering has been taking Kiko for her usual daily walks but the dog, her sweet dog, seems to be less energetic and more tired when the trail is over. Dove-Whispering and Michelle are both concerned about their pet and want to get a medical checkup to see if everything is okay with Kiko. Dacia meets Dove-Whispering at the veterinarian office to act as emotional support, although both girls are sure that the checkup will be excellent. "Well, Dove, what did your mom say about bringing Kiko to the doctor? Is there something wrong or hurting the dog? The dog looks okay."

"I think things are fine. Kiko needs a little checkup to let mom know that she's alright. Her last checkup was fine. We've had her for a few years, but I'm not sure how old she is now. She was pretty cute as a puppy, but I sure do like her as a full-sized dog too. She always likes to run and climb when we go hiking." Both girls give Kiko a good scratching behind her ears while Kiko responds with a low-toned howel. While petting Kiko, Dacia slowly changes the topic of the conversation; making sure to keep her voice low so as not to attract the attention of others in the waiting room. "Dove-Whispering, did your mom talk to you about the meeting between your grandma and my mom? Your grandma came here to Colorado and met with my mom at our friends café. I guess that it was to talk about my mom and your grandpa. Everybody has been making trips and talking about things in our family. Even when we talked to Ms. Walters in the science room that day, we didn't discuss our feelings. I think there's still a lot of secrets in our family. Yuck, it freaks me out when I think about the creepy school counselor being my grandma." Dacia changes her position to kneeling in front of Kiko and is intensely massaging the dog's neck and body. Kiko is trying to avoid the exuberant sign of affection but without much success.

"I try to listen when all the adults talk about us and how the DNA shows that we're related. Their discussions always come back to my grandpa. You and I were best friends long before we decided to compete in the science fair, but now that we added our genetic connection our friendship will be forever. I like the Idea, and I think that you also do. It's a mystery why the adults are having such a hard time with this. If we like each other why don't they? When I listen to what they say and watch their body language, sometimes the two things don't match each other. I hear my grandma say things like 'sure I would love to talk to you Pamela' but then I watch her hands while she's talking, and she's clenching them into a fist in front of her face. What's goin' on with that?" Now Dove-Whispering is also vigorously rubbing and massaging Kiko's neck and upper body as if there is a magical oil on her fur that will invigorate the mature dog back into a youthful puppy.

"Well, Dove-Whispering, I have a plan. Let's show the old people in our family how we want them to act by acting that way when we're around them. It's simple. They will watch us and then they will do the same thing. We can start a movement. A movement; that's what it is a movement."

Dacia stands up in the waiting area with her arms stretched out over her head as though she is advertising a fantastic, new, miracle product just arriving for sale on the public market. She then shouts, "We are best friends forever and are showing our family how to be happy and talk nicely to each other." Kiko barks loudly in agreement; not sure what the new arriving product is but confident that she too wants some of it. Just then the veterinarian assistant calls the trio back into the exam room for Kiko's appointment. The three soldiers march through the door as though following orders to advance to the front lines.

CHAPTER TEN

Transformation

"*Yes, your transformation will be hard. Yes, you will feel frightened, messed up and knocked down. Yes, you'll want to stop. Yes, it's the best work you'll ever do.*" – Robin Sharma

"*BECOMING HURTS.*"
   – Kat Howard "*From Greatmess to Greatness.*"
   – De philosopher DJ Kyos

"I'M TAKING a trip to Wray, Colorado. It's for personal reasons and won't be a long journey. Telling you the purpose of my travel reveals too much information so,

I'll say that I'm using some personal leave for the trip and don't know exactly when I'll return." The high school counselor and the science teacher stand in the teacher's lounge contemplating the consequences of Bernice's trip. Neither one wants to know or divulge too much information.

"Well, I'm sure that you will enjoy the change of scenery and take advantage of the opportunity to gather some desert flowers and plants. As I remember, Wray is pretty isolated and has an infamous history. There are a few stories of the 'good ole' days' where cowboys tried to escape the law in Denver and hid out in that small town. So, whatever you're going to do, take some time to relax." Erica's offering tokens of friendship to this cloistered staff member in the hopes that the suggestion will foster a better relationship between them.

"I appreciate your regard, but this trip's earmarked for something other than pleasure." The school counselor files her leave paperwork before leaving the school building. Her final look back toward the buildings' front door reminds her that her life has been devoted to hiding in dark shadows and hallways to observe and track the movements of both her child and grandchild. After this trip, she will no longer need to hide either of those activities.

Bernice decides to take a train trip to the small,

isolated town. It will be a slow, lonely sojourn but she'll have time to reflect on her sketchy childhood and troubled adulthood. The terror occupying her body is mummifying. What will she find? Does she need to rummage through the debris of her childhood? When the attorney notifies her of the legal document naming her as a claimant, she's surprised and ill-prepared for the explanation; 'when your mother died she wanted to provide for you.' Bernice's mother was a good friend of Mattie Silks, and when the infamous madam bought her ranch in the small Colorado town, Bernice's mother did likewise. Even though Mattie accumulated thousands of dollars through her illegal business, she was virtually penniless upon her death. However, Bernice's mother didn't face the same determination. She invested well. Her illicit income was invested in mining speculation and showed a healthy profit. Upon her death, Bernice's mother was a wealthy woman; albeit lonely. Her life of arranging love interludes and amorous exchanges hadn't offered her a chance at eternal love. Her entire fortune is left to her child, Bernice.

Views of the sparse scenery from the train window seem foreign to Bernice. She's familiar with the lush hills and valleys of Denver. Traveling the rails offers a rhythmic rocking that calms her nerves as the train approaches not only her mother's home but the reality of her relationship with her mother. Views of the Republican River also seem to quiet her concerns. Bernice often removes her jewel-winged glasses so that she can focus on a crisp view of the countryside.

A rather stoic looking gentleman meets Bernice at the railroad station. "Well, good afternoon Ms. McKim-DePue. I hope that you had a pleasant trip. I know that train travel isn't the most comfortable mode of travel these days. However, I understand that you may have wanted to view some of your mothers' land holdings as you were coming into the city. You know, everyone is taking expensive train trips these days." The lawyer extends his hand accompanied by a slight bow to establish a professional relationship with his most prestigious client.

"Uh, excuse me, sir. Did you say land holdings?" Bernice absentmindedly shakes the lawyer's hands as he escorts her off of the train.

"Why, yes, mam. I'm sure that you will want to see the real estate as well as all of the other items that your dear mother bequeathed to you in her will. We all thought very highly of her in this town. She was one of our first prominent citizens. She bought property here in the late 1880s just when our little town was becoming a little town. She moved here a few years later with her friend, Mattie." The lawyer helps Bernice with her luggage and places it into his late model Mercedes; only the best accommodations for his prominent clients. "I'll get you settled into your hotel room; we can discuss business after you have time to rest."

"Sir, I don't remember your name. You contacted me about my mother's will, but in confusion, I neglected to focus on your name."

"Miss, my name is Mr. Sylvester Smith, Esquire. I was your mother's attorney for many years. She was a dear woman and thought highly of you and your accomplishments."

"Well, how did you know where I lived?" Bernice is astonished that this person she has never met knows intimate details of her life.

"Your mother kept track of your adventures. When you left the brothel, she begrudgingly knew that it was the right decision for your future. Staying would have ensured your path as a prostitute in your family home. She hired me to find you and secretly monitor your movements. There were emotional discussions about contacting you, but she knew that her torrid background would damage your future; she physically stayed out of your life but monitored your progress through surveillance. It was a painful process for her in every way." Mr. Smith is uncomfortable talking to Bernice in a public area. He fidgets with his key bob and focuses his attention on small floor objects during the conversation.

"We need to talk about all of this, Mr. Smith. This new information overwhelms me." Bernice unceremoniously sits on a large hotel couch in the front lobby.

"Miss, McKim-DePue, we'll do that tomorrow. Get some sleep; I'll pick you up tomorrow. We have an ample conference room at the law office that provides room to review documents." The counsel, and the claimant part company.

"As we discussed yesterday, Ms. McKim-Depue, your mother bequeathed to you, as her sole heir, her worldly assets. These include land holdings here in Colorado, financial investments and holdings in the mining industry. Which would you like to look at first?" The attorney has neatly displayed a variety of paperwork on a richly adorned, dark oak table prominently arranged in his legal office.

"Mr. Smith, I want to say before we begin that all of this information is new for me. You're well versed in my mother's matters, so I'm going to leave that question to you." Bernice takes a seat at the end of the long, legal table suspiciously eyeing the array of assembled legal documents.

"Bernice, I'll read the will first. That way you will understand your mother's thinking. She wanted you to know that you were loved and she greatly desired to care for your family."

"How did my mother know that I had a family?" Bernice is at full attention anticipating the attorney answer.

"Remember Bernice; your mother was monitoring your life. That's all that I can tell you." Mr. Smith averts direct eye contact, therefore, avoiding any additional conversation.

The attorney reads the strong will to Bernice as she listens in uneasy silence. It's obvious to this foundling of lavish lewdness that even though she escaped a life of prolific prostitution in a four-star establishment, her childhood home was indeed notorious. It's also glaringly apparent that remaining in the brothel may have prevented her from establishing her own family. The path that her life has taken since leaving her childhood home was unimaginable at the time and looking back on the journey seems just as improbable. Bernice is jarred back into the present moment as she hears the attorney speaking in a loud tone.

"Ms. McKim-DePue are you listening to me? Did you hear what I was saying? You are a wealthy woman. You inherited land and money from your mother. Your family is financially comfortable, and if you manage the money well, that security will last for generations. The money given to you by your mother will certainly make ripples in the coming generations of your family."

Bernice sits quietly, trying to absorb the emotional information. The numbing revelations make her believe she is an invader swimming in an ocean of stingrays injecting a paralyzing toxin into every muscle, nerve, and tendon rendering her helpless. 'How could my mother let me languish in such a cruel world, alone? Why didn't she contact me at the birth of my daughter? Surely she knew about her granddaughter? Did my mother love me? I don't understand all of this.'

"I heard you. Mr. Smith. I'm rich. My family has money and land. I heard you."

"As I told you, Ms. McKim-DePue, your mother was a charming woman who was liked by many in this small town. I'm sure that some form of public funeral would be appropriate. This community would like to say good-bye."

"Mr. Smith, from your letter and your manner, I assumed that my mother's buried. Why didn't you tell me her body wasn't interred?"

"Your mother is buried. I'm talking about a public

goodbye for everyone. Something that they can recognize as a farewell."

"Yes, of course. Can you organize it? You know the community well. I'll attend. My leave from my job requires that I return in a few days, so the ceremony needs to be within the week. Can you manage it?" Bernice still doesn't realize that she has no need for continued employment at the high school; she's independently wealthy.

"Surely, Ms. McKim-DePue, I take care of everything. Let me ask if you have a personal attorney who manages your financial affairs. The reason I inquire is that there are intricate details involved in managing this large sum of money, land leases and mineral rights. You may also need someone versed in real estate matters. Your mother acquired both residential and commercial property, and the management for these is somewhat different."

"No, Mr. Smith, I don't have a financial advisor. I will definitely be looking for a competent manager."

"Well then, may I offer my services since I'm personally acquainted with the finer details of this fortune. Excuse me, your fortune. Ms. McKim-DePue you will also pardon me if I ask if I may call you by your first name. Your mother and I were on a first name basis, and I would like to do business with you in that same capacity. I don't want to seem too familiar, but it may be easier for us to do business. However, it is your choice." Mr. Smith busies himself with arranging the variety of legal papers on the beautiful oak desk.

"Mr. Smith, I'll consider that later. Right now I'm comfortable addressing you as, Mr. Smith. I'm a bit overwhelmed with all of this information and don't feel that I should make any other decisions." Bernice busies herself by visually scanning the assembled legal documents.

"Well then, I'll introduce you to some of our prominent citizens. They will arrange the public recognition for your mother." Both Mr. Smith and Bernice leave the attorney's office and spend the day touring the city and greeting several notable community members. Everyone is gracious and remembers Bernice's mother in a friendly manner. A grand recognition in the public square honors Bernice's mother, and Bernice is asked to deliver a short yet solemn speech. Her oration is generic as though she is addressing an unfamiliar, unrelated stranger. This display of sentiment is puzzling to the citizens since they hold her mother in high regard. It's evident to everyone that Bernice must be in the depth of grieving for her sainted mother and 'not herself.' Following the ceremony, Bernice is greeted with warm wishes and graceful gestures.

Bernice rushes to her hotel room seeking solace so

that she can review activities of the past few days. 'Her life is transformed by words written by a woman who supposedly abandons her to the cruelty of life.' These thoughts continually circulate through her tired brain refusing to settle into a logical idea. The past week shows her that this same woman, this infamous lady of ill repute, this madam of Holladay Street, is indeed her gracious, protective mother providing for not only Bernice but future generations of their family. The idea is too big, too intense, too overwhelming for Bernice's brain and emotions. Whether it's the exhaustion or the recent revelations or Bernice's inability to accept her mother's protective embrace, she doesn't know, but she can hold back the tears no longer. Her fatigued body collapses into the soft bed welcoming her to release her emotional confusion out into the comforting universe. Bernice sobs quietly at first to restrain the volume from other fellow hotel guests. However, her internal angst overtakes her restraint, and a rush of tears intermingled with low-toned moans, and melancholy gnashing of teeth explode from this dowdy-clad, bee-hived hair-styled, middle-aged, secretive woman. The detonation lasts for a countless time. Complete physical and mental exhaustion consume this keeper of secrets, this shadowy figure, this secret observer.

Bernice's first thought upon waking is that she is

like her mother. Bernice too has been observing her daughter, Pamela and granddaughter Dacia from afar before revealing their real relationship. Bernice chuckles at the age ole' saying, 'like mother like daughter.'

Bernice is acutely aware of her ravenous hunger and need for a refreshing shower; accomplishing this, she calls Mr. Smith and arranges her final business appointment before scheduling her trip back to BigTon and her life at Dakota Flats High School. However, there is one last errand that Bernice decides to complete before her train trip back to her hometown.

"Mr. Smith, do you know a woman in town who owns an exclusive dress shop?" The attorney is momentarily stunned by the phone request from his recently acquired client. However, he can't deny the need for its urgency. He too believes that Bernice could benefit from a slight adjustment in her physical attire. "Why yes, mam. I do know someone like that. She owns the most exclusive shop in town, and I'm sure that she would be most happy to meet your needs. When would you like to visit her shop?"

"Well, I'm returning to BigTon in two days so I would like to visit the shop later today or early tomorrow." Bernice holds her phone close to her ear to detect any verbal sounds from Mr. Smith. Without hesitation, the attorney answers.

"Miss Violet is very exclusive, but I'm sure that she will be happy to serve your needs. I'll contact her now and arrange an appointment." Mr. Smith ends the call quickly so as not to become involved in a conversation concerning female clothing and unmentionable garments; this is the daughter of a whore house madam after all.

"Good afternoon, Miss Bernice. Mr. Smith arranged an appointment for you today. I'm sure that we can serve your needs. We work with most of the prominent women in the community, and they often return with a request that we strive to fill. Do you have any particular needs or desires to start with for today?"

Bernice breathes deeply, inhaling the sweet fragrance emanating throughout the exclusive boutique. Her eyes focus on the fine china and delicate flower arrangements that adorn the front sitting room of the elegant shop. "Miss Violet, I'm happy to meet you. I prefer to sit here and relax for a few minutes. I do so enjoy looking at your attractive sitting area. It refreshes my senses and reminds me of what a private French garden might look like."

"Mam, I understand. Your mother sat in that same chair admiring the flower arrangement." She too had a fanciful imagination."

Until that very moment, Bernice hadn't realized that her mother might well have visited this same salon. Her mother may have talked with Miss Violet. Her mother probably purchased elegant outfits from a design collection displayed in this shop. "Miss Violet, did you know my mother well? Did she come into your store often?" Bernice anxiously waits for the biased answer.

"Oh my yes, mam. I believe that you and your mother have a similar body type. Your choice of clothes may also tend to be in the same fashionable trend, but we will see about that. Shall we proceed to the salon and try out some designs?" Miss Violet gently guides Bernice into a new, fashionable world complete with boom-town history, feathered regalia, and pelf possibilities. Early afternoon melts into twilight while the two women are busily engaged in trying on and assessing appropriate garments to assemble a wardrobe for the town's most prominent member. Ms. Violet also requests the assistance of the respected Mr. Jones, of the excellent haberdashery shop, to outfit Ms. Bernice with elegant shoes, purse, gloves, and coordinated belts. Additionally, Suzy Mae, from the sophisticated Brazilian boutique, is summoned to assist with a fashionable hairstyle to accompany Bernice's new apparel. Suzy Mae is successful in restoring Bernice's fiery-red, curly hair to its former luster. The hairstyle is reminiscent of her childlike locks; when the brothel workers saw her running in the sunshine, they remarked that her hair resembled tentacles from a fire-breathing dragon.

Bernice's excitement has offered little chance to sleep, and so she's ready early for her departure. She nervously waits in the lobby for her ride to the station. The morning train to BigTon leaves early, and she doesn't want to miss Mr. Smith. The attorney enters the front door of the hotel, passes Bernice and walks directly to the elevator. He pushes the elevator button and patiently waits for the requested elevator door to open. He offers no welcoming glance or morning greeting toward Bernice. When the elevator door opens, Mr. Smith enters the elevator and proceeds up to Bernice's room. The attorney quickly returns to the front desk and learns that his new client has already checked out of the hotel. Mr. Smith is puzzled, 'Bernice is supposed to wait for a ride to the train station, where is she?' The attorney is leaving the hotel when an alluring, well-dressed woman approaches him introducing herself as Ms. Bernice McKim-DePue. Mr. Smith stops walking, physically backs up, looks at the woman speaking to him and responds.

"Excuse me, miss. I'm meeting someone here this morning, and I'm not in the mood for jokes or whatever you're selling. I can call the security guard if you persist with this intrusion." The attorney side-steps away from the irritating female and proceeds to the front desk to leave a message for Ms. McKim-DePue. Bernice follows him to the front desk.

"Excuse me, sir. I wish to leave a message for Ms. McKim-DePue. It seems that she has checked out early and I'm supposed to give her a ride to the station." The front desk clerk responds with a bewildered look in response both to the attorney's request and the presence of the attractive woman standing beside him.

"Uh, uh. I don't know what to say here, sir." Mr. Smith, obviously quite annoyed by this time, repeats his request. "I need to leave a message for Ms. McKim-DePue. She has checked out of this hotel early." This requisition again meets with an astonished stare from the desk clerk. Finally, Bernice, standing next to the attorney, nudges Mr. Smith.

He turns and stares into the eyes of someone faintly familiar. A few seconds lapse before the attorney realizes that the stare of the woman standing next to him is associated with his newest client, Ms. Bernice McKim-DePue. "Oh, my good, golly, gosh. What, who, when, I don't know, what." The jumbled sentence spoken by Mr. Smith is a foreign language to Mr. Smith. "Bernice, excuse me, when did you? Is that you, Ms. McKim-DePue?" The befuddled attorney takes a seat in the chair nearest to the front desk, shaking his head and wiping his brow.

"You were right, Mr. Smith. Ms. Violet was just the right touch. We all had a wonderful time. I gained new friends in a great atmosphere and learned lessons about beauty and charm and elegance. My account at the boutique is always available, and Mr. Jones at the haberdashery wants me to tell you that it's time for you to get a new pair of shoes." Bernice saunters in front of the main lobby desk so that both the desk clerk and the attorney can assess her new persona. Both men agree that her new alluring image is both attractive and genteel.

"Well, I'll be, you look wonderful," is all that Mr. Smith can say. "Let's hurry to the station before the train pulls out, and your schedule gets rearranged." While the attorney is escorting Bernice from the hotel lobby, the porter is scrambling with multiple pieces of new luggage.

Mr. Smith bids Bernice good-bye to his new client. "I will be making a trip to BigTon. I want to meet your family and see how everyone is settling into their new lives."

"What do you mean, new lives?" Bernice shoots the attorney a quick, questioning look.

"You certainly don't imagine that your daughter and granddaughter are going to maintain their current lifestyles after you introduce them to their inheritance, do you? Remember, your mother's will lists all of your family. That also includes extended family members. As I remember, Pamela has an uncle, and you have a brother-in-law. Also, wasn't there a recent DNA science fair project revealing another relationship? Those genetic relationships are also family members."

"You can't be serious! My first thought is for myself, Pamela and Dacia. The others are too far down in the family line." Bernice turns a shoulder toward the attorney as though to offer no thought to his last comment.

"Ms. McKim-DePue, I read your mother's entire will. It stipulates that you and your family are provided for in the proceeds of the will. By law that pertains to all genetically-related family members. It's specifically outlined in your mother's legal papers." Mr. Sylvester Smith, the Esquire, resumes his legal posture so that his message is fully received.

"Hum, maybe I do slightly remember a little clause like that, but I can't recall the specifics," Bernice mumbles a few more unintelligible words.

"Don't worry about the details. I'll follow-up with those details. Have a pleasant trip back to BigTon and give my regards to your family and friends. I can't wait to hear about their reaction to your new appearance. By the way, you haven't told me what you think about 'the new you.'" Mr. Smith looks directly at Bernice anticipating a positive response.

"It's a total change. I'm not sure how I feel. I didn't expect to reveal myself to myself. It scares me. The train ride home is slow so it will give me time to prepare myself to face myself, both inside and out." Bernice offers Mr. Smith a firm handshake as the two part company, each positive that they will meet again.

Ms. WALTERS RECEIVES a call in her classroom to come to the principal's office to talk with a visitor at the high school. The science teacher is a little annoyed at the interruption since the regional science competition is a few days away and the qualification guidelines are explicit. "Okay sir, I'll be right there. Do you know the visitor?"

"No, it's a woman who says that she's from your past and knows you very well. I think that she is a very handsome lady. She must be prominent; looks like money to me."

Erica Walters hustles to the principal's office thinking that the visitor has come at a most inopportune time. "Why do these interruptions always happen when I'm busy?"

Entering the office, the science teacher senses a familiarity with the visitor. The principal is right; whoever this woman is, she is a handsome, cultured lady. Approaching each other, the visitor politely extends her gloved hand. Erica tentatively receives the greeting. "I have the feeling that we've met before. Do I know you?"

"I would say that you do. You know me very well, Erica. I have been working with you for many years." Bernice's eye contact with Erica relates an unbelievable story; complete with its own set of questions.

The science teachers' gut instincts instantly respond; "Stinky-Poo? What? Who are you? Not? What? I don't know you, do I?" Erica grips Bernice's gloved hand with such intensity that the seams of the glove are threatening to make permanent indentations in Bernice's skin.

The school principal is observing the interchange. "See here mam. You can't come in here and impersonate a staff member. I'll call the police if you don't leave. Our counselor is on a personal leave, and you are obviously taking advantage of that to commit some felony. You better leave right now."

The science teacher raises her hand to interrupt the principal's speech. "No, wait a minute, sir. I know this lady. I have seen her somewhere. She's familiar to me. Look at her eyes. I don't understand what is going on with her but let's talk to her." Erica invites the woman to take a seat in the principal's office so that the group can talk in privacy.

Bernice graciously takes a seat at the far corner of the principal's office. When everyone is seated, she begins her revelations. "I'm Bernice McKim-DePue, your school counselor. You're right. I was on personal leave but have returned. I traveled to Wray, Colorado to be present at the reading of my mother's will. Mr. Sylvester Smith, my mother's attorney, related her history in that small community." Bernice then relaxes her posture and waits for her colleague's response.

Both colleagues compete to answer. The science teacher responds, adjusting her position so that she faces the mysterious school visitor. Wait. Are you telling us that you're Bernice? You want us to believe that you are the school counselor? I admit that you resemble her, but your appearance is entirely different. You must be a family member; maybe a sister or aunt. I don't want to insult your family, but Bernice is well, shabby and old. She wears black glasses, and black clothes and oh gosh, that bee-hive hairdo. Well, what can I say? Bernice is old. You are handsome, genteel and beautiful. You can't be Bernice. There, I said it." The principal staunchly nods in agreement.

"So, both of you agree that I'm not Bernice or as you so aptly said, 'Stinky-Poo.' Huh, what shall I do? Let's see. I can tell you both about the intricate details of the science fair and all the DNA background. I can relate stories about Mr. Menendez and his involvement in the Henry family. My most favorite memory is the close relationship between Dacia and Dove-Whispering. However, watching my daughter Pamela grow up and become an independent, prosperous adult woman is probably my greatest joy."

"Stinky-Poo, what happened? You are 'Stinky-Poo'. I'm so sorry Bernice, I don't mean to insult you but what happened to you? You went on leave, and now you are here and different. It's amazing and shocking and confusing." Erica is rambling and uncharacteristically unscientific.

"So, you recognize me. I'm still Bernice but also 'Stinky-Poo' yet also Ms. McKim-Depue. I'm all of them in one person. When you mix all of those characters up into one person, you come up with the same person who looks different. When I went to Wray, Colorado and learned about my mother and her life after leaving the Holladay Street environment, I decided to embrace the life that she left for me. It's one of privilege and luxury. However, it's also a tragedy built on illicit sex, high-end brothels, political intrigue, smitten railroad executives, contraband liquor and infamous back alleys. I can't deny that my mother was a madam in a Denver brothel on Holladay Street, but I can acknowledge that history, blend it with her legacy and develop my legacy. "

Both school employees sit dumbfounded listening

to their colleague recite the exploits of her recent leave adventure. The principal breaks the silence. "So, Ms. McKim-DePue does this mean that you're not returning to your position as a counselor here at Dakota Flats High School?"

"I appreciate your directness. I'm a woman of financial means. Even though I truly love my position here at the school, I'm officially tendering my resignation. I came to the school before notifying my family because I want to sever my financial ties. My daughter, Pamela and granddaughter Dacia will enjoy hearing about their new status. Will you call Dacia to the office for me, Ms. Walters?"

"Of course Ms. McKim-DePue. Will we see you at our school functions? Will Dacia continue to attend our school? I'm assuming that Dacia will participate in the upcoming science competition." The science teacher attempts to maintain a relationship with this shadowy, infamous and now famous employee.

"That is totally up to my granddaughter. She's old enough to make that decision. We'll see." Bernice remains uncommitted.

The two best friends are found in the science class, as usual, when Ms. Walters enters the room. "Well, girls, I don't quite know how to say this next statement. Dacia, there is someone to see you in the front office. You know this woman, but she has changed dramatically since you last saw her." As Ms. Walters is talking to her students, an announcement comes over the room speaker. 'Excuse me for interrupting, Ms. Walters but can you ignore that request for Dacia. Her mother will talk with her at home. Thank you.'

"Okay, I'll do that."

"What's going on? Is something wrong?" Dacia moves closer to Dove seeking support for some impending doom.

"It's not a medical urgency. I think that your mother will want to talk to you. Dove, I imagine that you may want to be with Dacia when she goes home. You may find the conversation interesting as well." The two friends rise in unison, gather their belongings and get their permission slips from Ms. Walters to leave the school campus.

"Ms. Walters, we can't go right home. Dove's dog, Kiko, stayed the night at the veterinarian office for observation and we're picking her up after school. Dove's mom, Ms. Henry is picking us up after school." Both girls look to their trusted science teacher for a solution.

"This is an interesting situation. Dove, your mother will also be interested in what Dacia's mother has to say. It seems like this situation is getting a little complicated. I'm not sure what to tell you, girls. I'll talk to your mother and let her know that she needs to pick you up a little early from school. When she gets here, I'll talk to her." Ms. Walters intentionally avoids eye contact since she's aware that her inquisitive students will detect any concealment of the full truth.

"Okay, we'll wait at the front door. Mom can take us to the vet after you talk to her." Dove and Dacia leave the classroom questioning the decision making ability of their ordinarily analytical teacher.

"Hi girls. I got an interesting call from Ms. Walters. If you wait for a few minutes, I'll talk to her, and then we can pick Kiko up from the vet's office. It shouldn't take long." Michelle's positive mood seems only slightly dampened by her questioning attitude since receiving a phone call from the school's science teacher.

"Ms. Henry, you need to make a detour on your drive home. Your first stop should be at Dacia's house. There's a visitor at her house who has important news that affects all of you. Since you have both of the girls with you and the information is relative to all of you, it's a good idea to see the visitor." The science teacher again diverts direct eye contact to avoid a lengthy conversation.

"Well, I have no idea what you are talking about, but it seems important to do this so, I'll do it. I'm not convinced about making the stop at the house, so I'm going to go into the house with the girls. There may be something going on here that isn't quite right." Michelle motions to Dacia and Dove to accompany her through the high school hallway; noting that the resident counselor isn't skulking around in the shadowy corners; her usual position.

CHAPTER ELEVEN

Revelations

"*D*o the best you can until you know better. Then when you know better, do better.*"
– Maya Angelou

"THERE IS *no agony like bearing an untold story inside of you.*" – Maya Angelou

"ONE FACES *the future with one's past.*"– Pearl S. Buck

THE KNOCK at Pamela's door reverberates throughout the front office of the Inn. While Bernice waits for someone to answer, she notices the inscription on the front sign: "You will love our Inn for generations." Bernice's anxiety and joy intertwine as she anxiously waits for her future to answer the door. Last minute clothes and hair adjustments help to calm her nerves.

"Yes mam, can I help you?" Pamela opens the front door almost as an after-thought since she is occupied organizing paperwork to keep a meeting with her financial advisor.

As the women's eyes meet, Pamela quickly dismisses a faint note of recognition. Bernice's gaze encourages Pamela to maintain eye contact. Recognition then becomes instantaneous for Pamela. "Bernice, what are you doing at my front door and why are you dressed like someone else? Why are you here? Shouldn't you be at school? I don't understand. You look like Ms. McKim-DePue, but you don't look like Ms. McKim-DePue. I still don't understand. Are you lost? Is there something wrong with Dacia at school? All this talk about our relationship bothers me. I know that there's something wrong, really wrong. It' getting to the point where I'm suspicious of everyone. Mr. Hernandez finally confided to me secrets that he kept for years. Are you going to hurt Dacia and me?" Pamela's body is shaking, and her hands fall limply to her side as she half-stumbles into the front office.

Bernice steadies her daughter and guides Pamela to a comfortable couch in the lobby. "Well, dear. I didn't intend to ambush you by showing up at your front door unannounced, but I need to talk to you, and this information is best delivered face-to-face. What I have to say will add to the information that you already know about our relationship. May I come in?" Bernice sits next to her daughter on the couch.

Still a little unsteady, Pamela answers in the affirmative. "Yes, sure, please do. I still don't understand why you're here. What is with the make-over? Don't be insulted because you look amazing, but it's a shock to see such a change. The other day I saw you at school, and you looked different – like the old Ms. McKim-DePue."

Bernice takes a breath and adjusts her position, smoothing her new finery. "Pamela you are my biological daughter. You were born out of wedlock, and Mr. Menendez arranged an adoption with Mr. and Mrs. Love. They were a gentle, hard-working couple unable to have children. I don't know the particulars of that affair, but I do know that you were cherished by a couple who wanted to provide security and prosperity for you." Bernice breathes deeply and tentatively makes eye contact with her doubting daughter. Seeing suspicion and disbelief in Pamela's face, Bernice continues. "I wanted to watch you grow but couldn't let you know the full extent of your lineage. Since Mr. Menendez influences this community, he secured a position for me at the grade school so that I could follow your educational progress and be close to you on a regular basis. I truly know that my past parentage is inexcusable and unforgivable, but there didn't seem to be other options at the time of your birth." Bernice relaxes her supporting arm around Pamela and softens her touch into a mother's concerning stroke to quell her daughter's stirring emotions.

"Wait, this is too much. Are you telling me that my whole life has been under surveillance and that people in the school and community know my secrets? As a child, I'm betrayed and talked-about by adults? Don't you think that William has already done enough harm to me!" Pamela lowers her head into her hands and sobs with an intensity that shakes her body and sends chills down Bernice's spine.

Physically comforting Pamela, Bernice finds herself joining her sobbing daughter. "Now, now child. We can face this."

"What do you mean, we face this?" Pamela grabs a tissue to catch sentimental fluids accumulating on her face. "It sounds like the only ones to face anything is Dacia and me. You are the person who has been keeping secrets. The adults in my life could have and should have done better as far as being role models for a young child. Didn't you think about me? What about me? What about Dacia? We are the ones that are being hurt and embarrassed and having our lives turned upside down. Speaking about turning things upside down, why are you dressed differently. You certainly have changed your appearance. Does that mean that what's on the inside is also changed?"

"Well, I took a train trip to Wray, Colorado because my mother died." Bernice tries to maintain a sense of dignity.

"Oh, here we go again. Now you're going to tell me all about a weird family connection that everyone in the world has known about for one hundred years, except me." Pamela has regained her composure and walks behind the front desk of the Inn's front lobby. That is when she has a shooting mental flashback – 'this is where I was standing when I met William.' It's interesting that Pamela doesn't think about her first meeting with William unless she is having an emotional moment.

Bernice follows her daughter to the front desk but stands on the opposite side. "Not exactly. What I have to tell you is about our family but it's convoluted. However, let us save that discussion until we have more time and privacy."

Pamela shoots Bernice a sharp-eyed look as if to say, 'don't tell me any more stories.' Pamela feels like she's suspended in a pool of disconnected alphabet letters that continually bombard her with incoherent, mismatched words and it's Pamela's job to organize them. "Privacy and secrecy seem to be something that our family is good at practicing."

Just as the conversation reaches a stalemate, there's a riotous entry into the front lobby. Dacia's boisterous, teenage girl voice declares, "Hi, mom. I'm home, and Dove-Whispering's with me. Her mom brought us home. There's something weird happening in the school office today. The principal and Ms. Walters talked to Dove's mom and then Ms. Henry said that she was going to see you when she dropped us off from school." All three visitors cease their socializing when they realize that Pamela is engaged in an emotional conversation with a hotel guest.

Pamela has visibly changed her usually calm persona and gentle tone; there's a sense of panic in her voice. "Of all the people who should come through the door at this particular time. Everyone, I would like you to meet Ms. McKim-DePue." Pamela extends her right hand toward the direction of Bernice while performing a slight, polite, bow as if to say, 'this will be interesting.'

Michelle instinctively extends her right arm out across the front of both girls, preventing them from any forward movement. "This beautiful woman can't be the school counselor. Dowdy, old 'Stinky-Poo' lurks in the corners down the hallway. 'Stinky-Poo' isn't like this woman. Besides, why would the school counselor be here in the front office of your business? Are the girls in trouble? Why didn't you notify me, Pamela, if there's a problem with our girls? You know that we're involved with protecting both Dacia and Dove-Whispering." Michelle walks toward the girls who have themselves huddled closer; unsure of the next interaction. The three sense that this alluring, demure visitor brings with her a substantial change in their lives.

"Michelle, I can assure you that this is indeed Ms. McKim-DePue. Her first name is Bernice, and she's my mother." Pamela motions for all three females to huddle with her on the lobby couch and help filter through the stunning knowledge.

Bernice takes advantage of the opportunity to begin slow pacing in front of the assembled group taking note that all four women are closely following each movement with a visual examination that rivals an x-ray machine. "I know that what you're hearing and seeing is shocking. That's why I want to talk to you in a less public environment." Bernice waits for the new sights and information to percolate into everyone's minds.

"You know me as a school counselor." Bernice starts her explanation by stating the obvious. " I've been in your lives since your birth, especially for Pamela and Dacia."

As Dacia and Dove-Whispering hear this statement, they can sit still no longer." What are you saying? We don't even know you, lady." Dove-Whispering jumps up from the couch and physically approaches the visitor with a posture that challenges the bold statement.

"Now don't worry sweetie. If you let me finish my story, you will agree with what I'm saying." Bernice attempts to pat Dove-Whispering's shoulder when Dacia also leaves her seat on the couch and motions for Dove-Whispering to regain her position. Both girls reluctantly recover their seats.

"I'll start from the beginning. Pamela, you have heard part of this story and were also amazed when you first heard it so I'll ask you to lock the front door and place the 'closed' sign in the window because this may take awhile." Pamela and Bernice exchange a glance of understanding.

Michelle stops the flow of the interaction. "The girls and I are on our way to the veterinarian office to pick up Kiko. She's there for observation. If I call the office, I can extend the time for pickup until tomorrow if this discussion is that important."

Pamela nods in the affirmative. "Yes, Michelle, call the office."

"Okay, as I was saying, I'm going to explain how we all fit into the same story. The DNA science project reveals how Dacia and Dove-Whispering are related. I think that the project is an issue that unearthed the hidden secrets of our family. I say 'our' family because as you will see, we are all related."

Bernice stops a moment to take a deep breath before continuing with the central issue of her tale. "I am indeed the school counselor, 'Stinky-Poo.' You do know me as the spooky, dowdy, dark lady who hides in the corners of the school hallway. However, I wasn't always 'that' person. Once, I was a vibrant, happy teenage girl with dreams of wonder and adventure. So, what I tell you now will begin to explain why I hid my life after my teenage years." Upon hearing this last statement, both Dacia and Dove-Whispering jump up from the couch in unison and move closer to the story-teller finding a comfortable seat on the floor next to Bernice.

"Although my choice would be to have revealed this information in a more appropriate and private setting, this front lobby where William and Pamela met each other somehow seems eerily appropriate. I'll continue by telling you about my childhood. I grew up in a brothel in Denver on Holladay Street."

Again, hearing this enticing information invites both girls to focus their attention on Bernice's story. "When I was about the same age as both Dacia and Dove-Whispering I left my mother's house for a life on my own. Staying with my mother would mean a life of debauchery and agony; much of it sanctioned under her watchful eye." Bernice stops briefly to peer into the crystal green eyes of her precious, naïve granddaughter sitting expectantly at her feet; Dacia's awareness is about to be shattered by a shadowy woman who has cautiously and lovingly observed her since birth. "As I was saying, my childhood was rather unusual. So much so that I needed to escape its influence so that my young adult years wouldn't be tainted by it. I shrouded my next few years in murky activities and was a success in hiding from my mothers' attention. However, one fateful night she, as a prominent member of the community, attended the local theatre and spotted me backstage. My incognito activities had failed. Fleeing Denver, I arrived in Bigton just as it was entering its boomtown status. That's when I met Mr. Menendez and his brother Jim."

Dacia and Dove-Whispering can stand it no longer. Both girls have listened in awe to an unbelievable tale involving a most unusual woman. Their brains are awash with confusion, half-truths, and questions. Dacia speaks first. "So, are you saying mam that you are 'Stinky-Poo' and you know my mom and you know Mr. Menendez?" 'Oh my god, you have been spying on me. Dove, she has been watching us in school. She knows all our secret stuff. Oh my god.' Dacia sits back down sharing a look with Dove-Whispering intermingled with shock and disbelief. Dove-Whispering squints her dark brown, almond-shaped eyes with such intensity that the resulting slits barely allows for vision.

Michelle, sensing that this discussion is following a vein of confidential family information, interrupts Bernice's talk. "I don't think that you, whoever you are, should be talking about family stuff in front of everyone. Maybe it would be better to talk with Dacia and Pamela at another time." Michelle has risen from her seat on the couch and walked toward Bernice.

"I understand your concern Ms. Henry, but if you listen for just a few minutes, you will see that my story does indeed include both you and your daughter." Michelle resumes her position and listens suspiciously.

"This next part is touchy, but it's part of our family, so I'll tell everyone. Jim, Dale Menendez's brother, assaulted me. I was their secretary in Bigton after my mother spotted me backstage at the theatre. Pamela, my beautiful daughter, is the result. Since I was a single mother without the support of a family, Dale Menendez arranged an adoption with Mr. and Mrs. Love. So you see, Mr. Dale Menendez is Pamela's uncle and Dacia's great-uncle."

Dacia quickly rises from her huddled position on the floor and nestles with her mother sitting on the couch. Dove-Whispering, mesmerized by Bernice's story, is transfixed, as though a statue, listening to the gallivanting journey.

"Yes, we're all related. The school DNA science project reveals that both of you Dacia and Dove-Whispering are related. That information also proved that Dacia is Dove-Whispering's aunt. We can all thank William for that connection. It's true that we are an odd, extended family but it's true never-the-less. However, I am getting ahead of my own story. I'll stop here and let you know a little more about my personal story." Dove-Whispering resists urging from Michelle to take a seat next to her on the couch.

"As I was telling you, Pamela was secretly adopted by Mr. and Mrs. Love. Therefore, Mr. Menendez and I and the Love's made a secret pact to withhold the facts of Pamela's true parentage from her. This secret secured the future for Pamela. Society at the time that Pamela was born wouldn't look kindly on an unmarried woman giving birth to a child. I could endure the suffering, but the child's life would be filled with torment and disgrace. We did it for the love of Pamela. The only way that I could remain in Pamela's life and not betray the secret that we all held in a sacred agreement was to take a position in the local school district. Mr. Menendez arranged that assignment. When Pamela graduated from grade school to high school, I changed my job to the high school.

Additionally, when William came into Pamela's life, and my granddaughter Dacia was born, I also followed her, through my position as a school counselor. Concealing my true identity so as not to draw attention to my activities. Everyone knows me as 'Stinky-Poo.' I notice the stares and hear the snide student whispers about 'the weird lady lurking in the dark shadows of the hallway.' Well, that 'weird lady' is me and yes I do 'lurk in the dark shadows of the hallway.' I do that because it is the only manner in which I can stay close to my daughter and enjoy the daily activities of my granddaughter. I am guilty of love, devotion, making secret contracts, holding truths in confidence, enjoying the pride of parenthood, expressing glee watching my granddaughter become a young ..."

Michelle jumps up from the couch and interrupts Bernice's supposedly captivating story. "Pamela, are you just going to sit there and let this lady, whoever she is, talk about you and Dacia like this? For all we know, it's made up to gain sympathy for herself and make a wedge into your life. She's probably lonely and looking for a family without having a true connection. How do we know that any of this is true? We should report this to the school principal. She has access to our children and may be mentally deranged. We need to do something right now, Pamela!"

Pamela rises slowly from the couch hugging

Michelle as much to calm her as to reassure her. "Michelle, Bernice or 'Stinky-Poo' or Ms. McKim-DePue or whatever name she uses is telling the truth about everything. She's indeed my mother, and yes, she's Dacia's grandmother. I recently learned this information and am still struggling to mesh it all together. I imagine that if our girls hadn't picked the DNA science project, this story would never be known. It's the spark that ignited the concealed connection between Dacia and Dove-Whispering. I don't know how long Bernice, my mother, would have concealed her past from not only us but herself as well; I just don't know. It's a big story, and yes, we're all related."

At this point, both Dacia and Dove-Whispering stand up, yell in unison and hug each other. Each competes to talk first since both are of the same opinion. Dacia wins the contest and loudly voices their sentiment. "Our science teacher, Ms. Walters tried to explain to us what the results of the DNA tests meant. We understand what the science tells us, but we're having trouble with what the genealogy means for us as friends. Now we don't have to wonder, we're related in every way; on paper, in blood and by what we call gentle genealogy. Now, no one can dispute that we will be friends forever. It's just fine with us. Now you adults, you old people are the ones who will be figuring out the future of our family. We already know that we'll be just fine." Both girls embraced in an entwined hug, settle back onto the couch ready to hear the rest of the tale of their fascinating family legacy.

Bernice's smile relates her happy contentment in revealing her family connections in this most unusual manner. "Well, I'll continue the update for everyone as to how I'm here today appearing is such a different form from my usual demeanor. I recently learned of my mother's death. She was living in the small town of Wray, Colorado after leaving Denver. My train trip to that area was both insightful and life-changing. Capitalizing on her exploits in running a successful brothel left her a wealthy woman. Her will gives her fortune to her only surviving heir; me. Traveling to Wray, Colorado was a life-changing experience. I discovered that my mother was not only wealthy but a prominent and respected member of the community. Members of the business population held her in high regard. She was a patron of the arts and contributed to the overall growth of the town, everyone I met or interacted with regarded my mother as a valued member of their community. I was astonished to learn about not only the generous personality of my mother but her acceptance into this rural setting. The scene still gives me pause to reconsider how I feel about my mother." Bernice, visibly affected by the emotion of reciting her life history, finds refuge in a lobby chair.

The assembled young women quietly sit pondering this rearranging information of their genealogy. The psychological effect quickly ripples throughout each member of the Henry family. Pamela speaks first. "So, my grandmother was a rich whore. Is that what you are telling us? She was good at what she did, and the money that she left for you is because her brothel was so profitable that our family can now live a life of privilege. Are you saying that?" Pamela is hovering over Bernice in a confronting stance as if Pamela is challenging her understanding of her lineage.

"Yes, that's what I'm saying, dear. It's a fact of our family. It's a dark, guarded secret that even I didn't fully understand until my trip back to examine my childhood. I've been living my shadowy life in a desperate attempt to conceal this torrid information from not only you but my beautiful granddaughter Dacia, as well. I made unscrupulous contracts in an attempt to bury the truth of my birth. The truth of your birth is fraught with suspicious details due to my evil past. Mr. Menendez is a co-conspirator in this intrigue. I'm not sure of his motives; probably self-serving."

"Do you mean that my great-grandmother was a

whore? Mom, did this beautiful, weird woman say that my great-grandma, whoever she is, was a whore and she ran a brothel? Mom, this can't be true. Mom, mom!" Dacia runs up to Pamela wedging herself in between her mother and grandmother."

Dove-Whispering, who has been transfixed by listening to her extended family's scorching history, rushes to Dacia's side hugging her in support. "Dacia, I'm here, it's okay. Your mom won't let anything happen to you. My mom's here too. They will help us. It's okay. It's okay. I'm here." Dacia and Dove-Whispering hug so tightly it seems as though they are one person, one inseparable from the other. Dacia's long, fiery curls and Dove-Whispering's long, raven hair intertwine and provide a protective, fibrous cocoon as though a legion of defensive spiders have been summoned to weave a shield around their coveted treasure.

Michelle responsively joins her Henry clan offering an encompassing hug. "It's okay girls."

KNOCK, KNOCK, KNOCK. "I wonder why the hotel is closed this time of the day. Surely, Pamela didn't forget about the Chamber of Commerce meeting. She's making a presentation about the impact of the history of the city on the current economy. I'll knock harder this time. I'm sure that she's at the front desk. She always in the office." KNOCK, KNOCK, KNOCK. Mr. Menendez's persistent pounding at the hotel door shatters the comfort that the cohorts of the Henry family are experiencing. Pamela hesitates to respond to the peevish pounding although she knows that her hotel normally maintains business hours during this time. She senses that even though this discussion has been emotional and intense, the initiation of an understanding between members of her family has begun. "Excuse me everyone, but I need to respond to whoever is knocking at the door. The hotel is normally open during this time. It may be a customer." Pamela adjusts her position to remove herself from the enmeshed group, straightens her clothing and posture as she approaches the hotel door.

"Well, Pamela, I thought that I might have the wrong time. Did you forget that your presentation for the Chamber is this afternoon? We can go together if you like. Do you have your speech ready?" Mr. Menendez stops at the threshold. He doesn't recognize the hotel guest sitting in the over-stuffed chair, yet she seems somehow familiar. However, he immediately recognizes the other visitors in the hotel lobby but isn't accustomed to seeing them together outside of the high school environment. "Did I interrupt something,

Pamela? We're you having a meeting about a school activity?"

"Mr. Menendez, come in. You'll be interested in the hotel guests and the discussion that we're having in here." Pamela ushers the hesitant, well-known, community leader into the hotel lobby.

Immediately, Michelle gathers both Dacia and Dove-Whispering closely around her in a protective mode. "We were just leaving, Pamela. I promised to take the girls to the veterinarian office to check on Kiko. I know that she's an older dog but may be okay, and we can bring her home tonight. "

"Yes, we're excited to see her. We've had her for many years, and she's part of our family. It'll be good to have Kiko back home." Dove-Whispering grabs Dacia's hand in a persuading gesture as the friends head for the lobby door. "Dacia will be with us if you need her for anything. Okay?" Dove-Whispering doesn't wait for a sympathetic response from Pamela, as she and Michelle usher Dacia out of the hotel front door.

Meanwhile, Mr. Menendez cautiously, yet politely, approaches the new hotel guest. "Good afternoon, mam. Are you staying very long at the hotel? I want to introduce myself. I'm Mr. Dale Menendez. I operate an insurance company in this community." As he extends his right hand for a friendly, yet business-like handshake, a sheet of recognition hits Mr.

Menendez as though someone just hit him with a raging river of freezing ice crystals. "Who are you? Do I know you? What's going on here? Pamela, what's going on here today? This lady looks like, could it be Bernice? Bernice, is that you? What?" Mr. Menendez slowly drops his extended hand, withdrawing his greeting to the visitor while repeatedly blinking his eyes in a vain recognition effort.

Bernice conspicuously rises from her chair, straightens her apparel, clears her throat and, facing Mr. Menendez, begins her introduction. "Dale, I'm formally re-introducing myself; I'm indeed Ms. McKim-DePue, a person you have known for most of my adult life. You know me better as 'Stinky-Poo' or Bernice." Bernice maintains her position in front of Mr. Menendez waiting for his response.

"Well, well, well, I never would have recognized you girl. What in the world are you doing in those clothes? Gee, you're all dolled up. What in the hell is going on with you? You sure do look spiffy. Is there some big, important party going on in the city or the school?" Dale Menendez drops his usual business-like manner as he questions his life-long acquaintance. The two stand motionless in the quiet lobby, each assessing the others' next statement. The lone witness to their interaction is the one person who has a familial invest-ment in both of their futures, Pamela.

Bernice's words perforate the silence as if a tool and die maker has designed a prototype for their following discussion. "I am Bernice. The same woman you have known intimately for many years. The woman you have dealt with and schemed with through an untold number of secrets. Yes, Dale. It's me."

"What happened to you, girl? You're beautiful. You left the school without notice and then I couldn't find you at your house. We do have things to talk about so you can see why I'm concerned." Mr. Menendez expects that his relationship with Bernice will continue as it always has been.

"Dale, what you and I have to talk about isn't something that needs to be discussed here in this setting. We will indeed talk about our concerns, and we will discuss how our relationship may be changing. However, we'll be doing all of this at another time." Bernice turns away from Mr. Menendez in an arrogant manner indicating to him that she is now taking the upper hand in their relationship. Not only has her outward apparel upgraded but Bernice's inward attitude toward her ties in covert family activities is refashioned; community members in Wray, Colorado would approve.

Pamela, taking the cue from her mother, chimes into the conversation. "Mr. Menendez I don't believe that I'll be making my presentation to the Chamber today. Here are my notes for the speech, you can make the points that I would highlight to the members. They will understand. Now if you will excuse us, my mother and I have a lot to discuss. Mr. Menendez, as you remember, you and I had our intense conversation about family relationships. I haven't changed my perspective."

Dale Menendez, unable to verbalize an appropriate response, grabs the Chamber of Commerce paperwork from his niece as he abruptly leaves the lobby office.

BERNICE AND PAMELA nervously pace on opposite sides of the lobby, each reluctant to make eye contact. Pamela's first to show acceptance of her mother's new personal attire by revealing a faint smile as she mentally recounts the conversation of the past few minutes. "Mom. Oh my god! I can't believe that I just called you mom. I never used that word except when I talked with Mrs. Love, and she's been dead for some years. Oh well, I've said it. I've used the word. It came from me involuntarily, so I guess that my brain accepts you in that way. I don't understand it because my heart isn't accepting it yet. I'm so confused about what to believe. Mrs. Love is my mother, and now you're my mother; it's very emotional and confusing."

"I know, dear. You've heard and listened to a lot of new information about our family in the past months. Even today you've had a shock about your mother. I imagine that's turned your world around in so many ways that it will never settle into any stable manner. However, it will settle dear; it will come dear."

Each woman walks to the middle of the front lobby, tentatively waiting for the other to react. Bernice opens her arms widely, offering an encompassing hug toward her beloved daughter. Without hesitation, Pamela rushes into her mother's open embrace. Both women entwine as though chameleon lizards are conspicuously blending and there's no discernible separation between either body.

"Oh daughter, I've waited for this moment since you were born. Concealing my true background and negotiating life in a shadowy format gave me such pain. I observed your life through a fenestrated veil, unable to interact in a meaningful manner. I love you my dear child and made decisions for you that I truly believed would keep you safe and happy." Bernice refuses to release her daughter now that she can publicly acknowledge her.

"Mom, you're squeezing me too tight; I can't breathe. You'll have to let me go for a while so that we can talk. I love you too. These past months have been very confusing." Bernice loosens her hold on her newly found daughter.

"You'll have to remember one thing, dear. People don't change who they are simply because we learn more about them. People are who they are. So, as you and I develop our relationship, I'm sure that we'll reveal life-long decisions that we would change if we had the chance. Based on that idea, I want to say that I'm available to be in your life and the life of Dacia for as much as you will allow me to be. It's obvious to me that Dacia, you and I form the basis of a new life story. We all bring heavy experience to our genealogy yet there are wonderful life experiences ahead for us to share. 'Stinky-Poo' will always be part of who I am whether I like it or not." Bernice turns her head to the side and slightly lowers her chin to break her eye contact with Pamela.

"Oh, mom. It's funny to hear you call yourself, 'Stinky-Poo.' But I do understand what you're saying about yourself. There was a time in my life when I learned that I was pregnant with Dacia that I considered calling myself Mrs. Henry. I thought that taking that name would protect both she and I. It's like using an umbrella of many colors to disguise yourself so that you can run to get out of the rain. Everyone looks at the beautiful shade instead of focusing on the person carrying the collapsible coverage." Pamela gently hugs her mother and slowly, silently begins a sob; her flood of emotional tension is releasing past scars and opening the gates to a functional, loving family.

"My dearest daughter. I have so much to tell you, not only about my past but about my transformation in Wray, Colorado and how it affects the future of our family. By our family I mean everyone that is genetically related to us; the DNA science project did more than satisfy the requirements for a science class assignment. I now realize that my actions concealing my identify were emotionally evasive. We'll all go forward from here and prosper into a new life, but let's not forget the lessons that we've learned."

"Of course mother. I'm so excited to hear about your childhood and your mother. I was about to say that you've missed a lot of Dacia's childhood, but then I realized that 'Stinky-Poo' hasn't missed a thing. Oh, mom, I love you." Pamela gives Bernice a gentle, secure hug.

"Daughter, loving you and Dacia has always been the reason for everything I have done. Let's go over to my home here in the hotel and spend the rest of the afternoon getting acquainted."

"GIRLS, I know that you're both excited and curious about seeing Ms. McKim-DePue in such a different appearance today. However, I'm sure there's a special story connected to why she looks like she does. I must admit that I was also stunned when I saw her standing in the front lobby. I believed that she was a new hotel guest. Her appearance is so stunning and different; no one would guess that she and 'Stinky-Poo' are the same. However, we need to focus on picking up Kiko from the vet's office. When I talked to the doctor, he told me that the tests would reveal any issues about her health. I'm sure, Dove-Whispering, that your pet will be fine and excited to see you today." Michelle tries to conceal her concern from her daughter. The discussion with the veterinarian when they dropped off their family pet to the office a few days ago indicated that Kiko might be ailing from the common issues that most older canines encounter.

The unison scream emanating from the back seat of the family's' SUV, pierces Michelle's ears. "Girls, girls, my ears. I need to drive the car. We need to get to the office so that we can pickup Kiko. "I know mom, but we are both so excited about getting that fluffy, big dog back with us. Both Dacia and I love her so much. She is almost like our best friend. She loves us so much too. Sometimes I think that she knows what we are thinking."

"Yes, Dove-Whispering is right. I'm going to rub her ears and ruffle her fur, just like I did when we dropped her off at the vet's office. She sure did like that when I did it." Dacia rubs Dove-Whispering's head pretending that she is Kiko and Dove-Whispering wiggles her lower back as though she is Kiko enjoying the rub from Dacia.

"Okay girls, settle down. I know that you both love Kiko but remember she is an older dog and maybe the doctor found out why she doesn't have as much energy as a few months ago. When we dropped her off, she did seem to be a little tired. But we'll see how things go." Michelle attempts at gently preparing the girls for possible health issues with Kiko, seem to go unnoticed.

"Oh mom, you worry too much. Kiko will be with us forever." Dove-Whispering gleefully remarks as she regains her position in the back seat.

"Good afternoon Ms. Henry. I see that your daughter Dove-Whispering and her friend are with you today. Can I have you wait for me in an exam room? I'll have the technician bring Kiko in to meet with us. I'll be there in just a few minutes. I want to get her medical file. I'll be right there." The veterinarian motions for the trio to wait in a patient care room.

Within a few minutes, a vet technician carries Kiko into the exam room and places her on the exam table. The dog appears tired and listless even though her tail is slowly waging when she sees both Michelle and Dove-Whispering.

Dacia immediately approaches the quiet pet and begins to stroke her ears and vigorously rub the thick fur on her neck. Kiko tries to respond in her usual excited manner but lays her head down onto the cold exam table, weakly waging her tail. "Dove-Whispering, what's happened to Kiko? Is she sick? Doesn't she feel good? Something wrong with her. Ms. Henry, what's wrong?"

Dove-Whispering rushes to the exam table and hugs Kiko. "I don't know, Dacia. Kiko is always glad to see us. Her tail wags so hard that she could hurt your leg if you get close to it. Kiko's eyes look sad. Mom, something is wrong. Mom, look." Dove-Whispering and Dacia, holding on to Kiko, both turn toward Michelle in a pleading manner as if to say, 'make Kiko feel better.'

Michelle hugs Kiko just as the veterinarian enters the exam room.

"Well, Ms. Henry, we performed a lot of tests on Kiko to check out her general health. I always like to tell the owners of my patients the full story of the test results. Kiko is in good general health for a dog her age.

She has had good care. Her teeth, eyes, and ears are in good shape. Now, I need to tell you the results of the other tests. Kiko has an inoperable tumor in her liver. She's in such good shape that her system has been able to compensate for the damage that the tumor is doing to her liver. When I say inoperable, it means that we can't operate on it and make it better. I'm sorry to tell you that Kiko has just a few weeks to live." The doctor is silent waiting for his worrisome words to settle into the minds of the trio.

A unison cry echoes so strongly throughout the exam room that two veterinarian technicians rush in to offer the doctor assistance. The call precedes another unison declaration. "That can't be. It's not so. You're lying. She's not going to die. You're making this up to get money. I, we, don't believe you. We're taking Kiko to another doctor. Another doctor will be able to fix Kiko. She's our dog, and she's fine. She's not sick." Dove-Whispering picks Kiko up from the exam table and lovingly cradles her as they sit in an exam room chair.

"It will be okay Kiko. We love you, baby. We love you, baby. Are you in pain? Mom, is Kiko in pain? She can't be in pain. We have to help her. She's our dog. She's part of our family." Kiko slowly licks Dove-Whispering's neck and cheek as if to say 'I love you too.'

Dacia sits on the exam chair next to Dove-Whispering and Kiko desperately hugging each one in an attempt to squeeze out the tumor that is sucking the life out of their precious pet. "This can't be, Dove-Whispering. This thing can't be."

Michelle's first inclination is to question the doctor. "Are you sure doctor about the test results? Sometimes these things show inaccurate results. I know you're trained, but are you sure about the results?"

"Yes, Ms. Henry, the results are accurate. I'm so very sorry. There is no easy way to tell people about these things. Kiko is a sweet dog. I can help you with whatever arrangement you want to make. I'll leave you alone for a while to discuss the results." The veterinarian leaves the exam room.

"Girls, the doctor is right. The tests are correct. Kiko is sick and won't be with us long. I'll go and talk to the doctor to see if she is in pain. If so, we can get something to make her comfortable. Kiko will be with us for a short time." Michelle leaves the exam room to discuss plans with the doctor.

Wailing and crying are all that Dacia and Dove-Whispering can do as they hold Kiko. The dog licks the hands of both girls and slowly wags her tail while attempting to wiggle loose and stand under her own strength. Accomplishing this feat, Kiko slowly walks toward the door leading out toward the main office. All three exit the exam room and meet Michelle in the front office.

"The doctor said that we could take Kiko home today. I have some medication to keep her comfortable and something to help increase her energy. So, we'll leave with her today but may be back here soon to see the doctor." Michelle doesn't want to discuss too much information about Kiko with the two girls until they get home. The three people and Kiko get into the SUV for their somber trip back home.

"Dacia, I'll drop you off at your home first. Dove-Whispering and I need to have some time together tonight to discuss and make some decisions about Kiko. I'm glad that you were with us today when we got the medical test results about Kiko. I know that you also love her. Dacia, let your mom know what happened here today. The structure and character of our family are changing. We're all going through transformations." Dacia and Dove-Whispering sit in the back seat cuddling Kiko between them.

CHAPTER TWELVE

Footsteps

"*S*uccess *always leaves footprints.*"
    – Booker T. Washington

"T*HE FOOTSTEPS A CHILD follows are most likely to be ones his parents thought they covered up.*"
    – James Dobson

"W*E ALL LEAVE footprints in the sand; the question is, will we be a big heal or a great soul.*"– Anonymous

"WELL, mom, have you heard from Michelle about Kiko? I know that she was taking the dog to the vet to see why she wasn't feeling well. That dog has been with Michelle and Dove-Whispering since Dove-Whispering was a baby. Grandpa William liked the dog too." Auntie Anne is visiting her mom Kaye to see if her sister, Michelle has contacted their mom about the health of the family pet.

"I'm waiting to hear from her at any minute. They're picking Kiko up this afternoon from the vet's office. Something tells me that the news won't be good. Kiko's getting older and sometimes older dogs have health problems." Kaye appears nervous transferring her cell phone from hand-to-hand.

"Mom, my phone's ringing. I'll take the call in the other room." Anne quickly answers the call from her sister Michelle.

"Hello, sweetie. We have been waiting to hear what the vet said about Kiko. Mom is waiting for your call. Where are you?" Anne is surprised to receive a call from her sister. Kaye was expecting that Michelle would notify their mother first about the vet's visit.

"Well, I couldn't tell mom what the vet said about Kiko. I had to call you first. Kiko isn't doing well. She has an inoperable tumor on her liver. We just got the news this afternoon. Dacia and Dove-Whispering were both in the exam room with me when the doctor gave us the results of the tests. The girls are both sad and emotional. I don't know how to talk to them right now. Those girls are so close to each other that they seem to know what the other is thinking without saying a word." Michelle ends her report to her sister and waits for consolation.

"Michelle, I'm so sorry to hear that result. Are you saying that Kiko is dying?"

"Yes, that's what I'm saying. Our dog, our pet, our loving, sweet dog is dying."

"I know that there is nothing I can say to make it better, but I'm so very sorry to hear you say those words. I love Kiko very much also. She's been in this family forever. She truly is part of us. So, the next thing is; telling mom. How are you going to do that?"

"I don't know, but I had to tell you first. My first call is to you."

"I understand. Do you want me to give the phone to mom so that you can talk?"

"Well, I guess that I have to have that conversation. Okay, give mom the phone."

Kaye picks up the phone, already knowing the message. "Hello, Michelle. What's the news on Kiko?"

"Mom, it isn't good. She has an inoperable tumor on her liver and not long to live. She'll be with us for only a short time longer. The vet gave us the news today with both Dacia and Dove-Whispering in the exam room. Everybody is sad today. I'm sad too, mom.

I need my mom. It's good to talk to you." Michelle's voice trails off in the conversation.

"I know that you're sad about Kiko. Age transforms everyone's body kiddo, even animals. It might be a good idea to start a journal. You and the girls can document your days with Kiko, and it will be a positive memory about your time together." Kaye's voice is scratchy as she suggests options to her grieving daughter.

"That's a good idea, mom. The girls and I will get a book and start making entries today. It will help in the process. Thanks, mom."Both women end their conversation with their traditional greetings of love and concern.

"Mom, why do we have to go shopping today? Dacia and I are working with Ms. Walters in the science class to get ready for the final touches of the regional science competition." Dove-Whispering follows her mom into the local greeting cards store. She watches as her mom walks up to the display case that holds a collection of scrapbooks and memory books.

"Sweetie, I want us to start a memory book for Kiko. It's like a footprint book for people, but this one will be one that we can put in a paw print from Kiko and then write-in thoughts and pictures of our time with her. It's a record of our life with our pet." Michelle hugs Dove-Whispering while they stand in front of the bookcase so that the couple can share a tender moment before beginning the farewell road toward their treasured family pet.

'Okay, mom. Whatever we get, I'll show it to Dacia and her mom." Dove-Whispering's tearful response is hardly audible.

The women purchase a book that contains both sketch pages and inserts for family photos. The insignia on the front cover is an engraved human foot-print interlaced with a dog's pawprint.

"My, my, Pamela, you certainly have a beautiful home here in the hotel. You and Dacia must be very comfort-able. I'm glad that I have the opportunity to ..." Bernice stops in mid-sentence so as not to upset Pamela by saying her next thought out loud.

"What were you going to say, mom?" Pamela questions her mother.

"I don't want to upset you, dear. I was going to mention William. This room is where he surely spent a lot of time in his life with you and Dacia. It's the first thought that popped into my thinking."

"It's okay. Don't worry about mentioning William. He was part of my life. Because of him, I have Dacia. So, you see, in some way I fondly remember him." Pamela tries to make her mother feel at ease.

"Well, I feel a little uneasy sitting here in your living room. I've observed you for so long from the shadows of the school hallways that to be able to sit in a cozy room and talk with you openly, feels unnatural. I've longed for this encounter, but now that it's here I'm not sure that I know how to handle it."

"I share your feeling. Even calling you 'mom' is unusual for me and uncomfortable. As time goes by, we'll both be more comfortable with this kind of conversation." Pamela wants them to feel at ease and fixes two cups of hot tea to enjoy during their visit.

"Dacia is doing chores in the hotel while we're here. I want to spend time with you so that we can speak freely before the three of us meet. Feel at ease to discuss issues with me. I don't know about your childhood or your life as a young woman. There are small pieces of information floating around the community about your life, and I must admit that I may have fostered some of them, and for that, I'm humiliated. I would like to know about you. You already know everything about my life." Pamela states the obvious.

"Dear child, my need for atonement is sizable. It's not because I'm necessarily ashamed of my childhood but because I made decisions out of fear; mostly fear of the unknown. My mother raised me in an uncertain environment exposing me to adult ideas early in my young life. Pamela, as you know, my mother was a madam in a brothel in Denver. She was successful in the trade that she knew best. I became accustomed to that lifestyle. I have vivid memories as a young child of lying in my bed at night listening to heavy footsteps tromping up and down the wooden staircase of our home. As I reached my teen years, those massive, nervous footsteps hesitated outside my bedroom door as if an evil Sasquatch monster might be ready to pounce into my room and devour me. I huddled cringing in my bed, terrified that the doorknob would turn and whoever was on the other side of the door would creep into my dark bedroom. I wasn't sure what the man would do to me if he entered my bed, but I knew that groans and wails came out of dark, shuttered rooms. One fateful night my consuming fears started slowly creeping through my flimsy door; the doorknob turned. I clustered my bed covers around me for protection against the intruder. That's when I heard a faint, familiar voice whisper to the intruder. 'Not yet, she's too young maybe next time.' Mother dissuaded the intruder. I knew that my mother was grooming me to follow in her footsteps. I listened intently to the whispers outside my bedroom door; terror filled my young body. Finally, the heavy, sluggish footsteps walked away from my door followed shortly by the light, yet determined, pace of my mother's footsteps. I huddled, shivering in my bed, surrounded by a dark, foreboding room and decided that I would leave home that very next morning. I waited until the house was quiet and all of the previous nights' activity had subsided. Gathering my few possessions, I opened my bedroom window, jumped onto the outstretched tree limb next to the window and shimmied down the tree. I was lucky because I knew the patrons at my mother's house. One of them was an actor in a local acting company. I knocked on his dressing room in the back of the production area, told him my story of escape, and he took me in for the night. He was an honorable man and developed a scene for me in their current production. One evening, my mother was sitting in the audience. After the presentation, she came backstage. I'm not sure if she wanted to congratulate the actors or because she recognized me. Whatever the reason, I knew that if she could, she would entice me back to the brothel. I decided to leave and find another job and another persona. That's when I met Mr. Menendez and his brother Jim Sleazy."

"Mom, stop your story right there. I know very little about this section of your life with Mr. Menendez and his brother, Jim. However, Mr. Menendez has been a kind and protective person for Dacia and me. Only recently did I learn about his part in my true parentage and adoption by Mr. and Mrs. Love. Mr. Menendez and I had a rather heated conversation about him withholding information about my birth and childhood. So, when you tell me the next part of your story, I am very interested in hearing the details." Pamela leans in toward Bernice and rests her chin on the palm of her right hand in an attentive posture that resembles the internationally known statue, 'The Thinker.' That bronze sculpture by Auguste Rodin seems an appropriate analogy to demonstrate Pamela's deep thought and focused attention.

"Yes, Pamela, the next part of my story is also your part of the story. I want to preface this next part by saying that I love you dearly and am honored to be your mother. So, let me tell you the rest of the details. My secretarial job with the brothers, who were unscrupulous land dealers, was short-lived and intensely violent. Dale attempted to subdue his brother Jim, but he was having none of it. Jim Sleazy was a riotous, rebellious, impetuous, scam artist. He cornered me in our office one fateful evening and violently raped me. Dale chased down his brother, confronted him in a dingy saloon where, seeing no options, Jim shot himself. That, my lovely daughter, is the story of your conception. That is also how you're related to Uncle Dale, Mr. Menendez, and in a perverted way, I'm a profane sister-in-law to that same man."

"So, you're saying that the man that I've known as Mr. Menendez my entire life is really my uncle because his brother, Jim, raped you?"

"Yes, that's what I'm saying. That's the family connection for all of us."

"I don't understand why Mr. Menendez didn't let me know of his family relationship. Why would he withhold that information? There were many times in my life that I needed the support of someone who knew and understood me. It would've helped me if he had said that he was a family member. I've had a discussion with him about his deceit, and now my discovery of this additional information is almost more than I can endure." Pamela's anxiety rotates on her hand-wringing repetition.

"Dear, my sorrow about the secrets that hide in the darkness of the lies conceived in the early days of our family, pains me to the core of my being. However, during the intense time that these torrid incidences occurred, Dale and I made a secret pact that we believed would protect and shelter you throughout your life."

"Mom, are saying that you agreed with Mr.

Menendez that I should be given away in a secret adoption and my true identity concealed forever?"

"Yes. I have no other defense or explanation; yes."

"Mom, I still don't understand. I'm your child. Was it because you were raped and looking at me every day reminds you of the rape?"

"Pamela, please understand when I say that you were born into a different social and political time. Society marks a single mother with a socially degraded stain. Her child also carries a shameful moral brand. I couldn't bear that life for you. My only option was to return to my mother's house; that's a life of debauchery I wouldn't consider for either of us."

"But why did you decide on adoption?"

"That's a convoluted story, Pamela. During the early settlement days of the Denver frontier, Mr. Menendez and his brother defrauded the prominent Love family in a land-grabbing deal. After Jim's death, Dale tried to amend partially for the brothers' dastardly deed. Subsequently, the childless couple agrees to adopt a foundling baby girl that Mr. Menendez had located during one of his many business dealings. The private adoption seemed to satisfy everyone's needs. Little did the couple realize that the baby's mother was a young, single woman living quite close to them. That young mother was me, and I knew that the Love family could provide a bountiful, loving childhood for you. That's the day that Pamela McKim-DePue becomes Pamela Love."

"Oh mom, that's so sad."

"I did have enough time to make prints of your little feet. You know the kind you see on the bottom of a birth certificate. Well, I used those tiny prints to make baby shoes that fit the size of the prints, perfectly. When I'm lonely, I take those little shoes with me to the beach and walk on the soft sand next to the tiny footsteps that I've made with the small shoes. I pretend we're walking in harmony on the shore; for a short time, we're together. Sometimes, looking back at the footsteps, I imagine that the impressions are real. It's a good day."

"Is that when you decide to watch me from a distance?" Pamela's thinking about what she, as a mother, would do if she had given up her baby for adoption.

"Dale and I devise the plan together. Being a counselor in the school district allows me to oversee you, and eventually Dacia, every day. I conceal my identity yet observe you growing and developing your talents within the community that I love. Its turned out to be the right decision because I know that you're raised by a loving couple who provide a stable family life for you. That's something I could never have given you." Bernice lovingly cuddles

Pamela's face between her hands allowing direct eye contact.

"Mom, I never knew the whole story. The sacrifice you made to protect me and provide a safe life is something that I'll never fully understand. Remnants of my embedded anger surrounding William's betrayal are still swirling around my heart, and that makes me too self-protective. That cloud conceals my heart from accepting love and support. Since learning about my true parentage and my family's nefarious background, I'm a sentinel for suspicious knowledge. So naturally, I become angry when sensing that someone is trying to undermine me."

"I knew that you would be furious upon learning about your genetic connection to both Mr. Menendez and myself. That's why I've always tried to be as quiet as an ant sitting on a cotton ball. That little, social insect quietly works to support both its family and multi-generational community to which it belongs."

"Thanks for explaining the full story, mom. I've felt alone. Someone secretly watching over me since my birth in some ways has given me two loving mothers. So, there's another question just screaming to be asked. Why do you look so different from the way that you did when you were a school counselor? It seems as though you've changed from an unlovely urchin to a cultured couturier. Mom, where did you go and what caused you to change so drastically?

"Child, I'm glad you ask that question. Surely, you've heard the saying that 'a journey starts with a single step' or is it a footstep, I can't remember exactly. Well, that's what I did. I took a step. It lead to a trip, and that lead to a journey. I ended up in Wray, Colorado. Wray, Colorado is the home my mother chose after she left her position as a madam in the brothel on Holladay Street in Denver. My trip to that city changed my life in every way. As you see, I physically look different. That's because of the information about my mother's feelings toward me that was revealed by the members in that town."

"Are you saying that my maternal grandmother was not only a madam in a brothel but also a respected community leader?"

'Yes, that's what I found out on my trip to Wray."

"Mom, my brain is swimming from all this stuff about our family."

"There is more information to come, Pamela." Bernice motions for Pamela to sit next to her on the couch.

"Your grandmother wrote a will. In that legal document, she acknowledges that I'm her child and she leaves all of her worldly possessions to me. All of her property includes her financial and physical effects.

Her lawyer stressed that there's a legal attachment to this document outlining specifics regarding the distribution of her assets. It states that all wealth should be divided "between all of her genetically related heirs."

"So, I'm confused. Didn't you say that you're an only child?"

"Yes, but in our family, we're all genetically related."

"Who do you mean by 'we'?"

"Pamela, I mean, me and you and Dacia and Dove-Whispering and her entire family and yes, Mr. Menendez. That's the 'we' of our family. Remember, genetics is what started the process of Dacia and Dove-Whispering understanding their relationship. Michelle and Kaye and Anne and Benedict are also attached to the genetics of this family." Bernice waits for Pamela to process her statement.

"Girl, that also means the coming generations of our family. What my mother has done effects people in our family that aren't born yet. She has sent ripples out into our generations."

"Well, what kind of things are you talking about, mom?"

"I'm talking about community respect and money."

"Your grandmother was a retired brothel madam as well as a well-respected community leader who freely invested in the Wray township. She and her friend Mattie seem to have found solace in that little city. Possibly, by leaving proceeds to her family, she wanted her lineage to discover that same solace and comfort themselves. Whatever the reason, Pamela, we're the recipients of her generosity."

"How do you know this information?"

"Mr. Smith, Esq., notified me; he's now our family attorney representing all of the legal concerns connected to my mother's will."

"Why do we need an attorney?"

"Dearie, we need legal advice to manage our fortune."

"What fortune?"

"Sweet daughter, we're wealthy. Not just rich but wealthy."

"Wealthy?"

"Yes, dear, wealthy."

"I don't understand."

"To put it plainly; your infamous grandmother ensured that her family would be financially secure for generations. We're wealthy. Every single one of us is wealthy. Our genetic relationship ensures our connection, and if we manage the wealth properly, it will attest to my mother's memory and ripple her generosity down through the generations." Mother and daughter embrace each other on the couch straining to absorb the understanding of their recent exchange.

"Oh my god, mom. So, Dacia and Dove-Whispering are wealthy too?"

"Yes, those beautiful, teenage girls are now wealthy, beautiful, teenage girls."

"Oh my god, oh my god, oh my god!" Pamela walks frantically around the front lobby reciting the primal phrase that expresses her feelings of surprise, disbelief, joy and intense happiness.

"Mom, what do we do? How do we handle things? What do we do next? Who do we contact? Does everyone know about this great money thing? Oh my gosh, I can't seem to think straight today. I still can't believe that I'm calling you mother." Pamela continues to wander around in circles in front of Bernice.

"Sit down Pamela. I've taken care of the fundamental issues. Our attorney has prepared all of the legal documents and papers transferring the property and financial concerns into our estate."

"Estate, what do you mean estate? Do we own property?"

"Yes dear, we own a lot of property. Most of it's in Denver, but some parcels are in other parts of Colorado. I'm sure that we'll be discussing the estate matters with Mr. Smith later this month. My significant concern is to make sure that both you and the girls are well provided for both now and in the future."

"I'm upset with Mr. Menendez, mom. His secrets did a lot of damage to my life. From what I'm hearing, he didn't do much to protect you when you're working for him and his brother, Jim in that small office." Pamela has regained her composure and is mentally reviewing some recent family revelations.

"Again, dear, I can't answer for Dale. He did rescue me when I was facing a lifetime identity as a 'scarlet' woman. Although, he shared responsibility for my condition since it's his brother who raped me and he would be the uncle of my soon-to-be-born child. I believe that Dale's a survivor but also someone who, when faced with making the correct moral decision, usually collapses into ethical decay. Whether or not he's sorry for his decisions, I can't say. However, I do know that Dale offered me a protected solution when you're born; I could watch you grow and ensure that loving parents adopted you. I suspect that he was also looking for some personal redemption. Either way, Mr. and Mrs. Love gave you their name and their heritage. In a way, you're like me in one respect. You're a female child of a family harboring secrets that are grounded in the early, uncertain settlement days of Colorado."

"He's tried to explain his actions, but I don't know the entire discussion between him and the Love's.

What would entice Mr. and Mrs. Love to adopt a child when they don't know the background of that infant? Could there have been some mention of my past? Did the Love's take me in exchange for something? Maybe they adopted me because they couldn't have children of their own? Was there a secret exchange between the Love's and Mr. Menendez?" Pamela continues with her litany of questions while she paces the floor in front of Bernice.

Bernice hesitates before revealing her intimate feelings about Mr. Menendez since Pamela is involved in a guardianship relationship with her uncle. "I don't know the intimate details of your adoption. I concentrated on my social standing in the community, your safety and my mother's ability to kidnap you after your birth; the only option for us was Mr. Menendez. He's involved in my story and the details of my pregnancy. Dale understood my desperation to shield myself and my infant from controversy and public persecution. I'm vulnerable, and the Love's may have been anxious to start a family. He's the kind of man who exploits rash opportunities. I know him well and can tell you that your Uncle Dale can be less than honorable if the opportunity arises."

"I know, mom. My discussion with him didn't end well. He knows my sentiments. Believing that he knew William's background and how it affected me will always be an issue that wedges between our relationship. He's my uncle, but I've learned that he can't be trusted. His involvement in our lives will always be an issue."

Bernice, sensing that the conversation is taking a morbid turn, switches the tone to a more positive focus. "How about we check on Dacia and the other girls. They're picking up Kiko from the vet's office, and that dog may pep us up for the rest of the day."

"Okay, mom. Let's go and see the girls and that beautiful, fluffy canine." Pamela proudly opens the front door of her office and prepares to escort her mother outside for their initial footsteps into public scrutiny.

"Mom, the first place we're going is to pick up Dacia. She's at Dove-Whispering's house. Dacia was with them when Michelle and Dove-Whispering talked to the doctor at the vet's office. Seeing that frisky pet will undoubtedly liven our spirits. Besides, Dacia always enjoys spending time with her friend, Dove-Whispering. It won't take us long to drive there. Moreover, we'll enjoy driving through town together viewing the city as mother and daughter. It'll be our introduction to society."

Pamela and Bernice pull up into the driveway of Michelle's house. Pamela helps her mother out from the passenger's side of the front seat. Both women approach the front door of the house anticipating the warm welcome they'll receive from both Dacia and Dove-Whispering. Pamela rings the doorbell; the women wait for an answer.

Michelle opens the front door with a sizable effort. Her flushed cheeks, teary eyes, and a sweaty forehead betray her attempts to hide the emotional turmoil saturating her body. "Oh Pamela, come in, will you. Who's with you? Is that the woman that was at your office?"

"Yes, Michelle, this is my mother, Bernice." Pamela turns toward Bernice and extends her hand in the direction of her mother.

"Good afternoon, Michelle. I'm glad to meet you although I've seen you many times." Ms. McKim-DePue extends her right hand as though to shake her hand in friendship.

"My goodness. Are you introducing me to the school counselor? You're telling me that the homely, sulky woman who tends to hide in the hallway corners, is this woman with you today? Pamela, it's hard to believe what you're telling me. But, as I look closer into her eyes, I see that there is a resemblance." Michelle guides the visitors into the living room.

"Oh, mam, I'm sorry. I don't mean to be rude, but

it's just a shock to see such a change in you, especially in this short of a time. I'm accustomed to seeing you as the school counselor. You'll need to tell me the story behind your drastic change." Michelle ushers both women to an over-stuffed couch.

"However, we're dealing with something just as shocking here today. Come in and be comfortable. I want to talk about a subject that affects all of us. Dacia and Dove-Whispering are in Dacia's room with Kiko. As you know, we brought the dog home from the vet's office today. Kiko isn't feeling too well. The doctor completed all the diagnostic tests and gave us the final word about her health." Michelle sits next to her extended family and after taking a quick breath and emitting a long, low, slow exhale, continues her explanation.

"Kiko is dying. She has an inoperable tumor on her liver. Since she's an older dog, her energy level diminished with age, and she's tired. The doctor let us know that the dog's dealing with pain and she's uncomfortable. Those two issues drain a lot of her energy. Generally, veterinarians give owners options when they're facing situations like this, but we have only one possibility; keep Kiko comfortable until she passes away. I've initially talked to the girls about that idea, but they both cried and yelled at me for just mentioning it. They're in the room, laying on

Dove-Whispering's bed hugging and talking to Kiko."

"I'll go in and talk with them," Pamela speaks for the assembled women.

"I think that's best. If the girls see Bernice at this point, the reality of her change might be too much." Michelle walks quickly toward Dove-Whispering's bedroom but softens her pace as she enters the melancholy room.

Michelle's gentle manner allows her entry into the somber, grieving trio as they huddle quietly in the shaded room. Kiko briefly lifts her head in a welcoming gesture followed by a slow, steady tail wag. Michelle softly pets the fur on the back of Kiko as much to offer comfort as to say 'hello.' "Girls I hear that the doctor gave us some sad news about Kiko." Michelle waits for the reaction of the emotionally groaning girls.

"Oh, mom. It can't be. Kiko being sick isn't okay. Kiko is our dog. She can't be sick. She can't be in pain. She's part of us. Remember all the things she helped us to do? We love her. She knows that we love her. It's like a person leaving us. We can't let Kiko abandon this family. We can't do that awful thing, mom. Mom!" Dove-Whispering hugs Kiko so hard that the fragile dog emits a short, low yelp saying, 'it's too tight, I can't breathe.' Dacia embraces both Dove-Whispering and

Kiko as if she's trying to ground their congealed levitation.

Pamela timidly joins her grieving family as much to console them as to lament their next decision. "Dacia, I know that everyone feels sorry about what the doctor at the vet's office told us about Kiko. However, it's not our decision to make; the choice is for Michelle and Dove-Whispering. We need to leave them alone for awhile so that whatever option they chose it's something that's comfortable for both of them." Pamela gently nudges Dacia away from her wedged position between Dove-Whispering and Kiko while guiding her out of the bedroom and toward the front door.

"I don't want to go away from you Dove-Whispering and Kiko, my loves. We'll always be the same. My heart is yours. My love is yours. My life is yours. Kiko, it'll be okay. It'll be okay. Oh, mom, I can't do this." Dacia embraces her mother in a choking squeeze and releasing her, frantically runs from the gloomy room.

Rushing toward the front door, Dacia abruptly stops; standing in the middle of the living room is the same finely-dressed woman she'd seen briefly in her mother's office. "Well, hello there young lady. I remember seeing you at your mother's hotel. We were rather formal at that brief introduction. However, I would like to introduce myself again." Bernice extends her right hand.

"I don't know what you want lady, and I don't much care right now. Our dog's dying. Can't you see that we're having a hard time with things?" Dacia tries to avoid any physical contact with Bernice.

Bernice, knowing well the emotional pain of her granddaughter and without regard to her resistance, grabs Dacia in an embrace hoping to convey her feelings of comfort and consolation. Initially, Dacia's vibrant struggles make it impossible for Bernice to maintain her consoling caress yet gradually Dacia's exertion weakens allowing granddaughter and grandmother to entwine. Dacia weakly whispers: "Grandma, I'm so sad like stones are hitting my heart. I love Kiko. I love her just like I love Dove-Whispering."

"I know sweetie, I know. It will be okay." Bernice releases her hold on her granddaughter.

Pamela joins her family in the living room. "We should return home. Michelle and Dove-Whispering should be alone with Kiko. We'll see them later at the burial. It's a time for them to be alone.

"Okay, Pamela, you're right." Bernice leads the exit through the front door.

Dacia quickly jumps into the back seat; not wanting to discuss her previous, embarrassing, emotional interaction with Bernice.

"Mom, I didn't expect so much commotion when we decided to travel to Michelle's house. I know that Kiko is a family pet and dealing with that terminal diagnosis is consuming all of Michelle's and Dove-Whispering's attention. It's a sad time for all of us." Pamela states the obvious.

"Exposing my status into the family, much less revealing my changed appearance, only adds confusion to the lineage of our family. I understand that fact. However, my ancestry may also bring added benefits for everyone; but we can discuss all of that later. Right now maybe we can all go back to our homes and think about what has occurred today, keeping in mind that each of our histories can be of value to everyone." Bernice holds her breath, hoping that her suggestion is relevant for everyone.

"That's great. I'll drop you off at your home. I'm sure that you're anxious to settle into your house with a new perspective." Pamela smiles as she agrees with her mother's suggestion.

BERNICE STANDS in the threshold of her front door facing her ornate, baroque living room. Memories of parental abuse, mistreatment from trusted confidants, molestation from colleagues flood her mind; all of the footsteps taken to arrive at this genesis, this beginning, are tracks that mark her journey. Miss McKim-DePue considers her next step; deciding to remove her shoes represents the imprints of her new life.

As Stinky-Poo's bare feet touch the floor, Bernice graciously assumes her new world of Miss McKim-DePue; the matriarch of the Henri family. Bernice's footsteps mark a descent from neglect and the tragic hypocrisy of prostitution and signal an ascent toward the accepting arms of her loving family. The hidden life of Stinky-Poo disappears, and Miss McKim-DePue assumes her role fully, entirely and responsibly.

There's much to be done. Bernice's first decision is to make a list; so much to do yet so little time. However, the once school counselor quickly realizes that she has all the time she needs to bond with her refound family. Taking a deep breath, Bernice stands in front of her walk-in closet staring at her varied collection of school-counselor wardrobe. The decision is simple; start changing her appearance to fit her new life. After stripping off her clothes and showering, Miss McKim-DePue dons a pair of shorts and a tee shirt to begin rummaging through her well-worn apparel. She realizes that there's little to keep from her previous life; no shoes seem appropriate, belts are out of style, dresses are too big and ill-sewn, nothing worth saving. Bernice makes a call to Ms. Walters, the high school science teacher because she works with the local home-less shelter; there's always a critical need for clothing in that community. Members of the collection team quickly fill the pick-up trucks with Bernice's discarded clothing.

The next step is to unpack her suitcase from her trip to Wray, Colorado. Exclusive outfits from Miss Violet's salon look comfortably placed in Bernice's closet. She chose well from the available options and arrived back in BigTon, Colorado with an ensemble fit for an elegant woman of genteel birth. It's evident that the women in the Henri family should wear clothes from Miss Violet's exclusive shop. The footsteps into Bernice's new life are uneasy yet focused. She walks forward.

CHAPTER THIRTEEN

Resolving Secrets

" *E* very obstacle yields to stern resolve."
— Leonardo da Vinci

"All journeys have *secret destinations of which the traveler is unaware.*" – Martin Buber

"Never give up, *for that is just the place and time that the tide will turn.*" – Harriet Beecher Stowe

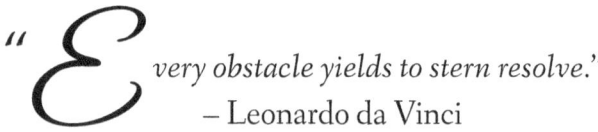

"Mom, I'm calling to let you know the final word. Kiko is dying. The doctor gave us the word. Dacia, her mom, Pamela, along with the school counselor and Dove-

Whispering and I gathered here at the house to spend some time together."

"Why was the counselor at your house? Was she helping the girls deal with their grief?"

"Well, in a way. But she also was present as a family member. She's Dacia's grandmother. I know that you have missed a lot since you live in Nevada, but things here in Colorado are moving pretty quickly as far as family relationships go. Dacia, Pamela, and Bernice, the counselor, were all in our living room when we brought Kiko home from the vet's office. It was a pretty sad scene in Dove-Whispering's bedroom. Even us grownups were teary-eyed. We'll meet again at Kiko's funeral."

"Oh, my dear. I'm sorry to hear about Kiko. It's like losing a portion of the family since she's been a trusted pet for so many years. Dove-Whispering got Kiko as a puppy. As we know, time passes, but sometimes it's painful when the reality of the passing touches you so closely." Kaye attempts to soften the blow for her daughter, Michelle, even though it's impossible to gauge the level of loss for someone else.

"Mom, I know you made a trip here recently but will you consider traveling to Colorado for a short time to be with Dove-Whispering? It will help her to deal with the loss. Besides, you love Kiko, and you'll have an opportunity to say goodbye."

"Of course, dear. I'll plan my travel and let you know. I'll drive to Colorado so that I can bring some of Kiko's old blankets and used toys for her to sniff. She may find comfort in those items. I know that Dove-Whispering and I will both want to spend time together with Kiko. The trip will be short because I know that you and Dove-Whispering will have some grieving to go through together. Give Dove-Whispering and Kiko a hug for me." Kaye sets down her 'heavy' cell phone; the bulk seems to have become instantly weightier, or maybe it's the information being delivered through the phone making it feel cumbersome.

"Anne, I have some disturbing news for you. That phone call from Michelle was to tell us that Kiko is dying. Michelle wants to know if we'll come to Colorado to spend some time with her and Dove-Whispering and Kiko."

"Oh my god, mom. That can't be true, not Kiko. She's been with us forever. Definitely, I'll go. When do we leave for Colorado?" Auntie Anne's kind heart and gentle demeanor suffer a sharp blow upon hearing the sudden life-changing status of the family pet; she too loves Kiko.

"I'm planning the trip now. My calendar's on the desk can you bring it so we can check our schedules?"

Kaye and Anne arrive at Michelle's house in the midst of funeral preparations.

"Oh grandma, I'm so sad it's like a real person is dying; Kiko isn't just our family pet, she's one of us." Dove-Whispering sympathetically hugs her grandmother while crying on her Auntie Anne's shoulder. "Auntie already talked to me about feeling sad and wanting to cry but my heart hurts, and I don't know what to do about it." Kaye and Anne both tighten their loving hug for the youngest member of their family knowing that the upcoming emotional stress is just going to be more intense.

"Sweetie, it's true our hearts are heavy, but I'll be awhile with grandma. We can talk. It's okay." Auntie Anne gently guides her niece toward the bedroom to spend their last bit of quality time with Kiko before the passing of their cherished family pet.

"Mom, our visit to the vet's office wasn't a happy affair; as I told you, Kiko's time is short. We're planning the funeral so that Dove-Whispering and Dacia have an opportunity to say goodbye to their cherished pet. Honestly, I'm as sad as the girls about Kiko and I have no problem showing my feelings about the loss. Dove-Whispering's right when she says that Kiko's more like a family member than just a dog; we've grown up with her." Michelle huddles with her mother and sister in an emotional conversation at the kitchen table.

"It's sad for all of us." Kaye, sitting next to Michelle, softly pats her other daughter, Anne, on the shoulder in a gesture of acknowledgment and inclusion.

"Pamela and Dacia were with us at the doctor's office when we received the sorrowful news. Both came here to the house expressing concern about our loss and offering their support. I'm sure they'll be at the funeral ceremony." Michelle's statement's interspersed with tears and nasal discharge.

"I wasn't aware that you and Pamela had grown so close in your relationship. She does seem to be a pleasant enough person but being at such a private family event may be something to think about."

"Oh, mom you know that you like Pamela. When you met with her at the restaurant, it ended up to be a good session. You know that's true."

"I know, but things are moving fast as far as personal relationships go, that sometimes it's hard for my brain to catch up with what's going on with everyone. Thinking about accepting new ideas and experiencing new ideas in your heart can be two different issues." Michelle, Anne, and Kaye join each other in a mutually-affirming head bobbing.

"I'll be here for an extended visit; it'll help Dove-Whispering and Dacia deal with the loss of Kiko. My work schedule's flexible; more than your time frame Michelle." Michelle fully accepts Auntie Anne's offer in a loving, sisterly hug.

"Okay girls, let's get things together for this emotional issue. Schedules will help us deal with the burning loss of Kiko. I'll make the initial move by calling Pamela and formally inviting her and Dacia to the funeral. Michelle, what did the veterinarian say about how much time Kiko has left with us?"

"The vet said that it'd be soon; we'll know for sure because she won't be able to digest whatever small amount of food she did manage to eat. She'll vomit everything she eats. That's the signal. We're supposed to call him, and if possible, he'll come to the house to give her some medication. The passing will be quick. The medication for Kiko that will make her more comfortable, and she'll just lay still and quit breathing. We can hold and cuddle her." Michelle visibly struggles as she relates the process of Kiko's death to her mother and sister.

"Mom, come quick. There's something different with Kiko." Dove-Whispering interrupts the kitchen table conversation by an urgent plea for Kiko's welfare.

"I'm coming, sweetie. What's going on? What's happening to her?" Michelle rushes to Dove-Whispering's bedroom, followed quickly by Kaye and Auntie Anne. Upon entering the pillow-strewn, darkened room, the three adults become melancholy realizing that the self-fulfilling prophecy has arrived.

"Mom, Kiko's vomiting. She ate a little of her food a few minutes ago. I put a little warm liquid chicken soup in her favorite dog food, and she licked some from the side of her bowl. It wasn't a lot of food, but I guess that she didn't like the soup. It's her favorite dog food, so I'm sure that it's the soup that didn't agree with her stomach. I bet if I call Dacia she'll come over to see Kiko. Kiko always likes it when both of us are with her. I'll call her now." Everyone senses Dove-Whispering uneasiness about leaving the consoling comfort of her place next to her lifelong pet, so Auntie Anne suggests a quick solution.

"I'll cuddle up next to Kiko there on your bed if that's okay with Kiko? That way you and Dacia will feel relaxed during your talk." Not only Auntie Anne but everyone in the Henry family household, look toward Kiko searching for a 'yes' answer.

Kiko slowly lifts her tired head and managing a weak tail-wag signifies, 'yes.'

RING, RING, RING. "Hello. Oh hello, Dove, (Dacia uses Dove-Whispering's school name). How is Kiko? I've been thinking about her all day. I didn't want to leave her side but everyone's tired, I'll come over if you need something." Dacia senses that her friend, Dove, is calling for support in dealing with the family pet whose captured the hearts of everyone spending any time with the friendly canine.

"It's more than that, Dacia. She's not keeping her favorite dog food in her stomach. It's coming up almost as soon as she eats. She's weak. She's not happy. I see the sadness in her eyes. You and I know her best. Can you come over? I know it's late, but Kiko would feel better if you're here." Dove makes no effort to hide her sullen emotions from not only her closest friend but the young woman who is nearly a virtual clone of her genetic organisms.

"I'll be right over. Since you and I have our drivers license, I can drive over myself. However, I'll talk to mom and see if she wants to come with me. Hold on for a minute, I'll ask her. I'll be right back." Dove patiently listens to muffled background noise while waiting for Dacia to return to their phone conversation.

"Hello, Dove-Whispering, this is Pamela. Of course, we'll be right over to your house. Is that okay with your mom?" Pamela wants to clear every decision with Michelle during this emotionally charged time.

"My mom won't mind seeing both of you."

"WE CAME AS SOON as we could." Pamela mixes an apology with a warm greeting upon entering the Henry household. Dacia races back to Dove's bedroom to give both her aunt and the dying canine a supportive hug.

"Oh Dacia, I'm so glad to see you. I think that Kiko is dying. She can't keep her food in her stomach. The doc said that her time was short, but I'm not ready for her to die, not yet."

"I know Dove. I love Kiko too."

"Dacia, I have a confession to make. I have been holding a secret inside of me. It has to do with Kiko. I'm ashamed to tell anyone else, but I know that you'll understand."

"Oh, I will."

"Every time I look at Kiko or smell Kiko or think about Kiko I remember my grandpa. You see, I got Kiko when I was a little girl; Kiko was with me when I was a little girl with my grandpa. Grandpa did bad stuff to your mom and my grandma, but I have some happy memories about my time with him; good times with him and Kiko swim around in my brain."

"Dove, you and I both know that the memory of my dad will be part our lives forever. Why are you talking about my dad now when Kiko is dying? I don't understand."

"I'm saying this because my memories of my

grandpa are all messed up with my feelings about Kiko. I feel that when Kiko dies my memories of my grandpa will die too. I haven't told anyone my secret. Only you know about how I feel. I'm scared that the way I feel will come true. Maybe, when I lose my dog, I will lose my memories too. Maybe just by telling you my secret, it will come true."

"Dove, memories don't die just because people or dogs die."

"Well, I know that Dacia but there's a part of me that wants the bad memories to die, the pain and hurt memories connected to my grandpa. I don't want everything to die just the bad stuff. Right now my brain has things about grandpa and things about Kiko mixed up together. I want Kiko to stay, but I want the nasty stuff to go away. It's confusing."

"Your secret is safe with me. It's resolved when Kiko passes. You'll see that your good memories of your grandpa are still with you. Remember, Dove, that your grandpa is also my dad and I know that my good memories of my dad will always be with me."

"I'm sure that you're right, but I just had to share my secret with you. Somehow sharing with you makes it real." Dacia and Dove encircle Kiko in an embrace, possibly their last.

"GIRLS, can you come into the living room? I want to talk to you about Kiko." Michelle wants everyone to be present when talking about Kiko's medical condition.

"Okay, mom."

Michelle, Pamela, Dacia, and Dove-Whispering, followed slowly by Kiko, gather for a somber meeting to discuss the inevitable demise of their beloved canine.

"The veterinarian at our last doctor appointment told me that when the end is near for Kiko the first physical sign that we see is when she starts to vomit up her food. The vomiting will let us know that her digestive system isn't working and her last hours are fast approaching. The doctor has medication for Kiko's comfort, and he's willing to come to the house to give it to her for her comfort." Michelle's statement intentionally trails off into a whisper since she's fighting back the tears of her own as she struggles to deliver the haunting news to other family members.

"Michelle I know that it's difficult for all of us but especially you and Dove-Whispering since Kiko is a part of your family. Dacia and I are sad for you so just let us know what you need and we'll do it." Pamela stands up from her seated position on the couch and ceremoniously stands in the center of the living room as though she is a loyal soldier waiting for her 'marching orders.'

"Well, not too much ceremony, Pamela, just a lot of emotion. I'll call the vet tonight and see if he'll come over tomorrow morning with the medication."

Upon hearing this response both Dacia and Dove-Whispering echo a blood-curdling wail rivaling the piercing cry of a trapped animal. "Oh no, it's too soon, not yet. We love her." Dove-Whispering and Dacia collapse onto the floor grabbing Kiko's fur as if trying to find security in a fierce wind storm. However, each girl quickly echoes another set of screeches when they see each of their hands full of Kiko's detached fur.

"Oh mom, you're right, it is time." Dove-Whispering looks into the sad, whimpering eyes of her cherished life-long pet. After inviting the veterinarian into their home, the Henry family gather for their final farewell to Kiko.

"Goodbye, sweet girl. We'll miss you dearly, but we'll always have our memories.

"Dove-Whispering I'm so happy to be here with you and your mom to say good-bye to Kiko. It's hard for all of us. Your Auntie Anne loves that dog a lot. Of course not as much as she loves you, but it's a lot. You know that I'm kidding you kiddo. Your Auntie loves you a thousand times more and more every day."

"I know grandma, but my heart still hurts. Losing Kiko is like losing a person."

"It'll hurt for a while, kiddo."

"I know, but at least we'll have our memories."

"Yes, we do, and from what I hear we're just about to make new memories. Remember we're all meeting with Miss McKim-DePue today to discuss her mysterious trip to Colorado. I don't know what she discovered in that town, but it changed her life." Kaye consoles her granddaughter Dove-Whispering while trying to nudge her thoughts into future possibilities.

"Grandma, I don't know about change; I need things to go in a positive direction. Dacia and I have been through so much in the past few months that the only thing left for us is a new future. Understanding all the old people in our family talking about bad stuff that happened long ago is a mystery. Maybe they have old memories or something – not sure what it is." Dove-Whispering sits quietly joining her grandmother in a few stolen moments of reflective thought.

BERNICE GINGERLY OPENS both sections of the front door revealing her newly remodeled home and with a grand hand gesture welcomes her assembled family members into the airy front sitting room. "Please come in. I'm excited to see everyone. Having my family in this house is truly an event to celebrate."

"Uh, mom, I'm not sure why we're here, but you wanted everyone to come over today to talk about your trip to Colorado. So, we all came." Pamela takes the initiative to speak for everyone and verbally state what seems to be the general thinking.

"Sure, everyone, come in. Have a seat, sit down; make yourselves comfortable." Bernice finds herself feeling nervous even though she has planned out the day down to the finest detail.

The parade of family members entering her home is a diverse collection of community leaders, high school students, business owners, and concerned kinfolk. Assembling this diverse group of clan members could only be accomplished by a person who herself has to lead a life of concealment and secrets.

"Everyone knows each other but having everyone here together as a family unit is something that needs to happen. It needs to occur because of the news that has been hidden but revealed today. Some of you know the fragments of the news, but I'm the only person who can tell the full story of our family. However, before I begin to explain the saga, I need to talk about the members of our family who are no longer with us."

Pamela and Michelle jointly interrupt Bernice. "Is

this part of the story that Dacia and Dove-Whispering should hear?"

"Yes, indeed. These young women carry us into the future. They can only do that by understanding the past; that knowledge gives both girls a clear picture of how to develop the pathway for our family. It's vital that they know this information." Bernice's conviction convinces both mothers that indeed their daughters are emotionally strong enough to learn the full truth of the Henry family.

"Besides, showing respect for these young women by treating them as adults it shows them that we value their place in our family." Bernice shoots a quick smile at both Dacia and Dove-Whispering.

"First, I'll tell you about Mr. and Mrs. Love. They're the sainted couple who adopt Pamela. She's a newborn destined to be a foundling, and I would've been a tainted woman. Although the Love's didn't suspect that Pamela's mother was a close member of their community, they never investigate her true parentage. Their love for Pamela forges them into a family, and you're a loved and cherished daughter."

"Mom, I never knew that you were so close to me while I'm growing up." Pamela loudly cries out.

"That's because you weren't supposed to know sweetie." Bernice shows her a loving smile.

"Now, let's discuss how Mr. and Mrs. Love came to acquire the land on which they built their hotel."

"Well, that's no secret, mom. They worked hard to make their money to buy the land." Pamela interrupts her mother.

"That's not the full story. We'll have Mr. Menendez talk about the land deal for the hotel. Well, Dale. It's your turn to speak."

Mr. Menendez, feeling embarrassed and intimidated, slowly stands and after clearing his throat begins to relate his dastardly deed. "As Bernice says there are a few people of our family that aren't with us today. One of them is my brother Jim Sleazy. Jim and I were in the land speculation business when Colorado was in the boomtown business. We're interested in making money whatever way possible. If that means cheating someone, then that person was cheated. Being honest wasn't something that bothered either one of us. That doesn't excuse anything that we did; it just explains the land deal with Mr. and Mrs. Love. This next part of our family story gets delicate. Bernice works for us in our land speculation office as a secretary. She's hiding from her mother after escaping from the brothel. One fateful evening my brother Jim raped Bernice. Pamela is the result of that rape." Dale stops his story here to take a large drink of water from a crystal goblet setting on a finely-carved wooden table positioned next to his chair. After taking a long, slow swallow, he notices that both Dacia and Dove-Whispering's attention is steadily glued on to his next sentence.

"I'll continue with the story. Jim became overwhelmed with his debauchery and shot himself in a local saloon. However, Bernice and I were indelibly bound. My solution is to approach Mr. and Mrs. Love for the adoption of the newborn. My perverted sense of justice tells me that this approach offers partial atonement for cheating the couple in the land deal."

"Let me interrupt you here, Dale. I was destitute. Surrendering my beloved child to a social service agency was unbearable. The private adoption fit everyone's needs." Bernice's attempt to defend her decision of abandoning her child is as useless as attempting to return fallen leaves onto an October tree branch.

"It helped me feel better about cheating the Love's in the land deal." Dale's words go unnoticed.

"Dale, tell everyone the rest of the story." Bernice urges Dale to stop feeling sorry for himself and focus on family issues.

"Yes, you're right Bernice. I'll continue. Mr. and Mrs. Love, Bernice and I make a pact. The agreement provides for the financial future of Pamela and her genetic heirs. As the Love's became financially secure and their property investment was paid off, they established a trust fund. The financial fund provides for long-term security for Pamela and her family members. Well, not just her family members but any genetic heirs. That means anyone genetically related to Pamela. In other words, all of us. All of us sitting here in this room today. We all share equally in the trust fund. It's a substantial, hefty trust fund and it'll support us for our entire lifetime." Mr. Menendez pauses to take another drink from the crystal goblet.

"Do you mean that we're rich? Are we rich? Are we rich?" Dacia and Dove-Whispering jump up screaming and hugging each other.

"Yes, girls. It means that we're rich. Bernice will tell you the rest of the story."

"Dale is right. I met with Mr. Smith during my trip to Colorado. He's our family attorney. He's managing the Love Family trust. I'll just let that information sink in for a while before I tell everyone the rest of the story."

"You mean there's more to the story?" Kaye can't contain herself. I can't believe that there's more information for this family after what we have just heard. It's amazing that this family receives such fabulous financial news." Kaye embraces Michelle and Dove-Whispering.

"Before you continue, mom. I want to clarify what I'm hearing. Are you and Mr. Menendez saying that you traded a baby for hush money? Are you telling us that you sold me for money to a barren couple that you already swindled in a land deal? Is that what I hear, mom?" Pamela rises from her comfortable chair and approaches her mother in a face-to-face confrontation.

"Again, mother, I ask you, is that what I am hearing? Was I sold?" Pamela assumes a firm, accusative position in front of her mother.

Bernice struggles to rise from her chair but finds it difficult to assume a standing position since her daughter intentionally positioned too close. "Uh, daughter, it isn't like that exactly. *Not sold*; you're privately adopted." Again Bernice attempts to find her stable footing.

"After all that I've endured, after all of the pain and lies that I've lived through, I now find out that the adults in my life used me as a bargaining tool, or a salve if you will, to soothe their guilty conscious. I'm a negotiation ploy."

"Oh daughter, it's not at all like that. I love you dearly. The Love's loved you. Mr. Menendez loves you. We all try to make the best decisions for our children. Your life would've been one of intense discrimination and bullying if we hadn't made the choices that we did." Bernice has struggled to her feet and follows Pamela over to the large picture window on the opposite side of the front parlor.

Pamela shrugs off her mother's comforting attempt. "Mom, I know that you love me but to 'sell' your newborn child is unthinkable to me."

"Daughter, listen to me. It's because I love you so dearly that I made the heart-wrenching deal with the Love's. I knew that you would be cherished and protected. That's something I couldn't do. I'm an unemployed, single woman with a lurid past. No one in the business community knew me as a reputable person; there are no references. My only saving grace is to work with Dale on a plan to keep you safe. Yes, you're correct. We did deal with the Love's for a private adoption, but it wasn't in exchange for the land swindle. Mr. and Mrs. Love don't know about the fraud in their land acquisition. Providing a loving family for a beautiful baby girl is their concern. That newborn is you." Pamela, seeing the desperation in her mother's face, realizes that the story is true.

"Mom, as I'm looking at Dacia and how these issues would surely tarnish her delicate life, I begin to develop an understanding of your anguish and distress in dealing with my adoption. The issue of placing your-self incognito by impersonating a shabby, ignorable, elderly school counselor is incomprehensible to me. The years of throbbing misery you endure to maintain even a distant connection to me is just now becoming painfully aware to me. I don't have your continence that's painfully obvious to me. I now understand how arrogant I am even to attempt to place any judgment on you or your actions." Pamela entwines her mother in a hug much resembling two bees communicating after a lengthy visit to a springtime botanical garden.

"I love you, darlin."

"I love you too, mom, and if I live forever, I still won't be as strong as you."

"Well, I have some additional news for everyone. Do you remember that I mentioned Mr. Smith that I met on my trip to Colorado?" Bernice waits until she has everyone's attention.

"Well, as I also mentioned he is our family attorney for the family trust. The reason that we need a lawyer is that there are many issues to address when people are dealing with large fortunes." Again, Bernice waits for everyone nod in the affirmative.

"As I mentioned, Mr. Smith's a competent legal mind. We may well need someone of his caliber to manage two large fortunes."

Kaye speaks first. "What do you mean, two large fortunes?"

"My trip to Wray, Colorado revealed that not only

did I inherit a fortune from my mother but all of my genetic heirs did as well. I informed Pamela of this windfall earlier but wanted to wait until we were all assembled to let everyone know the full extent of the inheritance news."

Again, Dove-Whispering and Dacia quickly bellow out a high-pitched scream, but their 'jackal-yell' ends abruptly when the two young women realize that their over-excited brains can't comprehend this additional financial news. "What do you mean grandma, when you say 'more money'?"

"I mean that you and Dove-Whispering are rich now because both of your family's ancestors were forward thinking and planning for their descendants. Each side of the Henry family, whether they be notorious or infamous, thought about their family members. They may not have done their planning in a traditional manner or with a legal mind but never the less; they knew that setting aside some manner of financial security would help their family. Because of that foresight, you girls will enjoy financial security." Bernice changes her position so that she sits cross-legged on her plush front parlor floor covering in front of Dacia and Dove-Whispering.

"Grandma is saying that we can buy whatever we want whenever we want from whomever we want."

Dacia excitedly grabs Dove-Whispering's arm and repeats her litany

"Dacia, take a breath, take a breath. Sit back down here next to me. Both of you girls need to listen closely to what I'm saying. Yes, there is glamour and opportunity with money, but the bigger issue is your responsibility."

"We're not responsible for stuff." Dove-Whispering and Dacia again answer in unison.

Michelle, Pamela, and Kaye all move in closer to the group sitting on the floor to add to the upcoming conversation. Michelle speaks first. "I believe that Miss McKim-DePue is trying to make a point about using our newly bestowed wealth. Remember girls, we were all struggling middle-to-low income people this morning, and now our status has changed. With that change comes, like she just said, both opportunity and responsibility."

"You're right. But before I continue, I want to invite Mr. Menendez to come and join us down here on the floor. Come on down here Dale; it's quite comfortable."

"Okay, here I come." The older guy struggles to adjust his body but doesn't match the limber position of the girl's flexible contortions.

"Well, my point is that as we investigate our new wealth, it will be exciting. We'll tingle and be giddy. At first, we might not believe our good fortune. Possibly there will be a period of anxiety about the large amount of money that is available to us. It will take a while for all of us to understand that our wealth is now our responsibility."

"Mom, I think that you and Kaye have extensive experience managing a tight budget. Maybe we should all designate you guys to manage this money." Pamela wants to defer the responsibility before the discussion progresses.

"Pamela I appreciate your concern, but I believe that the amount of money that we're talking about here is more than just managing a monthly bank statement." Kaye bounces the implied responsibility back into the hands of another family member.

"Everyone take a breath. This anxiety is what I mean. Don't get excited. We have time to deal with our fortunes. Besides Mr. Smith will be at the helm in that area." Everyone joins in a nervous laugh.

"As I was saying to the young women in our family; our lives are now different, enriched and beholden."

Dove-Whispering, who's been sitting listening intently to Bernice's recent explanation, stands up. "I still don't understand who gave us the money. One day my mom and I are struggling to make every dollar count and the next day we have more money than both of us can ever use. So, who gave us the money?"

"Oh, my sweetie. It's like Ms. McKim-DePue just said, the money came from people in our family who have passed away. One fortune is from her mother and the other collection of wealth is passed down from Pamela's adoptive parents, the Love's."

"So, it's like when Kiko died, but since she's a dog, there wasn't any money to give us." Dove-Whispering is clearly overwhelmed by the emotional upheaval of recent events in the Love family. Michelle nuzzles up close to her daughter, reassuring her.

"The subject of money connected to the history of our family can certainly be discussed at another time. Why don't we all go back home and review every-thing? It's a lot to consider." Bernice assists Dale rise to his feet; unexpectedly he also gets help from Dacia and Dove-Whispering.

"Thanks, everyone, I appreciate you helping me get back on my feet."

"We're all in the same family now, so it's okay." Dacia gives Dale a gentle pat on his shoulder as he heads toward the front door of Bernice's home. Dove-Whispering locks arms with her aunt as the two young women merrily prance out of the front parlor.

"Wait just a minute, girls. I thought that you might like to see my redecorated home. It's been a long time since I've entertained visitors and I would enjoy taking you both for a tour through my house."

"Uh, sure, yes, wouldn't we Dove-Whispering?" Dacia still isn't entirely comfortable being alone with her maternal grandmother.

"I guess, sure."

"Let me ask your mother if she would like to join us girls. I'll be right back."

While the two young women wait for Bernice to return, they begin investigating their brilliant surroundings by touching, smelling and looking at the ornate furnishings in 'Stinky-Poo's' home.

"Who knew that 'Stinky-Poo' lived in such a great place," Dove-Whispering speaks in a whisper since her attention focuses on exploring the finery in Bernice's home.

"Well, the last time I was here the house looked a lot like 'Stinky-Poo.' It was dull, drab and forgettable. I'm not sure what happened, but this house now looks more like a rich lady's palace. I guess that when 'Stinky-Poo' redid herself, she redid this house too." Dacia pretends that she knows a bit of the secret life of her grandmother even though the two haven't had a quiet opportunity to speak.

"This is a good day because Pamela, Kaye, and Michelle are all going to join us girls for the tour. Let's go. You've all seen the front parlor so strolling through the rest of the house will be a similar pleasure." Bernice conducts an informative tour through her refurbished home as though she's presenting it for a nationally televised broadcast.

"Mom, I have to say that you certainly live in grand style." Pamela seems to speak for the impressed group.

"I'm giving a party next month for the whole town. Invitations are going out to everyone. I don't know who'll attend, but you never know. It should be fun. We should all go shopping for really nice looking outfits. I know this elegant dress shop in Wray, Colorado. The proprietor, Miss Violet, will be happy to outfit all of us. The trip by rail is very relaxing."

"You're inviting everyone in our town to a party here in your house? What do you mean by a 'dress shop in Wray, Colorado'?" Kaye looks at Bernice with a questioning expression as though she is pondering a perplexing motive.

"Yes. Ms. Walters and the administrators at the high school are helping me with the invitations. When do we all want to go to Wray? Dale, you can come too. There's a nice haberdashery shop."

Kaye, Michelle, and Pamela line up as though waiting for feeding time at the public zoo. "Ms. McKim-DePue I don't know how to respond to your statement. Neither my daughter nor I am accustomed to such finery." Michelle struggles to add a further response.

"Don't worry my child. We'll each go back to our own homes, discuss all the things that we learned here today. You'll discover that the more you review everything, the more you become comfortable with your new lifestyle."

"The first thing I'm doing today is talk with Auntie Anne. She's waiting in Nevada to discuss what we did today. I can only imagine how she'll feel when I tell her about 'our fortunes.' I'm going to go back to Michelle's house and order an airplane ticket for Auntie Anne right away. It'll be exciting to have all of us together while we enjoy this adventure. I can't wait."

"Okay, mom. I'll get Dove-Whispering, and we'll leave right away. Boy, will my sister be surprised." Michelle is so excited that she stumbles to remember which end of Bernice's house faces the street access. Michelle, Kaye and Dove-Whispering leave 'Stinky-Poo's house in a flurry of activity leaving Dale, Pamela and Bernice standing at the front door trying to get their 'bearings.'

"Bernice, our lives are going to be different that's obvious. Our conversation started me thinking about activities that occurred years ago. It made me realize that I haven't apologized to you. My brother violates you in every way, and that violation changes your life; your strength in surviving that trauma leads to our meeting today. Whatever path we take from this moment depends on the courage and desires of the young woman in our lineage. We made our decisions, be they right or wrong, however Dacia and Dove-Whispering know enough about our past to determine which direction they want to steer the future of this clan. We're resolving the secrets of our history. Those secrets that sent ripples into the next generations are affecting the current lives of innocent people who don't carry the scars of our actions. That's why Dacia and Dove-Whispering can view the world with open eyes and clear minds. I'm confident that they'll lead us all into a bright future."

"Dale, I've never heard you talk like this before. Your words seem to be coming from someone who has learned valuable life lessons. Is that the case? Could it be that you, Mr. Menendez, are turning over a new lease in life?"

"I don't know about all that stuff, Bernice; I feel different. I'm positive for once in my miserable, little life. Sometimes, I wish I'de never had a brother named Jim Sleazy or ever met William Henry. Both these men brought out the raw side of my character. Now I'm looking forward to seeing what two positive, young women in our family will do."

Bernice and Dale embrace as though each is reintroduced to a lifelong friend.

"GEE, this is my first train ride. Mom says that the town's people are waiting for our entire family. Can you imagine, Dove-Whispering, we got a pass from school and a great trip on this fabulous custom train car so that we can visit my great-grandmother's home. I'm excited." Dacia's body protrudes halfway out of the train car window while the quick 'click-a-t-clack' of the rails sway she and Dove-Whispering into a rhythmic dance as the steaming locomotive heads steadfastly toward Wray, Colorado.

"Dacia, I'm nervous about all of the changes in our lives. Sometimes when things move fast, we make mistakes. I want us to always check with each other when making decisions. You and I are going to meet Mr. Smith, the attorney for our family trust funds. He'll be helping us manage our money. I agree that it's exciting, but I can't help feeling that something else is going to happen in our lives; something that will add even more difference." Dove-Whispering often relies on her pensive Native American ancestry to guide her when emotional issues seem to overwhelm her ability to manage her options in life. That reliance has always led her toward a path of understanding and helped her make logical choices. It's also an ability that has tempered the excitability of Dacia when the two friends meet new situations.

"Okay, sure. We'll have fun in this little town. I'm going to get some nice clothes. Both of us will go back to BigTon lookin' good." Dacia hugs her friend; mostly to reassure her but also to help calm her almost unbridled excitement.

Bernice reserves an entire scenic train car for the Henry family to accommodate their travel from Bigton to Wray, Colorado. Auntie Anne arrives from Nevada at the station just as the train is leaving. Everyone settles in for a journey that's destined to change their lives.

Michelle waits for everyone to find their comfortable area before telling them just one more secret. "I've been waiting until we're all together before letting everyone know about the recent news concerning Dove-Whispering."

Again, Michelle waits until she holds everyone attention. "A few months ago I submitted a DNA test for Dove-Whispering to verify her Native American lineage. Dove-Whispering's father left her a legacy based on that lineage. That legacy isn't only the proud lineage of being Native American but the ancestry of sharing an Earth-based knowledge. Genetics and family history verifies her genealogy, and she's heir to her father's legacy which was established long before his death.

Dove-Whisperings' Native American bloodlines of Cheyenne and Blackfoot are bestowed upon her by her maternal great-grandmother, grandmother and father. Both tribes' nomadic migration begins in the Canadian territory and evolves into settlements throughout the Northern Great Plains. The Cheyenne and Blackfoot belong to a larger group known as the Algonquian family. The Blackfeet Indians are prairie people moving swiftly in large groups, making long journeys to wage war and hunt buffalo. Their adopted name of 'Blackfoot' comes from the fact that they discolor their moccasins with the ashes of prairie fires.

The Cheyenne are plains tribe people living a life of hunting and building teepees. The Cheyenne perfected the art of communicating with sign language and trading with local tribes. They're widely known to be tenacious and will fight to the death protecting their people. Both Native American tribes are physically handsome people. Dove-Whispering's 'people' are registered at an old Jesuit mission in Montana. I met Dove-Whispering's father when he moved to Colorado."

The assembled Henry family sit in mute transfiguration listening to Michelle's rendition of Dove-Whispering's family tree; each mentally formulating their questions.

"Gee, does that mean Dove-Whispering is an American Indian? Is she going to attend some weird Indian school?" Dacia's first reaction takes the form of innocent, unscripted questions.

"The answer to your question, Dacia, is both yes and maybe. Dove-Whispering's a proud member of both the Blackfeet Tribe and the Cheyenne Tribe. Her percentage of American Indian blood isn't large in either tribe, but her pride in both is considerable." Michelle proudly hugs her daughter.

Dacia's next question is predictable. "So, Dove-Whispering, where's your dad?"

"My father's dead just like your dad Dacia." The sharp tone of Dove-Whispering's answer surprises Dacia.

"I didn't mean to hurt you, kiddo. Remember, we're best buddies?"

"I know, but everybody seems to be dead. I guess that I'm still thinking about Kiko."

Michelle, seeing the emotionally charged atmosphere between the two closely-knit friends, quickly picks up the conversation. "Dove-Whispering's father died before she was born. He was a quiet, gentle man who married me when both of us were in our early 20's. Dove-Whispering has inherited her father's beautiful Native American features and intellectual abilities. I often see her father's characteristics in her mannerisms and attitudes. If her father were alive today, he would be beaming with pride for his precious daughter."

'Oh, mom. You always tell me that same ole' story. Someday I'm going to start believing it." Dove-Whispering shyly answers her mom's litany.

"That's a cool story about a girl and guy, almost our age, falling in love and having a baby. Dove-Whispering, I love the story. You should have told me that story long ago. It's adorable." Dacia enthusiastically hugs her very best friend with lifelong gusto. The two friends sit quietly in their seats talking in hushed tones for the remainder of the train ride to Wray, Colorado.

Pamela, Bernice, Kaye, and Anne have been listening intently to Michelle's family history lesson. However, Mr. Menendez finds it necessary to pass the time by taking advantage of the chartered trains complimentary beverages. Half-way into their journey, it's evident that Dale is drunk. "Aw, that's hogwash. Everyone knows that all Indians are savages. None of them are any good. There's no good to come out of an Indian!" Dale staggers from the bar into the observation area to loudly address the female members of his extended family. At which point he's quickly silenced by being physically tied up and gagged by the woman for the duration of the trip.

"Oh, I hope that the girls didn't hear any of Dale's rantings." Bernice quickly protects Dacia and Dove-Whispering and chastises Mr. Menendez. "He'll never learn to keep his stupid mouth shut. I guess that his little show of atonement was just that, 'a little show,' for all to see. Well, we'll go on to Wray and maybe leave him on the train to travel endlessly." The women shake their heads in agreement.

Pamela prods Michelle to share additional information about Dove-Whispering's father. "Please tell us more."

"Well, as I said, he's a gentle man with well-developed spiritual senses. Maybe that's where Dove-Whispering gets her ability to observe and understand events. Although, when he sees an injustice he's quick to bravery in voicing his opinion, which expresses his Cheyenne heritage; Dove-Whispering is so like her father in that way also. My daughter's striking physical beauty is a tribute to her combined German and Native American heritage, and as she grows into womanhood, I see the strength and pride of her father growing stronger within her."

"Michelle, it may be painful and private but how did your husband die?"

"You're right, it's painful to remember that fateful

day but the memories of our time together help to soften the rough reflections."

Michelle takes a moment to center herself before continuing with her family saga. "My husband's walking down a country road on his way to work for a local farmer. The driver of a speeding car hit him from behind and sped away without stopping to see if my husband needs help. Our doctor says that his death was instant and painless. However, that gives me little comfort since I'm pregnant with Dove-Whispering and about to give birth. Raising my daughter as a single mother makes the parenting job difficult; I'm an adult dealing with the past while looking toward my daughter's future, and as Dove-Whispering gets older, I see more of her father reflected in her. I love her dearly, but I still miss her father."

"Oh, Michelle. I understand what you mean when you speak about being a single mom raising your child alone. It's as though you're both drifting in a small, salvaged, wooden canoe in the massive ocean hoping that a huge luxury liner doesn't appear out of the fog and crash into your survival craft."

"Pamela, you're so right, living in two opposite realities is difficult."

Kaye and Bernice each hug their daughters and in a joint rendition say, "You girls are doing a good job, and things will turn out just fine."

Auntie Anne yells out, "I think that we're coming into a small town. There's something up ahead on the tracks." Everyone rushes to the train windows to verify her announcement. Even Mr. Menendez's bondage is released just in time for him to witness the prospect of his future slowly appearing down the tracks in the form of Wray, Colorado.

"You're right Anne, but I'm not sure what's next to the tracks." Kaye wonders if the tracks are under repair and the train won't be able to pull into the station.

"Oh, heavens that's just the committee," Bernice announces in a rather off-handed manner.

"What committee?" is the joint response from everyone in the train car.

"The Welcoming Committee arranged by Mr. Smith to greet us." Bernice can't pass up another opportunity to encompass her family in their upcoming acceptance ceremony.

Auntie Anne overwhelmed with excitement, runs to the front of the train car to get a sharper look at the quick-gathering crowd assembling around the train station. Just then the train conductor announces, "Next stop is Wray, Colorado."

———

"WELL, Miss Bernice McKim-DePue it is so very nice

to see you again. I hope that you and your family had a pleasant trip. Train travel is certainly the luxurious way to journey these days." The distinguished Mr. Smith, Esq., dressed is an elegant, finely-tailored, business suit greets Bernice and assists her as she steps off the train. As 'Stinky-Poo' steps onto the train station platform the local fire department band bellow out their traditional rendition of 'For She's a Jolly Good Fellow.' This joyous merriment quickly mingles with the light-hearted cheers from members of the Welcoming Committee and the local Chamber of Commerce dignitaries. Bernice revels for several minutes in the town's heartfelt greeting.

"Mr. Smith we did have a pleasurable ride from Bigton to Wray, and I thank you for asking. Also, I would like for you to meet the other members of my family. I'll introduce them as they exit the train. Each of them is precious to me, and each is looking forward to their stay in your beautiful city." Bernice takes her time to focus her attention on each member of the Henry family making sure that the prominent members of the community greet the adults and both teens with respect due to visiting dignitaries.

"Mr. Smith our business is to meet with you in your office and discuss the trust fund provisions. However, our first order of importance is to visit both Miss Violet's Salon and the Haberdashery. We have a

Mr. Menendez in our family who can certainly use the services of a well-heeled men's boutique."

"Whatever your family needs Miss Bernice McKim-DePue I can arrange to address personally." Mr. Smith, Esquire, politely offers his arm to escort Bernice to Miss Violet's shop. The Henry family parading down the main street of Wray, Colorado sends out ripples of unanswered questions to future generations.

– THE END –